A NOVEL

NEW YORK TIMES BESTSELLING AUTHOR
DEBORAH BLADON

Also by Deborah Bladon

Chapter 1

Arietta

"Are you skipping your coffee break again?"

I glance up at the sound of the cheery voice of one of my co-workers. Bronwyn Kirby flashes me a dimpled grin.

"Yes." I sigh. "I can't leave my desk. I have too much to do."

Undeterred by my answer, Bronwyn waves a chocolate bar at me. "I picked this up yesterday at a candy store in Times Square. Take a break, and we'll split it."

Chocolate is one of my weaknesses. It's the perfect partner to a hot cup of dark roast coffee.

I'm tempted to drop everything to satisfy my sweet tooth and caffeine craving, but it's not worth facing the wrath of my boss.

I point at the stack of file folders on the corner of my desk. "Mr. Calvetti wants all of those updated before he gets back."

Bronwyn's gaze drifts to the files. "You have time to squeeze in a short break."

She says it with enough confidence that I almost fall victim to her ploy. I know she doesn't want to spend the next fifteen minutes alone in the break room. The chocolate is a compelling lure, but avoiding Mr. Calvetti's disappointment bears more weight.

I shake my head. "He made it clear before he left for his meeting that I needed to get through all of that. I want to avoid angry Dominick today."

1

Bronwyn tucks a lock of her brown hair behind her ear. "I convinced Judd to switch everything to electronic form. When I have to make an update to a client's file, it takes two seconds flat."

I don't need the reminder that her boss is the opposite of mine. We're both executive assistants working for the same company, but Bronwyn reports to Judd Corning. He's known to smile most of the day, dole out a few compliments each week, and the bonus he handed her during the holidays was in the low-five figures.

Mr. Calvetti has resting scowl face. He wouldn't know a compliment if it hit him in the side of the head, and my December bonus consisted of a ten-dollar gift card to a bodega.

Bronwyn unwraps the chocolate to snap off half. She offers it to me with a grin. "You look like you could use something stronger, but this is the best I can do at the moment."

Taking a bite, I close my eyes and lean back in my chair. "This is incredible. It's so good."

Bronwyn laughs. "You act like it's better than sex."

My eyes pop open. "What?"

"It's chocolate, Arietta." She takes a bite of the piece in her hand. "It's good, but even bad sex is better than this."

I disagree. I've never had sex that has been as satisfying as this chocolate.

"If you change your mind and decide to sneak away from your desk, I'll be all by my lonesome in the break room." Bronwyn pushes out her bottom lip in a pout. "I'd tell you not to work too hard, but I know you have no choice."

She's right. I don't have a choice. I have to get my to-do list done before my boss's meeting uptown comes to an end.

***

An hour later, I finally close the last file folder on my desk. I have no idea how I managed to get it all done, but I did. I pop what's left of the chocolate into my mouth.

I turn my attention to all of the messages that have been left for Mr. Calvetti this morning. I need to sort through those now.

It sounds simple enough, but in his world, nothing fits into that category.

He made it clear that any message from a woman who is not related to him or looking for investment advice is to be tossed in the trash.

I search through the fifteen pieces of paper in front of me.

I pick out three.

I read the first to myself. "Tell Dominick that I have his tie. If he wants it back, he's going to need to fly to Norfolk to get it out of my bed."

My gaze drifts to the name I jotted down during my brief conversation with the woman. *Teagan.* Next to that is a phone number with a Virginia based area code.

I open the bottom drawer of my desk and tug out a manila envelope. I push the paper with Teagan's message into it, cramming it in with the dozens of others I've put in there since I started working for Mr. Calvetti.

I do the same with the other two messages I plucked out of the pile.

Even though Mr. Calvetti has told me repeatedly not to take messages from the women he knows "*outside of the office*" (code for has sex with), I always do. Tossing them in the trash feels cruel. If a woman is putting herself out there, I can't ignore that, even if Mr. Calvetti always does.

I'm not okay with being the bearer of bad news, and I refuse to be responsible for a stranger's broken heart.

Since two of the three messages I just put in the envelope are from women in Virginia, I'd say that my boss did more than handle business on his trip there last week.

I wish he'd jet off again. The offices of Modica Wealth Management are peaceful when he's not here.

When he spent months in Italy courting new clients, it was almost perfect.

He did wake me often in the middle of the night to do menial tasks for him, but whenever I sat behind this desk, I didn't have to glance into his office and see the stern expression on his gorgeous face.

Speaking of which…

I bolt to my feet when I hear the telltale whispered warnings from my co-workers that Mr. Calvetti is back from his meeting.

Pushing my eyeglasses up the bridge of my nose, I suck in a deep and uneven breath. I've got this. I can do this.

Mr. Calvetti promoted me because he knows I'm capable of great things.

I convinced myself of that as I was signing my employment contract. I knew it wouldn't be easy, but the best things in life come with a challenge and a commitment to overcome anything standing in your way.

My gaze hones in on him when he steps around the corner and turns in my direction.

Perfection in a three-piece charcoal gray suit is headed my way.

Did he get even better looking since he left the office this morning?

His dark brown hair is a touch longer than when he hired me, and his brown eyes look even more soulful.

I shake my head because I'm being blinded by how handsome he is. Dominick Calvetti doesn't have a soul. Greed sits in the place where his soul should be.

He breezes past me, leaving a trail of expensive cologne in his wake.

"My office now," he says in a clipped tone. "Follow me, Miss Voss."

I grab the messages and my tablet from my desk and fall in step behind him, hoping that the rest of the day flies by.

Chapter 2

Dominick

Arietta Voss looks as though she stepped out of a finger painting done by a four-year-old. Every color of the rainbow is represented in the patterned blouse she's wearing.

Her sense of style has never been on point.

That's one of the reasons she was promoted a few months after being hired as a junior analyst.

My last two executive assistants were women as well. They dressed to impress. They both caught the eye of my single male clients. Many of the married ones were just as enamored. It was a distraction my business doesn't need, so when it came time to find a new executive assistant, I perused the company employee files while paying close attention to the attached photos.

Arietta stood out in the simplest way.

She puts minimal effort into her appearance. Today is a perfect example of that. Her blonde hair is wound up in an uneven chignon. The bottom hem of the oversized skirt she's wearing skims the top of her sensible black shoes, and the blouse she has on is not only a mishmash of colors; it's at least two sizes too large for her.

I've heard people in the office comment behind Arietta's back about how she's the youngest grandma they've ever met.

My grandmother, Martina Calvetti, would have a word with them about how a woman's age shouldn't dictate her wardrobe choices.

I agree, but I don't have the time or inclination to defend Miss Voss's attire.

I care about her intelligence and competence. The clothes she puts on her back keep my clients focused on their portfolios and not on her.

I consider that a bonus.

"How has your day been so far, Mr. Calvetti?" she asks as she follows me into my office.

"Fine," I answer brusquely.

"And the meeting? How was that?"

"Fine," I repeat, leaving it at that.

She doesn't expect me to ask her anything. I know what I need to know. She's twenty-two. She has a degree in business. She skipped the fifth and tenth grades. Her IQ is higher than mine, although that's a fact neither she nor anyone but me is aware of.

I take the seat behind my desk. "I want a coffee in my hand in..."

"Ten minutes," she finishes my sentence. "I've emailed you a proposed schedule for the remainder of the day. I contacted Mr. Morano, and he was happy to reschedule his appointment to tomorrow afternoon at four. That gives you the time you requested so you could leave the office an hour early."

I look up when I hear the subtle shift in her tone as she says the last two words. Her face gives nothing away. Her gray eyes lock on my mouth as I study her.

If she's expecting an explanation or a smile, she'll be disappointed.

"Good," I offer.

The corners of her mouth edge up toward a grin.

Have her lips always been that full?

"Mr. Corning would like to see you as soon as you have a free moment." Her gaze drifts to the window to my right. "I did ask what it pertained to, but he wasn't forthcoming."

I'd bet my entire fortune that it's about a client we've been trying to persuade to sign with us. We want to manage her hundreds-of-millions. She wants us to work harder for the privilege.

Going into business with my two closest friends from high school seemed like a good idea at the time. I was eighteen, full of hope, and blinded by lust for a future bank account with a six–figure balance.

Sixteen years later, I've leapfrogged that to a comfortable eight-figure investment portfolio, an apartment that overlooks Central Park, and a villa in Italy. Hope fell by the wayside during my freshman year of college when I realized dreams could only take a man so far. Hard work and ruthless determination have been the keys to my success.

Daniel Lawton, a third of our trio, moved to Los Angeles two months ago to handle our growing list of clients on the west coast. Judd Corning, who sits in an office down the hall from mine, brings his unique talents to the business. He balances out Daniel's and my strengths.

We've nurtured relationships, made connections, and proven to our clients that if you want your wealth to grow, we'll make it happen.

"I'll see him now." I glance at Arietta. "Tell him I have fifteen minutes, and that's all I can give him."

I can carve out an hour for Judd, but I've already read through a string of text messages that he sent me today. His latest effort to convince Clarice Blanchard to agree to a meeting with us to present our investment strategies was met with silence.

It's a calculated move in the seemingly unending game of cat and mouse that we've been playing with her for weeks.

"I'll do that," Arietta says. "Is there anything else you need?"

"That's all. Thank you."

She tilts her head as if she's trying to comprehend what I just said.

This may very well be the only time I've thanked her for anything. I'd say it slipped out, but good intentions take effort. I'll never be the gentleman my father is, but an attempt at good manners now and again can't hurt.

A full smile graces her lips. "You're welcome."

"Your call to Mr. Corning, Arietta…"

"Of course." She takes a step toward me before she backs up several inches. "Since you are leaving an hour early today, I was wondering if I could too?"

"No," I answer without hesitation.

Again, her expression gives nothing away. If she's disappointed, she's hiding it behind a smile.

"That's all, Miss Voss."

She places a stack of papers on my desk. "These are your messages, sir. There were others, but I took care of them."

I read between the lines. Arietta tossed any messages left by women I've had encounters with.

"Good." I don't need to thank her for that. It's part of her job. "My coffee, Arietta."

She nods. "I'll call Mr. Corning and grab a coffee for both of you. If you need anything else, you know where to find me."

Indeed I do. She'll be where I pay her very well to be. That's behind her desk, keeping my professional life in order.

Chapter 3

Arietta

"I will never understand how Mr. Calvetti grew up with that woman as his grandmother." I wave a finger in the air toward where Martina Calvetti is standing near the kitchen of the restaurant that bears her surname. "She's a saint. He's the devil."

My roommate, Sinclair Morgan, glances in the direction I'm pointing. "Marti has like a bazillion grandkids. You can't expect them all to be winners."

I let out a stuttered laugh. "There are a lot of them, but I think it's under twenty total."

Sinclair shrugs her shoulders. "Maybe The Dick didn't spend enough time with her during his formative years."

I almost choke on the forkful of ravioli I just shoved into my mouth. I chuckle as I chew. "I haven't called him that in a long time."

The Dick is the nickname I gave Mr. Calvetti after I worked with him for a week. Although I appreciate that the man has the weight of the world on his shoulders since he's managing the financial portfolios of some of the world's wealthiest people, his one-on-one skills are lacking.

Or at least they are with me.

He pays me enough that I don't take his rudeness to heart.

Sinclair runs a hand through her long brown hair, pushing it over her left shoulder. "Speaking of dicks, how is online dating going?"

"I thought we agreed to finish dinner before we talked about men."

Sliding her now empty plate to the side, she points at my almost empty bowl. "We're done. Are you ready to take the plunge and meet that guy you've been talking to online?"

Sinclair means well. Since we started living together a few months ago, she's been helping me wade through the muddy waters of online dating. In my case, it's app dating. Three weeks ago, I downloaded an app that matches singles in the five boroughs with each other.

I've had six matches so far, but only one is someone I'd consider meeting in person. Lowell Wellington is good-looking, funny, and building a career in finance. So far, we have loads in common, and our chats on the messaging system built into the app have been hours long.

He may be the ideal guy for me, right down to his close-cropped black hair, blue eyes, and eyeglasses.

"Soon." I sigh. "We're building up to it."

"Building what? Courage?" Sinclair glances at Marti. "If you're not that into him, why not ask Marti if she has a spare, hot-as-heck grandson she can set you up with?"

"That will never work. What if we hit it off and I end up marrying him?" I run a fingertip over the clasp of the silver bracelet I'm wearing. "I'd be related to Mr. Calvetti forever."

With a smile blooming on her lips, Sinclair shakes her head. "What if you end up marrying The Dick one day? Anything is possible, Arietta."

I finish the last of the red wine in my glass in one gulp. "If he were the last man on earth, I wouldn't…"

"If who were the last man on earth?" Marti appears next to our table. "Are you two talking about your boyfriends?"

I shake my head vigorously. "No."

"Maybe." Sinclair smiles at me. "Arietta is planning a date with a new guy."

Marti turns her attention to me. Warmth settles over her expression. I've never seen her with anything but a smile on her face. The day she found out I worked for her grandson, she hugged me and welcomed me into her extended family. She's the epitome of what a grandmother is, but her loyalty lies with Dominick, and I don't need my boss to know anything about my personal life.

"Tell me about him," she encourages as she picks up the bottle of wine from our table to refill my glass. "Is he cute?"

"Very," Sinclair offers. "He has a Clark Kent vibe."

Marti nods. "My late husband did too."

I have to take her word for it since I've never seen an image of him. Mr. Calvetti doesn't have any family pictures sitting atop his desk or decorating his office walls. The space is as cold as he is.

"Dominick has a different vibe," Sinclair says.

He sure as hell does. He fits the part of the villain in every superhero movie I've ever seen.

"He looks better than ever." Marti beams. "He left a little while ago. I told him to come early today, so I could spend an hour hugging him before I gave him a big piece of lasagna. It's his favorite."

His desire to leave the office early today suddenly makes sense.

"He always looks good." There's a hint of amusement in Sinclair's voice as she subtly winks at me. "You have a beautiful family, Marti."

"I do," she admits with a sigh. "It's getting bigger all the time. I hope one day my Dominick finds a woman who can handle him. He has the same wild streak his grandfather did. It took me to tame it."

There isn't a woman on this earth who can tame The Dick.

The three women who left messages for him today couldn't. He must have taken all of them to bed. Maybe he was with the two from Virginia at the same time.

I need to change the subject because a fire always gets lit inside me when I think of Mr. Calvetti having sex.

Bringing the wine glass to my lips, I take a small swallow. "What do you recommend for dessert, Marti?"

Stepping closer to the table, she rubs her palms on the white apron tied around her waist. "I'll get you both a piece of the honey ricotta cheesecake and an extra slice to take home to share for breakfast tomorrow."

"That's perfect." Sinclair claps her hands together. "It's my all-time favorite."

If a smile could be cashed in for currency, Marti's would be worth millions. "I'll run and get that now. You two stay put."

Sinclair clears her throat as soon as Marti disappears into the kitchen of the busy restaurant. "You drifted somewhere when she was talking about The Dick finding a woman who can handle him."

"I didn't." I punctuate the words with a shake of my head.

"You did," she counters. "Maybe you should step into his cage and see if you're the one who can tame him."

I'm as far from Mr. Calvetti's type as a woman can be. I laugh off the suggestion. "Me?"

Sinclair doesn't crack a smile. "Yes, you. Don't sell yourself short. You're beautiful. You're smart, and you're one of the most badass women I've ever met."

Pointing my index finger at her, I grin. "I can say the same about you, so I will."

"Look at us." She sits back in her chair. "We're two hotties stuffing our faces with Italian food. The men of this city have no idea what they're missing. That includes The Dick."

I don't think Dominick's missing anything.

Right at this moment, he probably has a woman pinned to a bed somewhere in this city while she screams his name.

"You're drifting again," Sinclair accuses. "Are you thinking about Dominick, or is it Lowell?"

It should be Lowell.

I want to daydream about him.

This seems like the perfect time to stop talking about men, so I circle back to what we were discussing on our way to the restaurant. "About that new phone I told you to get. When is that happening? It's been three days since you lost yours."

"I didn't lose it. I misplaced it," she corrects me. "It's too soon to get a new one. It might turn up. On the plus side, I'm getting a lot more work done now that I don't have a phone. There are zero distractions."

"At least use my tablet. Emailing me from your computer isn't working."

She laughs. "It's working fine for me."

It's not for me. Since she refuses to download a messaging app to her laptop, we've been stuck emailing each other. "I write enough emails a day for and to Mr. Calvetti. I need you to get a new phone, so we can go back to calling and texting."

"I'll do that soon." Sinclair picks up the wine bottle and empties what's left into her glass. "I know what you need more than anything."

"What?" I ask hesitantly.

"New lingerie."

"Why?"

"Because the night you meet Lowell, you want to be wearing something that will blow his mind before you blow him."

I laugh. "I'm not having sex with him on our first date."

"You never know." She lifts her glass as if to toast me. "Here's to wearing pretty lingerie and taking chances on first dates."

I raise my glass and tap it against hers. "Here's to good friends."

"Cheers!" she exclaims. "I want a preview of the lingerie so I can approve it before the date."

"Deal," I agree with a nod of my head.

New lingerie can't hurt, even if I have no intention of doing anything with Lowell before our third date.

Rules are rules, after all, and I always follow the ones I set for myself.

Chapter 4

Arietta

Cursing under my breath, I roll over in bed when I hear *it*.

The sound of fingernails dragging across a chalkboard means that Mr. Calvetti has sent me an email. I got used to hearing the alert from my phone at all hours of the day or night when he was in Sicily. I'm surprised to hear it this late since he's back in Manhattan.

The hairs on the back of my neck stand at attention.

The sound itself is jarring. I downloaded it after Sinclair directed me to an app that contained a catalog of audio clips, including what sounds like someone vomiting and another of a woman screaming.

I feel Dudley stir at my feet. He's a sweet Yorkshire Terrier. Technically he belongs to Sinclair, but we agreed to share custody. He's supposed to be in his kennel in the kitchen, but I snuck him out and brought him into my room after Sinclair went to bed.

I pick up my eyeglasses from the nightstand so I can see the time display on my phone.

It's almost midnight.

My boss's message sits on top of at least a dozen other work-related emails that have arrived since I left the office.

I slide my finger over the screen to find out what Mr. Calvetti wants.

Subject: Tomorrow A.M.

Miss Voss,

Arrange the delivery of an assortment of breakfast items to the office by 8 a.m. tomorrow.

Skip the place you used the last time as the croissants looked dry, and the berries were at least a day past their peak freshness.

Also, pick up two coffees from Palla on Fifth on your way to work. One is for me. The other for Mr. Fetzer. I trust you remember how he takes his coffee.

I expect you at the office at 7:45 sharp.

Signed,
Dominick Calvetti

Dropping my phone on the bed, I turn on my side, gather the pillow next to me in my hands, and scream into it.

For good measure, I scream a second time, adding a litany of curse words to the end of it.

My mom wouldn't be proud, but she'll never know that I tossed my swear jar in the trash when I started working for Dominick so I wouldn't go broke.

My boss could have given me a heads-up earlier that he wanted muffins, croissants, bagels, and fruit at the office first thing tomorrow. He's not going to touch any of it. I doubt Mr. Fetzer will either because he never remembers to put in his dentures before he comes to the office for his last-minute early morning meetings.

Seeing as how I have no choice but to fulfill his request, I scroll through the contact list on my phone.

There's one person I know will make Mr. Calvetti's breakfast wish come true.

Leta Conyers.

She's the assistant manager at one of the nicest hotels in Manhattan. She's also one of my neighbors. She lives on the third floor of this building.

Since I saw her less than an hour ago when I went to take Dudley for his last walk of the day, I'm confident that she's still awake.

She told me in the lobby that she left a boring date so she could binge-watch her newest Netflix obsession.

Hoping that she hasn't drifted off next to a big bowl of popcorn, I call her number.

She picks up on the first ring. "Arietta! Did you take my advice and start watching this show? The male lead is delicious, isn't he?"

"I'm going to start watching tomorrow night," I answer honestly. Sinclair and I are always looking for recommendations to add to our must-watch list.

"We'll compare notes." She laughs. "Don't say I didn't warn you. This guy is tall with dark hair and brown eyes. He's built for fulfilling women's fantasies. I wish men like that existed in real life."

They do. I work for one.

I skip past my personal, confusing thoughts about my boss and get to the reason I reached out to her at midnight. "I'm sorry I'm calling late, Leta, but I need help."

"I'll come up." I hear movement. "I've got your back, Arietta. If you need an alibi, you can count on me."

What the hell?

"An alibi?" I question with a half-laugh.

Leta giggles. "I'm sorry. Blame it on the show. Legal thrillers are my weakness."

Mine too. Her recommendation just shot to the top of my must-watch list.

"What do you need?" she goes on. "Whatever it is, I'm here to help."

"Food," I admit. "My boss sent me an email five minutes ago with a request for a breakfast spread eight hours from now. I ordered from a bistro in midtown last time, and he wasn't a fan."

"He'll be a fan of our breakfast," she says confidently. "Are you looking for pastry items or more?"

Since my co-workers and I will be the ones enjoying the food during our coffee breaks, I list a few of our favorites. "Muffins, donuts, bagels, croissants, some fruit, and maybe a few of those mini parfaits with the Greek yogurt you let me sample."

Leta welcomed me with open arms when I stopped by the Bishop Hotel one morning to greet a client who flew in from Boston the night before to meet with Mr. Calvetti. While I waited for the client to finish getting ready for the day, Leta sat me down in her office and brought me several breakfast items to try. The yogurt parfaits were my favorite.

"Done and done," she chirps.

"I can pick it up on my way to work."

"We'll deliver it to your office," she offers. "I'll bill it to Modica."

"Add a fifty percent tip since this is last minute." I rest my head back on my pillow. "You're a lifesaver, Leta. Thank you."

"Anytime." She yawns. "I'll send a text to the chef to get this ready for delivery first thing in the morning. Your boss will be happy, Arietta. I promise. Goodnight."

"Goodnight," I say before ending the call. Looking at Dudley, I place my phone back on my nightstand. "Leta can promise all she wants, but food won't make The Dick happy. Nothing will."

All I can hope for is that Mr. Calvetti will be semi-satisfied with the breakfast that awaits him, even if it never touches his lips.

I close my eyes and drift off, trying desperately to ward off thoughts of his perfect, full, kissable lips.

Chapter 5

Arietta

"You're the most beautiful young lady in this city."

I glance at the man showering me with that compliment. "That means a lot coming from you, Mr. Fetzer."

He flashes me a gummy grin. It makes him even more charming than he already is. With a slow wink of one of his light blue eyes, he points at the two trays of food that Leta had sent over. "Did you stay up all night baking for me?"

I sneak a glance at Mr. Calvetti, but his gaze is pinned to the screen of his phone. I didn't expect a thank you when he arrived at the office five minutes after me. He looked over the food, took a sip of the coffee that I had set by his chair at the head of the table in the conference room, and told me to bring Mr. Fetzer in to see him as soon as he arrived.

I nodded. I was tempted to say good morning, but I turned and walked away. I've learned to read the subtle nuances in my boss's body language. Today, his jaw was tight, and his shoulders tensed under the tailored navy blue suit he's wearing. Something or someone pissed him off. I don't think it's me. At least, I hope it's not.

"I can't take credit for any of this." I give him a soft smile. "I can cook, but I'm not a very good baker."

"My Eudora was a great baker." He looks at the tarnished silver band on the ring finger of his left hand. "Her pineapple upside-down cake never failed to make a bad day brighter."

I've heard countless stories of Mr. Fetzer's late wife. I listen to each one with wonder because their love story spanned sixty-five years. It's a real life fairytale with a tragic ending. She died from a heart attack one day before his eighty-eighth birthday.

"Why don't you take a seat?" Dominick pockets his phone as he gestures toward a chair at the table. "Miss Voss has work to do, so let's get down to business."

It's Mr. Calvetti's not-so-subtle way of telling me to get lost.

Mr. Fetzer sighs. "I'll stop by your desk on my way out, Arietta. Remind me to tell you about the blueberry banana muffins Eudora always made on our anniversary."

Shooting my boss a glance, I smile. "I can't wait to hear about that."

Dominick lifts a brow. I get it. I know when I'm not wanted.

I turn on my heel and march out of the conference room, closing the door quietly behind me.

***

"Let me guess," Bronwyn says as she crosses the break room to where I'm standing. "All of this was for Dominick's meeting with Mr. Fetzer?"

Nodding, I smile. "All of it. They didn't touch any of the food."

Their meeting took less than an hour, and when I went into the conference room to clear it, I immediately saw that the expensive trays of food were exactly as I'd left them.

I hummed a happy made-up tune as I carried the trays one at a time to the break room. The smiles on my co-workers' faces as I passed their desks told me everything I needed to know. I chose correctly when I asked Leta to handle this. She's my go-to now whenever Mr. Calvetti wants to impress a client with an array of breakfast treats.

"I want one of everything." Bronwyn grabs a small plate from the stack I placed next to the trays. "I'm so hungry lately. It must be that yoga class I'm taking. The more energy I exert, the more calories I need to consume."

She punctuates that by popping a mini lemon tart into her mouth.

Judging by the look of bliss on her face as she chews and then swallows, I'd guess it's even more delicious than the chocolate she gave me yesterday.

"Speaking of yoga." She wiggles both her dark, perfectly arched brows at me. "Tag along with me tonight. We had a lot of fun last time, remember?"

The last time I went to yoga with Bronwyn, she sat to the side texting on her phone while I worked my ass off. I twisted my body into poses I'd never done before.

The next morning, Sinclair had to help me tug my dress over my head.

I've limbered up since. All the yoga I do now is in my living room. Finding a yoga course online for free has always worked best for me.

"I can't. I have plans tonight."

Bronwyn's gaze drifts to my face. "You do? With who?"

She's as determined as Sinclair is to find me a boyfriend. After I had a disastrous blind date with her cousin, Bronwyn agreed to stop setting me up. She kept that promise for less than a month.

Every time she starts a conversation by telling me she found the perfect guy for me, I stop her mid-sentence with a shake of my head and a hand in the air.

I won't have to do that this time. "No one tonight, but I am going to buy lingerie for when I go to dinner with a guy I've been talking to on a dating app."

Her brown eyes widen. "Arietta! Why am I only hearing about this guy now?"

"I haven't even met him in person yet," I admit. "It's new. We're still getting to know each other."

She reaches for another lemon tart. "That's the way to do it. I've known the guy I'm seeing now for a couple of years. When things heated up a few months ago, we knew it was the right time."

I don't bother questioning her about who the guy is because I know she'll shut me down. She's keeping the details of her new romance quiet because she's worried she'll jinx it.

Bronwyn has convinced herself that's why her marriage ended. She boasted about her ex-husband to everyone who would listen until the day she went home from work early and found him in bed with one of her closest friends.

Glancing at my watch, I let out a huff. "I need to get back to my desk."

"Whoever the guy is, he's lucky. I hope he realizes that."

I hope so too. My history with men hasn't been stellar.

"You'll let me know how the date goes?" she asks with a grin. "I don't need all the behind-the-closed-door details unless you feel like sharing."

Laughing, I start toward the corridor that leads back to my desk. "It's going to be our first date. Nothing will be going on behind closed doors, Bronwyn."

"It might," she calls after me. "You wouldn't be buying new lingerie if there wasn't a chance for some action."

Smiling, I tug on one of the sleeves of the cream colored cardigan I'm wearing. I'm buying lingerie because I want to. Lowell will see it when I'm ready. I haven't decided when that will be yet, but it doesn't hurt to be prepared.

Chapter 6

Dominick

I watch Arietta take a seat at her desk. I should thank her for the work she did to get the food delivered to the conference room this morning, but I won't.

She was assigned a task that she completed.

I pay her to do that. Any accolades above and beyond that are unnecessary.

Judd considers his executive assistant, Bronwyn, a friend. Daniel views his right hand man, Paul, the same way.

Crossing the line between business and friendship muddies the waters. I can count my friends on one hand, two of them being the men I own this firm with. I'm satisfied with that.

Arietta glances in my direction. "Do you need something, sir?"

I've never *needed* anything beyond food, sleep, and a roof over my head. I've wanted things. I've craved experiences, but need is a beast I've been able to steer clear of.

"I take it that your fellow employees enjoyed the food?"

She smiles. Why the hell do I want to smile back at her?

I've seen this woman smile at me hundreds, if not thousands, of times. Something is different about it now. Or perhaps it's my reaction to it. If that's the case, I have to ignore the desire to respond to her smile with one of my own.

"They loved it." She claps her hands together. "I trust that you were satisfied as well?"

My mind twists those words into something that has absolutely nothing to do with food because that's not how I find satisfaction.

I drop my gaze to the purple eyesore she's wearing that she considers a dress and the pale cardigan that covers it.

"It was fine, Arietta."

When I glance back at her face, the smile is still there. It's less vibrant, more restrained, but it's just as genuine as it always is.

"Is there anything pressing you need me to do?"

"Reach out to Mrs. Blanchard," I direct. "In the event she answers, invite her to tea at the Waldorf the day after tomorrow. The afternoon works best for me."

Her eyes stay glued to my face. "You have back-to-back meetings booked the day after tomorrow."

"All of which can be rescheduled to accommodate Mrs. Blanchard."

Arietta knows about the woman I'm trying to snare in my net. Since her financial advisor is retiring, Clarice is on the hunt for another. I'm going to land that account, regardless of what it takes.

"You're determined to get her to sign with Modica, aren't you, Mr. Calvetti?"

Surely, that question is rhetorical, so I don't answer it. Instead, I watch as Arietta tugs on the sleeve of the cardigan that is swallowing her small frame.

"She will," she announces with a nod of her chin. "I'm confident she will, sir. "

"I'm the only man for the job. The sooner Clarice realizes that, the better."

"I'll do whatever I can to help," she offers.

"Call her, Arietta." Pushing back from my desk, I move to stand. "Call and arrange that meeting. Or at the very least, leave a message asking Clarice to contact me."

I feel her gaze pinned to me as I breeze past her desk on my way to the elevator.

"You're leaving?"

I turn back at the sound of her voice. "I'm meeting someone for lunch. Don't interrupt me. If anything pressing comes up, call Mr. Corning."

Without batting an eyelash, she smiles again. "Of course, sir. I hope you enjoy your lunch."

I won't.

***

When I enter the crowded diner, I spot the man I'm meeting right away. His left knee is bouncing up and down as he sits in an old wooden chair. His right hand is tapping an uneven beat on the circular table he's next to.

Anyone watching him might think he's anxious to eat his lunch, or a nicotine craving is hitting him hard.

I know better.

Taking a deep breath, I approach him.

Once he catches sight of me, he rises to his feet. His outstretched arms are an invitation I'd prefer to decline, but persistence is part of his DNA. If I don't accept the embrace, he'll push it until I do. I learned that when I was a kid and he'd come over on Saturday nights with his wife to play cards with my folks. His friendship with my dad reaches back to their grade school days.

I half-hug him quickly before I drop into the chair across from him.

"Dominick." My name leaves his lips with an air of disgust wrapped around it.

I recognize it. He's embarrassed. Shame taints his movements and the tone of his voice. No one who runs a multi-million dollar business wants to find themselves in his shoes even if they cost several thousand dollars.

"Brooks." I'd offer more, but we both know why he texted me this morning to ask me to meet him here for lunch.

Brooks Middlestat, sole heir to the Middlestat fortune, husband, father, and grandfather, has brought me here so he can plead, try to persuade, and eventually, threaten me to release part of his fortune so he can gamble it away.

He drops his head. "I need a favor."

Leaning back in my chair, I gesture to the approaching server to stop. She tosses me a look of confusion, so I point a finger sending her in the direction of another table.

"No," I answer succinctly.

He rakes a hand through his short gray hair. "I didn't get a chance to explain."

"You didn't need to." I lower my voice. "You got your allowance at the beginning of the month, Brooks."

His blue eyes hone in on me. I see desperation looking back at me. "I need more."

There's no reason to humiliate him by asking what he needs the money for. We both know the answer to that question. It's for a table game. Today it might be poker. Last month it was blackjack.

It's a dance we do regularly. Brooks invited me here because he knows I'll take the lead. He's paying me to. Part of the contract we both signed included an agreement that I'd supply him with a set allowance on the first of each month.

It's generous. It affords him enough to pay his bills and lavish an expensive gift on his wife on her birthday and their anniversary.

If she's not wearing a new set of earrings or a bracelet in the days after a special occasion, I notice.

"If you don't give me the money, I'll get it from someone else."

A threat this early in the conversation is concerning. It's not critical. We're not there yet, but it's time I bring out the game changer.

"Think about your grandson." I lean my forearms on the table. "How old is he now? Three months or is it four?"

His hand jumps to scrub the back of his neck. "Don't bring him into this, Dominick."

I tap my fist on the table to draw his gaze to mine. "You know I have to. You want that kid to be proud of you, Brooks."

I'm using his words against him because it's a weapon that has yet to let me down.

"How will he ever know if I hit up the casino today?"

"You'll know."

Guilt is a powerful tool when used wisely.

I agreed to keep Brooks on track in exchange for two percentage points more in my fee. It seems inconsequential, but with a fortune as vast as the Middlestat estate, it's substantial.

"I want to void the contract," he lies. "Let's go to your office and rip it up."

Desperation can drive a man mad.

Since the option of ripping up our contract is not based in reality, I offer an alternative. "Let's go to a meeting. There's one in Tribeca in an hour and a half. We'll eat something for lunch here and then head over there."

His gaze drops to the expensive watch on his wrist. The only reason it's still there and not in a pawnshop in Midtown is that it's an inheritance piece from his grandfather.

"You'll stick around while I'm in the meeting?"

I always do. I keep the schedule for every Gamblers Anonymous meeting in Manhattan in the calendar on my phone. When I was in Italy, my cousin, Nash Jones, stepped up to help out because his addiction brought him face-to-face with Brooks in a meeting two years ago.

I nod my head. "I'll be there."

Some of the weight that has been bearing down on his shoulders melts away. "Food would be good. The meeting will help. Thanks, Dominick."

I accept his gratitude with a nod of my chin. Brooks trusted me to handle his fortune. He needs me to keep him on course, so he doesn't blow through it at breakneck speed. I've come to accept that means that I'm at his beck and call.

I learned a long time ago that if I wanted wealth, it came at a price.

I'm more than willing to pay it.

Chapter 7

Arietta

I pretend to type out a document as I steal glances at Mr. Calvetti. He's standing ten feet from me, having a hushed conversation with one of his clients. Mr. Morano arrived just after Dominick got back from his hours long "*lunch meeting.*"

Those unexplained last minute meetings pop up every few weeks.

Mr. Calvetti disappears for hours at a time before he returns looking exhausted.

I try not to think about where he's been, but my mind never cooperates with that.

Today, I imagined it was a brunette with long legs and expensive perfume. Dominick couldn't resist the urge to be with her, so he rushed out of here to meet her at his apartment. Or maybe the desire was so overwhelming that they ended up in a bed in the hotel that's half a block from here.

I drop my gaze to my laptop screen.

Nothing I typed during the last five minutes makes any sense, so I close the document, deleting it in the process.

I shift my attention to all of the email messages I need to get through before the end of the day.

Any email directed to Mr. Calvetti through Modica Wealth Management's website contact form is my responsibility. I'm to use my discretion when deciding whether to forward any to Mr. Calvetti's private email.

I rush through the first three emails waiting in the queue. All are from potential clients, so I respond to those with Modica's standard questionnaire. No one is granted a meeting via phone or in person with Mr. Calvetti unless they meet specific criteria. It's his way of saying they need to be filthy rich.

The current size of my bank account disqualifies me. Sinclair's does too, since she works as a ghostwriter. She hasn't had a high-profile client yet, but she's determined to change that.

We share that in common. We've both set our long-term career goals high.

"Arietta?"

I glance up when I hear the unmistakable wheezy tone of Mr. Morano's voice.

I keep my focus on his face even though my impossibly sexy boss is standing right next to him. "Yes, sir?"

"Dominick won't confirm it, but I suspect that you're responsible for the bouquet that was sent to my daughter last week." A wink accompanies his sly grin. "She was delighted when she saw the flowers. It brightened her day."

My gaze shifts to Dominick. He's as stoic as ever.

He didn't ask me to send flowers to Melody Morano, but everyone deserves some sunshine after having four wisdom teeth pulled. When I was a kid, my dad brought a handful of artificial roses to the dentist's office the day I had a stubborn primary tooth removed. I still have those flowers. They're in a vase on a shelf in my bedroom.

I opted for fresh white and pink roses for Melody.

"Thank you for that, Arietta." He bows. "You made a young woman with a very sore jaw incredibly happy."

I take pride in knowing that. "I'm really glad, sir."

Dominick's expression hasn't changed since this conversation started. If I hadn't nicknamed him The Dick, Poker Face would be the next best choice.

"I'll be in touch tomorrow, Dominick." Mr. Morano slaps my boss on the shoulder. "Your advice is invaluable."

That's not true. It comes at a percentage of Mr. Morano's wealth. In his case, it's a steep percentage.

"Of course," Dominick dips his chin. "I'll speak with you tomorrow."

Mr. Morano takes that as the cue that it is and sets off toward the elevator.

Without a word to me, Mr. Calvetti heads down the corridor toward Mr. Corning's office.

"Grump," I whisper under my breath as soon as he rounds the corner and disappears from my view.

***

I stand outside Liore Lingerie on Fifth Avenue, gazing inside one of the windows. I've been here before. Sinclair has, and my other close friend, Maren, has too. Maren is Sinclair's sister-in-law, and both of them have invited me here in the past, but I've never tagged along with them.

It's not that I don't like pretty panties and bras. I do. I have many. Along with chocolate, I have a weakness for lace lingerie.

My mom took me to buy my first bra. We made an entire day of it, enjoying breakfast at a pricey café, followed by manicures, hair appointments, and finally a stop at a lingerie store her friend owned.

I picked out a pale blue lace bra that I hand washed as soon as we got home.

I wore it to school the next day under my sweatshirt. It made me feel grown-up. I felt pretty even though it was hidden from everyone.

I take a breath and pull open the door to the store. The bell hanging above the door signals my arrival. A woman in a wrap dress turns toward me. She raises a hand in the air. "Good evening. Welcome to Liore Lingerie."

I do feel welcome.

Smiling, I raise a hand in return. "Good evening to you too."

She makes her way over to me. Each tap of her heeled sandals on the floor sounds through the elegant space. "Are you looking for something in particular?"

Her warm smile puts me at ease. "Something pink. Maybe a shade lighter than your dress?"

She glances down before her gaze wanders over my shoulder. "A matching bra and panty set? That's what you bought the last time you were in, if I remember correctly."

I'm taken aback enough that my breath catches. "That was at least three months ago."

"Arietta, right?" She smiles. "I remember you because of your name. It's unique, just like you."

I take it as a compliment. "And you're Chantelle."

The nametag pinned to the front of her dress gave it away, but she still nods. "You're right. Are we picking out something for a special occasion?"

"A date," I answer quickly. "It's a first date, but he probably won't see it until a few dates later."

Her brows perk. "Playing hard to get is how I landed my husband."

I'm not playing. I may be hard to get, but that's because I'm worth the wait.

"Follow me." She starts across the showroom toward a display of lace bras. "I think I have something perfect for you."

Chapter 8

Arietta

The sound of a rooster crowing startles me enough that I almost spill my coffee all over my lap.

I glance toward Mr. Calvetti's office, but his gaze is stuck on the screen of his laptop.

If he heard the cock-a-doodle-do coming from my phone, he would have glanced in my direction.

I tell myself that as I switch my phone to silent before opening the email app.

I already know that the sound means Sinclair is writing to say good morning. She was still asleep when I left for work.

Stifling a laugh, I read the subject line before opening the email.

Subject: Lingerie for Lowell

Hey Arietta,

I'm awake!

Tell me that you bought new lingerie last night for your date with Lowell. Better yet, tell me that this date is going to happen soon.

The notes for this memoir I'm ghostwriting are the most exciting things in my life right now. Since I'm contractually obligated to keep the details to myself, let me just say that there is a 79-year-old woman in this city getting more action than either of us.

Her life story is so much better than mine – or yours!

You and Lowell need to hook up, and I need to hear about it.

Sinclair

"Miss Voss."

My head pops up at the sound of Mr. Calvetti's deep, rough voice.

Shit.

I look at his face since he's standing next to my desk.

"What was that sound I heard?" He taps his ear as if I'm unaware of how hearing works.

"What sound?" I play dumb, which in itself is a dumb move because that never works with my boss.

He glances at my phone. "That sound coming from your phone."

I drop my phone on my desk, screen side down. "It was a notification of an incoming email."

Based on the fact that his brows are drawn together, I doubt my answer satisfied his curiosity.

"It sounded like a rooster," he says. "Is that what it was?"

How the hell am I supposed to explain that my roommate grabbed my phone and set that sound to notify me of her incoming emails? Sinclair has a habit of whispering, "cock-a-doodle-do-me" whenever we see a guy with a noticeable bulge in his pants.

She giggles every time she does it, so I've never told her to stop because I love the sound of laughter.

The quickest and least painful way out of this is telling the truth, so I do. "Yes. It's a rooster."

"Why?"

What? Am I supposed to answer that question?

Do I come clean and tell him that Sinclair points out men with big packages before she tosses her catchphrase at me? Do I lie and say it's a reminder of all the mornings I woke up on a farm even though I've never stepped foot on one?

Just as I'm about to open my mouth to allow a string of lies to fall out, the office phone rings.

I owe the person on the other end a big thank you.

Glancing up at Mr. Calvetti's face, I answer the call. "Mr. Calvetti's office. How may I help you?"

"Is he there?" A woman's breathy voice floats over the line. "Please tell me he's there."

It's Teagan. Again.

"I'm sorry, but Mr. Calvetti is busy at the moment."

"You're serious?" Teagan grumbles. "How is he busy all the time? When he was here, he sure as hell made time for me. Put him on the line."

"I can't do that."

"Yes, you can." She raises her voice a notch. "Just do it."

My boss taps my shoulder. "Who is it?"

Nestling the phone's receiver against my chest, I whisper, "I'll handle it, sir."

That's enough of a hint to signal that I'm talking to a woman who wants more of whatever he was handing out in Virginia.

He takes a step back, nodding as he does.

My gaze falls from his face to his chest, and then it trails down, all the way to the front of his gray suit pants.

Cock-a-doodle-do-me. That's a bulge. A very nice-sized bulge.

He turns and walks into his office, so I turn my attention back to the phone.

"I'm sorry to keep you waiting," I say even though I gave her no indication I wasn't listening to her rant about how she needs to speak to Mr. Calvetti.

"When you get a chance, tell him that Teagan got something very special pierced, and it's not my ears." She giggles. "I need him to come and kiss it better."

Before I can stammer out a response to that, she ends the call.

I look to where Dominick is standing. He's gazing out one of the windows in his office.

Teagan has no idea that she's a distant memory to him by this point. All of the women he's slept with are.

I pick up my phone to put it away so I can focus on work. A notification from the dating app I've been using flashes across the screen.

I hurriedly open it.

My face lights up in a smile when I see Lowell has reached out to me.

Lowell: *Arietta! Have dinner with me tomorrow night. I can't go another day without seeing your beautiful face in person.*

I respond immediately. I need to take this chance. I doubt like hell Lowell is the type to fuck and flee like Mr. Calvetti does.

Arietta: *I'd love to.*

Shoving my phone in my desk drawer, butterflies flutter in my stomach. This is a big step, but it feels like the right one.

When I look into Mr. Calvetti's office again, he's moved.

He's standing near the open doorway with his gaze locked on me.

"Is there something you need, sir?"

"No," he says before he shuts the door without another word.

37

Chapter 9

Dominick

The last thing I expected to hear in my office was a goddamn rooster.

The sound took me to my feet. I waited for a moment after hearing it to see if Miss Voss would signal where it came from.

She did when her gaze immediately dropped to her phone.

Curiosity drove me to her desk, but before I could say a word, I was hit by the scent of her perfume.

It reminded me of the wildflowers that grow in Sicily in early spring. I closed my eyes and inhaled before I asked her what the hell was going on.

The look she gave me told me that I'd stepped into something personal. I was tempted to demand an explanation, but the incoming phone call interrupted that.

A series of soft knocks on my office door straightens me in my chair. "Yes?"

The door opens cautiously before Arietta peeks around it. The dark-framed glasses on her nose slip down. She pushes them up with her index finger. "Mrs. Glassman is here, sir. Her appointment isn't for another hour, but she's wearing a watch that isn't keeping time."

I watch as Arietta skims a hand over the red blazer she's wearing. The shoulder pads are from another decade. The yellow dress underneath was likely popular back when my mother was in her twenties.

"I'll see her now."

She nods. "If it's alright, I'll take her watch to the jeweler she bought it from. They are just down the street. Mrs. Glassman doesn't have anyone to help her with things like that."

Kindness always drips from my executive assistant.

"Fine," I answer. "Before you do that, get Mrs. Glassman a mug of..."

"Peppermint tea with honey," Arietta interrupts. "Bronwyn started on that for me. She'll bring it into your office the moment it's ready. I also emailed her the details regarding the upcoming meeting with Mr. and Mrs. Cunningham. She'll see to it that Mr. Corning has those in his hand immediately."

Was Judd's assistant the person emailing Arietta earlier, or was it a man?

I shake that thought away because why the fuck would it matter if it was a man?

A knot sits in the pit of my stomach. It has to be hunger. I skipped breakfast after my morning workout. Once this meeting is over, I'll head out for a coffee and a bagel sandwich.

"Are you sure it's okay if I go to the jeweler, sir?" she asks to confirm. "I can take care of it after work if you need me here."

"Go." I wave a hand at her. "Show Mrs. Glassman in and go get her watch fixed."

A broad smile lights up her face. "Thank you, sir."

I should thank her for taking such good care of my clients.

"I'll pick you up a coffee from Palla on Fifth and two egg whites on a whole wheat bagel on my way back."

What the fuck?

Arietta must spot the look of confusion on my face because she clears her throat. "I didn't mean to overstep. But I have that same look on my face when I'm craving something."

I scrub a hand over my forehead while I try to determine if I'm that predictable or if my assistant is a goddamn mind reader.

"Or I can skip the stop for your coffee and bagel if you prefer."

"No." My voice comes out deeper than I intend. "Make that stop, and thank you, Arietta."

That lures a broader smile to her mouth. "You're welcome."

She doesn't say it, but we both know that I've thanked her twice in three days. It stops now before she decides she deserves a raise for her good work.

"Show Mrs. Glassman in," I say, pushing to stand.

"Yes, sir." She nods before she turns to walk away, almost tripping over her own feet.

***

Forty minutes later, my assistant comes storming down the corridor toward my office with her hands full.

A cardboard beverage tray is in her left hand. In her right is a white paper bag with Palla on Fifth stamped across it. Under her right arm is a large box, and on that same shoulder is her oversized purse that she carts everywhere with her.

On top of that, she's soaking wet, as is everything she's carrying.

I desperately try not to crack a smile as I push back from my desk and stand.

Giggling under her breath, Millicent Glassman rises to her feet. "I swear she's the most precious thing in the world. Just look at her."

It's impossible not to.

Arietta approaches us with a grin. "I'm back."

The announcement is unnecessary, but I don't point that out.

Placing the tray on the corner of my desk, she drops the paper bag next to it. "I got a warm tea for you, Mrs. Glassman. It's just the way you like it."

Millicent claps her hands together in delight. "Thank you, dear."

"I also got this." Arietta tugs on the cardboard box under her arm. It's a puzzle of a zebra. "I saw it in a toy store window on my way back to the office. I thought your grandson would like it since he's into zebras right now."

How the hell does she know that?

"Arietta! It's perfect! He's going to love this!"

My assistant sighs. "Now, about the watch."

Millicent's smile vanishes. "Was there a problem?"

After fishing in her purse blindly, Arietta produces a watch box. "I have it."

"I don't understand," Millicent says as she takes it in her hands. "Why is it in a box?"

Arietta sweeps a hand over her forehead to push back a few strands of wet hair that have fallen from her lopsided bun. "The owner of the store tried to tell me that the watch didn't have a lifetime warranty."

"They told me it did when I bought it."

I saw the watch. It's a hundred or perhaps a two hundred dollar piece. That's a drop in the bucket to Millicent. She's frugal, which is one of the reasons she's amassed the fortune she has.

"They have a sign hanging in the store window which claims that every watch comes with a lifetime warranty." Arietta drops her purse into one of the chairs that face my desk. "He pointed out the fine print at the bottom of the sign that states exceptions apply."

Millicent's back straightens. "Mine was one of the exceptions? You didn't have to buy me a new one."

Arietta smiles. "I didn't."

"Then how did you get this?" Millicent questions as she opens the watch box.

"I asked to see a list of exceptions," Arietta says. "He couldn't produce it, so I pointed out that under New York State Law, that warranties made orally are binding."

I'm just as mesmerized as Millicent as I listen to Arietta state her case.

"He decided it was in his best interest to replace the watch. He included a new lifetime warranty in writing and free cleaning and battery changes when I told him I was going to contact New York State's Division of Consumer Protection to lodge a complaint."

Stunned speechless, I stare at Arietta.

Millicent launches herself at her. "Thank you! I can't thank you enough."

Arietta hugs her. "There's no need to thank me. It was the right thing to do."

My assistant has a habit of doing the right thing. That's only one of the many ways we differ.

In my hand, the watch would have landed in the trash. Yet now, my client is happier than I'm ever seen her, and Arietta is the person responsible for that.

"I'm going to clean up." Arietta runs a finger over her chin. "I'll be back at my desk shortly, sir."

She picks up her purse and heads out of my office. I stare at her back while Millicent once again sings her praises. "Hold onto this one, Dominick. I like her better than any of your other assistants."

I'd never admit it out loud, but I'm beginning to as well.

Chapter 10

Arietta

Since I crawled out of bed before dawn, it's no surprise that I was the first to get to the office today. I didn't plan on it, but the nerves bouncing inside of me because of the anticipation of my date tonight kept me on the move.

I took Dudley for two morning walks before I cracked open Sinclair's bedroom door to let him sneak inside. I could have put him in his kennel in the kitchen, but she likes to cuddle with him as much as I do.

I could still hear Sinclair typing on her laptop when I went to bed at midnight. I didn't want to disturb her then or this morning as she slept. I know she's on a tight deadline to get her most recent manuscript turned in.

Even though her oldest brother, Berk, is the owner of the publishing company that contracted her to ghostwrite the book, Sinclair never asks for extensions or favors. She takes her job seriously.

I do too.

I have a mountain of work to get through today. I'm starting that with a large coffee and another phone conversation with the very persistent Teagan.

"Listen." She sighs heavily into the phone. "I need you to give him a message for me. Promise me you'll do that."

How can I keep that promise?

Before I have a chance to relay that to Teagan, she starts talking again. "Tell him his lips are the purest form of pleasure this side of the Mississippi."

The pen in my hand tumbles to my desk.

"Pardon….um…what did you just say?" I stutter out the question.

She repeats what she just said word-for-word at a snail's pace, enunciating each syllable.

I follow along, writing it all down. I read it again and then again. Is she talking about the way he kisses or oral sex? Is Mr. Calvetti that good at eating a woman out that it's pure pleasure?

"Repeat it back to me," she demands.

Um. No. That's not happening.

"Hold please," I say to give me a second to catch my breath.

I have a date tonight with Lowell. I can't be thinking of Mr. Calvetti with his face between my thighs. No, Teagan's thighs. It was Teagan's thighs, not mine.

Just as I'm about to take Teagan off of hold so I can end this call, the elevator dings in the distance, signaling its arrival on this floor.

I dart to my feet. There's only one person who would show up this early.

I brace myself for it, but I'm still not prepared.

My heart does that flip-flop thing it always does when Mr. Calvetti comes into view.

Today he's wearing a dark gray suit with a light blue button-down shirt and a striking royal blue tie.

If he didn't manage billions of dollars, he could be a model.

For the briefest of seconds, I imagine him cruising shirtless up and down a runway at New York Fashion Week wearing a pair of board shorts with a T-shirt slung over his shoulder.

"Miss Voss," he calls out to me, ending my fantasy. "You're here early."

I nod my head up and down, trying to knock the vision of him half-naked out of my mind.

A red light on my desk phone starts blinking. It's a reminder that Teagan is still waiting on hold.

I bite the bullet and pass on the message because I don't think she's going to give up until she gets another taste of his lips. Or his lips tasting her. The gist is that she wants his lips and him.

"Sir, there's a woman on line one." I suck in a deep breath. "She's called numerous times. She wanted me to tell you that ..." I glance down at the message pad on my desk. "Your lips are the purest form of pleasure this side of the Mississippi."

He stops mid-step just mere feet from my desk. "What did you say?"

Seriously? Why does everyone want me to repeat that sentence?

I rip off the message and shove it at him. "Here."

He doesn't glance down.

Balling the paper into his fist, he leans toward me. "I have told you repeatedly to ignore all messages left for me by women who are not related to me or those in need of financial advice."

He tosses the crumpled paper toward the wastebasket next to my desk. Naturally, he makes the shot. "Is that clear?"

"Yes," I whisper, not bothering to add '*sir*' on the end of it because he's more of a selfish jerk than a man who deserves respect right now.

"Good." He starts toward his office door. "I want my coffee in..."

"Ten minutes," I interrupt because we do this same song and dance almost every morning.

Without so much as a glance back at me, he walks into his office and shuts the door behind him.

I drop back into my chair and pick up the receiver of the phone. For the first time, I can finally tell Teagan the truth, even though it's bound to give her false hope. "Sorry to keep you waiting. I gave Mr. Calvetti your message."

"You did?" Her voice is giddy. "What did he say?"

"He has a busy morning." I close my eyes, wishing I could tell her to forget about him because he's undoubtedly forgotten about her.

"I'll wait to hear back from him."

Since I can't tell her that she'll be waiting for the rest of her life, I end the call by wishing her a good day.

I sure as hell hope mine improves.

So far, this Friday is turning out to be a flop.

Chapter 11

Dominick

Scanning her from head-to-toe, I take the cup of coffee that Arietta offers.

Black sensible shoes, a green and white striped skirt, and a black turtleneck are quite the look for a spring day.

Again, as always, her hair is pinned into a makeshift up-do.

"Is there anything else, sir?"

My gaze drifts to her face because there was a subtle bite of venom coating that last word as it left her tongue.

"I need you to draft up an email to Mrs. Blanchard since our previous attempts to connect with her have gone unanswered."

Arietta glances at my laptop. "Do you have an outline for that, or should I wing it?"

Wing it?

I bow my head to hide the grin that has popped onto my lips.

"I mean, if you don't have a general idea of what you'd like the email to say, I can craft something with a friendly tone that might garner a response from Mrs. Blanchard."

That's what I'm looking for, so I nod in agreement. "Do that."

She scuffs the toe of one of her shoes against the floor. "I'll start on that now."

"Send it to me once you have a draft complete," I instruct. "I'll fine-tune it before we send it to Mrs. Blanchard."

It's a simple task. I expect she'll be done within the hour. If it hits a chord within Clarice, there is a chance I'll hear from her today.

That's the goal.

"Is there anything else?" Arietta asks again out of habit.

She's accustomed to me assigning her at least a dozen tasks each morning. Since I sent her an email last night with a number of them listed, I have nothing new to add now.

"Get the draft of the email done first." I point a finger past her toward where her desk sits outside my office. "Once that is complete, you can begin work on everything else I outlined in the email I sent last night."

Since she hadn't responded to it before I went to bed, I can only assume that she read it.

"All right." She takes a step back. "You know where to find me if you need anything."

I won't need anything, so I drop my gaze to my desk. "That's all, Arietta."

The next sound I hear is the door of my office softly clicking shut.

I turn in my chair to face one of the windows that offers a view of Lower Manhattan. The sun is rising in the distance. Many of the millions who call New York City home will be getting their days started. Living life in this city should offer a daily respite from solitude, but for me, it never has.

It never will.

***

Two unnecessary telephone conversations later, I finally lean back in my chair. A potential client called. They easily passed the initial criteria for a phone meeting with me, but I won't be taking them on.

Their ideas for smart investments don't align with mine.

48

I refuse to work with someone who believes it's wise to sink a quarter of a million dollars into a dog acting class run by their mistress.

When said client called back after I explained that he should find another wealth management company, he called me a '*loser*' and hung up on me.

Substantial wealth at a young age rarely comes without issues.

He's twenty-six and already making mistakes that will cost him for years, seeing as how he confessed in a hushed tone that both his wife and mistress are expecting babies.

I wake up my laptop with a touch of the trackpad.

My email program immediately comes into view. I scan the new messages, stopping at one that arrived from Miss Voss less than fifteen minutes ago.

I read the subject line once and then again to make sure I'm not seeing things.

Shaking my head in disbelief, I click on the email to open it.

Subject: The Dick

Hey Sinclair,

Mr. Calvetti is as ornery as ever today.

He scolded me for taking a message from a woman who asked me to pass along this to him – "*your lips are the purest form of pleasure this side of the Mississippi!*"

She may not be a poet, but she is obviously head over heels for him, so I thought I'd play cupid and give him the message.

Dominick (The Dick) Calvetti told me once again to ignore all messages women leave for him.

He's a cruel bastard with a gorgeous face and rock hard abs. I imagine he has those. He's 6'3" and works out every morning. He has to be built under those suits, right? I know that the nickname I gave him is based on his attitude, but I sometimes wonder if it "fits" in other ways if you know what I mean. Even if it does, I still loathe him. He's the worst boss on both sides of the Mississippi.

I attached a picture of the lingerie I bought for my date tonight. I snapped a selfie in the mirror this morning since you were still asleep.

Let me know what you think, roomie.

Arietta xoxo

P.S. Tomorrow we're getting you a new phone. I miss texting. Emailing is for old people like The Dick.

What the fuck is this?
The Dick? Arietta nicknamed me The Dick? She has no idea how apropos that is.
Against my better judgment, I let curiosity take control as I download the attached picture meant for her roommate's eyes.
As soon as I get a glimpse of Arietta in a pale pink lace bra and panty set, all the air leaves my lungs.
I stare at it, at her with her long blonde hair draped around her shoulders and the eyeglasses she always wears perched on top of her head.
Jesus Christ.
My heart is racing. My mind is trying to comprehend what I'm seeing, and my dick is as hard as stone.

My executive assistant's body can drive a man down to his knees.

I close the picture, willing myself to forget I ever saw it, but I can't.

The image of her full round breasts covered in lace, her toned stomach, and those pink panties will forever be burned in my mind.

I snap the cover of my laptop closed and push back from my desk.

The urge to fire her is strong. The desire to fuck her is stronger.

I won't do either.

Instead, I move to the window and stare out of it, willing myself to calm down enough to figure out how the hell I'm going to handle this and her.

Chapter 12

Arietta

"What time did you get to work this morning?" Bronwyn asks as she slides half of a poppy seed bagel across the table toward me. "You can eat this if you didn't get a chance to grab breakfast."

"Thank you," I say softly. "I was here before the sun came up."

She takes a bite of the half bagel in her hand. "Did Dominick dump extra work in your lap again?"

That's an ongoing thing. He always assigns me more work than he thinks I can accomplish in one day. I've never fallen short of completing it all.

It feels like a competition, even if Mr. Calvetti would never admit that's what it is.

"It's not that. I'm nervous," I confess.

Bronwyn gazes around the break room. Since three of our co-workers are sitting at a table less than ten feet away, she lowers her voice. "Why?"

I pick up my half of the bagel but set it back down on the paper napkin before I take a bite. "I'm going out for dinner with that guy I told you about."

Bronwyn sits up straighter in her chair. "Tonight?"

I nod. "I'm excited, but there are a million butterflies in my stomach right now."

She pushes the bagel closer to me. "Eat, Arietta. You don't want to pass out tonight right before the good stuff happens."

I can't tell if she's joking, so I perk both of my brows. "What?"

"Sex uses a hell of a lot of energy." She chuckles. "Good sex does, so eat up."

I'm not hungry, and I'm not in the mood to remind her that I don't have sex on the first date.

I glance at the clock hanging on the wall behind her. "I need to get back to my desk soon."

Her gaze drops to the watch on her wrist. "We have seven minutes."

I pick up the bagel and take a small bite. Chewing it slowly, I wait for her to say something.

She adjusts the collar of the pristine white blouse she's wearing. After clearing her throat, she grins. "I know that you're not comfortable getting physical with a guy right away. I get that, but don't let that get in the way of a great goodnight kiss."

The corners of my lips curve up in an uncontrollable smile. "I do like kissing."

"Me too." Her eyes widen. "I thought my first kiss was amazing until I grew up and realized what a great kiss is."

The sudden jarring sound of fingernails racing down a chalkboard startles us both.

Bronwyn cringes. "What the hell was that?"

Laughing, I point at my phone on the table. "It's the notification I set on my phone for Mr. Calvetti's incoming emails."

That lures a giggle from her. "That's ingenious, Arietta."

"It's fitting."

She smiles at me. "I know I lucked out when I landed my job. Dominick isn't anything like Judd."

That's an understatement.

I glance at my phone. "I should read the email, but I already know what it's going to say."

"What?"

I lower my voice, trying to mimic Mr. Calvetti's gruff tone, but I fail miserably as soon as I say my name. "Miss Voss…"

Bronwyn lets out a laugh so loud that the people sitting near us turn to look. They join in, not knowing what they're laughing at.

Once the laughter fades, I lean in toward Bronwyn and whisper, "I had to draft an email to Mrs. Blanchard to try and convince her to meet with Mr. Calvetti. I sent him the draft before my coffee break. He likely changed ninety percent of it and sent it back to me."

"The email I sent on Judd's behalf two days ago didn't even garner a response from her."

I'm not surprised. Mrs. Blanchard is making Judd and Dominick work hard to get her attention. Her attorney intercepts every phone call, and all the emails we send go unanswered.

I looked her up online in the hopes of gaining some insight into what she likes or what's important to her, but I came up empty. There was a brief mention of her in an article about her late husband, but that's all that my search garnered. I wasn't surprised. Many of Modica's clients keep a very low profile. Wealth comes with benefits, but it comes with risks too.

I glance at the clock on the wall again. "I better get back."

"Finish the bagel while you read the email," Bronwyn suggests. "That counts as work, right?"

I half-shrug my shoulder. "In my book it does."

I pick up my phone and glance at the screen. I'm not surprised to see a string of notifications. There are several for emails from clients, one for a text message from my friend Maren, and the most recent is an alert that Mr. Calvetti has indeed sent me an email.

I click on that one first.

I blink when I read the subject line. Confused, I read it again and then a third time. That's the subject line of the email I sent to Sinclair right before I took my coffee break.

With my stomach twisting and my heart in my throat, I click open the email.

Subject: Re: The Dick

Miss Voss,

Thank you for your email.

I hardly think 34 is considered old, and for the record, I'm 6'4".

Details matter. Sending an email to the intended recipient matters more, especially when you include a sensitive image exposing so much of your body.

Also, cancel your date, as you will now be working late tonight.

And report to my office. Immediately.

Signed,
THE DICK

"XOXO"

My phone tumbles from my shaking hands into my lap.

This is bad. This is *I've-ruined-my-life* bad.

How the hell did Mr. Calvetti end up receiving the email I sent to Sinclair?

"Arietta?" Bronwyn asks quietly. "You look pale. Is something wrong?"

I don't raise my head to look at her. I can't form one word in response to her question.

I screwed up so badly. All of my dreams are disappearing from my grasp.

Why did I write Sinclair an email when I was preparing the one for Mr. Calvetti? I must have opened and closed them both so many times that I got mixed up and typed the wrong messages into the drafts.

"Do you want a glass of water?" Bronwyn pushes to her feet. "I'll get one."

Water won't help me. Nothing will.

I've destroyed my life. I should leave the building now before Mr. Calvetti has the chance to fire me.

I pick up my phone and reread the email.

He wants me to work late, so there's still hope.

Maybe he won't kick me to the curb for calling him a dick.

A million thoughts race through my mind as I try and come up with an excuse for the nickname.

"Drink this." Bronwyn shoves a glass half-filled with water at me.

I swallow it all before I push to stand. "I need to go see my boss."

She rests her hands on my shoulders. "Was there something in the email you sent him that he didn't like?"

Answering that question would take at least an hour. It's time I don't have to spare.

"I need to discuss that with him." I hug her quickly.

"All right," she says skeptically. "I'm down the hall if you need me."

I won't need her. I need courage.

I have to face a man I called a dick who has now seen me dressed in nothing but underwear.

This Friday just went from bad to catastrophic, and it's not even ten a.m. yet.

Chapter 13

Dominick

I tug on the collar of my shirt. It feels tight, my tie is knotted too stiffly, and my cock is still waging war against my common sense.

I've looked at the picture of Arietta in her lingerie three times since I first opened the email.

Deleting it would be the right thing to do, but I have never done the right thing, so why start now?

A soft knock at my door sends my pulse racing.

I have to face my meek assistant, who parades around the office in clothing that doesn't fit her. She's been doing that since she was hired, all the while hiding lush curves underneath it.

I fucking hate the bastard who has a date lined up with her tonight.

Jesus, I feel like I've stumbled into a time machine and shot back to high school when my dick directed everything.

"Come in," I say in a strangled tone.

The door opens slightly, but there's no one in view.

If this is the game she wants to play, I'll go along with it. I have all day and night to deal with this.

She finally steps into my sight.

I'm surprised that there's no evidence that she's cried. I assumed that she might burst into tears after reading my reply to her email.

"You wanted to see me, sir," she says as if it's any other morning.

"Close the door behind you, Arietta."

She steps in just far enough to swing the door shut behind her. Once she's done that, she backs up until her ass is resting against the door.

Her ass.

If it's as curvy as the rest of her, it's perfection.

I wish to hell she had offered her roommate a view of that in the form of a picture.

I shake off that thought.

"I'm sorry, sir." Her voice remains steady, calm even. "That email was supposed to go to my roommate. I was frustrated when I wrote it. I don't think you're a dick."

I fight to ward off the smile I feel inside. "I've been called much worse, Arietta."

"You have?" Surprise taints her tone.

I won't go into specifics, but I know my reputation. I haven't gotten to where I am in life by making nice with everyone I meet. The world is a cold place designed to reward those who fight for what they want. I've done that, and I've been compensated kindly for it.

"I didn't mean it when I wrote that you're a cruel bastard either." She tests her luck by sneaking that in. "I felt frustrated because of the woman who called earlier."

There's no way in hell I'm diving into a conversation with Arietta about a former lover of mine.

"She likes you a lot, sir," she persists. "I think she feels something special for you."

Since I feel nothing for whoever it was, it's irrelevant.

I am crystal clear with the women I spend time with. We have dinner. We fuck. We say goodbye.

They know that before they take their first sip of wine.

"I appreciate your concern, Miss Voss," I lie. "However, my personal life and how I conduct it is not up for discussion."

Speaking of which, realizing how hypocritical it is, I still ask the question that's been perched on my tongue since she walked into my office. "Did you cancel your date for this evening?"

Her gaze drops to the phone in her hand. "Not yet. I believe that whatever you need me to do tonight, I can finish before six. This date is important to me, sir."

"Is it with your boyfriend?"

No part of that question is related to my position as her boss. I want to know if she's seeing someone.

"Lowell and I haven't met yet," she says his name, and I immediately feel the hairs on the back of my neck stand up.

What kind of name is that? He's probably coasting along at an Ivy League school thanks to his old-money family.

"You haven't met yet?" I repeat her words back.

"We've talked for hours." Her eyes dart up as her lips curl into a grin. "We connected on a dating app."

She's searching for a man on a dating app? She's brilliant, well educated, insightful, and kind. Any man would be fortunate to be in her presence.

What the fuck is wrong with the men in this city?

"I shouldn't say anymore." She levels her gaze on mine. "You said our personal lives aren't up for discussion."

I sure as hell did not say that, but I admire her for pushing back.

"Tell Lowell that you need to postpone." Disdain drips from my tone as I say his name. "I need you to restructure the filing system. I want every client's file entered into the computer."

Her mouth drops open. "Tonight?"

"You'll start on it tonight. I expect you to have it all completed by Monday."

"I have to work all weekend?"

"You've been asking for this for months, Arietta." I'm not above pettiness. She did call me a dick and a cruel bastard in that email. "Didn't you say it would streamline our system?"

Her gaze drops to the floor. "Yes, I did say that."

I open my laptop. "Get started now, Miss Voss."

Mumbling something under her breath, she nods before she turns, opens the door of my office, and walks out.

Chapter 14

Arietta

I shove another piece of ginger beef into my mouth as I watch the expression on Maren's face. It turns from shock to concern almost instantly.

"Arietta," she says my name in one long slow breath. "You could have been fired for sending him that email."

Sinclair nods her head. "That's what I said."

Both of my best friends were kind enough to buy dinner and bring it to my office. I've been here since seven this morning, and since it's now twelve hours later, I needed food and friendship. This time in the break room with them will give me the energy I need to power through the next few hours until I head home to bed.

Maren slides her fingers through her curly red hair. I catch sight of her wedding rings. I always feel happy when I see them. Maren fell in love with her boss Keats Morgan, and now they're married and expecting their first baby together.

She's always joked to me about how I will marry Mr. Calvetti.

He may be dreamy to look at, but he's not my type at all.

Yesterday proved that.

Spite is drove him to assign me the task of shifting the entire filing system to electronic mode. He never wanted it before I sent that email. His goal was to steal my weekend away from me. He succeeded, but I feel like I won our latest battle.

I still have my job, and the new filing system makes that job much easier.

"It was a mistake." I run a paper napkin over my lips. "I messed up. He forgave me, and we'll never talk about it again."

I hope.

When Dominick left the office last night with a smug grin on his face, he wished me a good weekend.

I did the same to him, but as soon as he was out of view on his way to the elevator, I flipped up my middle finger.

It was childish and harmless since he couldn't see it, but it made me feel better.

"He's seen you without your clothes on," Maren points out.

I was going to leave that out of the story about what happened yesterday morning, but Sinclair piped up and added it in.

I can't blame her. She's Maren's sister-in-law. They share everything with each other.

"I was wearing a bra and panties in the photo." I stab another piece of beef with my fork. "Besides, the picture was grainy, and the lighting was bad."

That's a fib.

Maren and Sinclair will never know that since I deleted the picture from my phone after realizing I sent it to my boss.

I lean back in the chair I'm sitting in and cross my legs. I'm dressed in a pair of black sweatpants and a white T-shirt. I'd never come to the office like this on a regular workday, but since I'm the only one who has been here all day, I knew my wardrobe choice wouldn't matter.

"Do you want to know what I think?" Sinclair asks with a glimmer of something mischievous in her eye.

Shaking my head, I answer first. "No."

Maren laughs. "Yes."

Sinclair points at her sister-in-law. "Good answer. I think Dominick Calvetti is hot for you. I think that picture did something to him. What man in his right mind wouldn't want to do you after seeing your body?"

I narrow my eyes. "Were you writing and drinking again before you came here?"

Maren barks out a laugh. "You do that, Sin?"

Shaking her head, Sinclair scowls. "Never. I took too much cough medicine once and tried to write, but that's a story for another time."

I laugh for the first time today. "Let's hear it now."

"No." Sinclair waves a finger at me. "Let's talk about how Mr. Calvetti has stroked out one or two to that picture of you."

I drop my gaze to my lap. "He hasn't."

"I'd bet money that he has." Maren reaches for my forearm and squeezes. "You have a gorgeous body, Arietta."

I agree. I love my body. I work to keep it toned and strong.

I don't agree with the idea that Mr. Calvetti found it alluring. The man has a different lover almost every night. That picture of me in my underwear did nothing for him. He didn't even bring it up when we spoke about the email.

It wasn't important enough for us to discuss, so it's a moot point.

"Lowell will agree with us once he sees it." Sinclair winks at me.

Maren turns to her. "Who?"

"He's the guy Arietta should have been banging last night." Sinclair arches a brow. "Calvetti put a stop to that, but Arietta is determined to get a piece of Lowell."

Chuckling, I add, "Lowell is a guy I met on a dating app, Maren. I was supposed to go out with him last night for dinner. It was just a dinner, but I had to postpone. I'll talk to him tonight to set up a new time for our date."

Maren rubs her small baby bump. "Do you think he might be someone special?"

I can read between the lines. Maren wants me to find the same type of happiness she did. She's six years older than me. She didn't meet Keats until she was twenty-eight. I should point that out, but I don't.

"Time will tell," I say with a grin.

"You'll tell me how your date goes, right?" She questions me before she shifts her attention to Sinclair. "What about you? Have you met someone on a dating app too?"

"When the hell would I have time for that?" Sinclair raises both hands in the air in mock frustration. "Berk works my ass off. I swear my brothers never want me to meet a man."

We all laugh.

"You two are the best," I say softly. "Thank you for the food and for coming down here. It means a lot to me."

"You mean a lot to both of us." Sinclair reaches for my hand. "If you're stuck here on a Saturday night, we'll stick around for you."

I push back to stand. "You should go home. I have at least a few more hours of work tonight. I'm determined to show Mr. Calvetti that I can do this."

Maren darts to her feet. "You will, Arietta. You're a superstar. There's nothing you can't do."

I believe her.

I'll finish this task, and then I'll reward myself with a night out with Lowell. That's a win-win for me.

Chapter 15

Dominick

"Just look, Dominick." Judd shoves his phone at me. "Look how beautiful that kid is."

I take the phone and look at the screen. I twist it sideways before I have it upside down in my hand. "What the hell am I looking at?"

I know exactly what I'm looking at. It's a sonogram picture. My youngest sister, Bella, send me a string of them when she was pregnant with her daughter. She even framed one that she presented to me when she asked me to be the kid's godfather.

"That's my daughter," Judd says, his voice shaky. "After three boys, I'm about to be a girl dad."

"Congratulations," I offer because I sense that's what he's looking for.

"You know what this means, right?" He lifts the bottle of beer in his hand as if he's about to toast to something.

I follow suit and bring mine to within an inch of his. "It means that there's a strong possibility that she'll date a kid who is just like you when you were sixteen."

All of the color drains from his face. "What the hell?"

Chuckling, I lightly tap my beer bottle against his. "Here's to years of you being an overprotective girl dad."

He downs what's left of his beer. "Jesus. What am I getting myself into?"

I can't offer an answer to that. He's a few months away from being a father of four. He started down this path ten years ago when his wife Judith gave birth to their first son.

"How's Judith feeling?" I ask, genuinely curious about how she's holding up.

Her third pregnancy was rough. She ended up in the hospital for weeks during her third trimester.

His mood shifts instantly. "You know Judith. She's thrilled."

I do know her. She was in my English Lit class during my senior year of high school. On the third day, she asked me who the blond guy with the ocean blue eyes was. I gave her Judd's number, and the rest is history.

I take another drink. "Good."

"You're falling behind." Judd motions for the server to bring another round. "You're not even married yet, and I've got a full house with another about to be born."

I glance around Durie's, the bar that Judd and I regularly meet up at. I catch the eye of a brunette. It's the second time since I walked in that I've glanced in her direction. There's an invitation there. I sense it. The question is will I accept it or not.

It's Saturday night. I've got nothing going on, so it should be an easy yes.

Leveling my gaze back on Judd's face, I lift a brow. "It's not a competition, Judd. We're not all destined to be husbands and fathers."

He glances over his shoulder. "That woman has her eye on you."

I ignore the comment to circle back to the reason I asked him here. "Give me an update on Clarice Blanchard."

Exhaling heavily, he shakes his head. "I haven't made any progress there. We need face-to-face time with her before she signs with someone else."

Indeed we do.

After the email mix-up yesterday, Arietta sent me her draft of my email to Clarice. It was charming and professional with an air of thoughtfulness woven into it. I sent it out immediately, but I'm still waiting for a response.

If we sign Clarice to our firm, she'll jump to the position of our number one client. Her wealth is vast. We'll make a mint, but we'll also provide her the best financial advice that much money can buy.

The server slides two beers onto the bar between us. "Here you go, gentlemen."

I reach into the back pocket of my jeans, pull out my wallet, and hand him a few bills.

He's not discreet about it. He fingers them, counting as he goes. "You're serious, man?"

Judd laughs. "He's a fucking show-off. Take it and run before he changes his mind."

"Thanks." The server tips his chin. "This is half my rent for the month."

Good service deserves a reward. I always tip well.

"You made his night." Judd takes a small drink from the fresh bottle of beer. "Hopefully, he doesn't spend it all on weed and video games."

Huffing out a laugh, I glance back at the server. He's excitedly showing his tip to a young woman dressed just as he is in a white button-down shirt and black pants. "He's not fifteen, Judd."

"He's twenty-one. Maybe twenty-two." He chuckles. "I had Judith to ground me when I was that age. You were a wild child still. The only thing on your mind was…"

I interrupt him with a hand in the air. "Making money."

"I was going to say pussy and beer, but I agree, you were chasing the almighty dollar even back then."

"I need to get in on this conversation."

Judd and I both glance in the direction of a breathy feminine voice. It seems the leggy brunette has invited herself over.

Her gaze settles on my face. "Is someone going to buy me a drink? Whiskey suits me just fine."

Still undecided whether I'll take this beyond the bar, I turn to find the server.

I scan the interior of the pub, but I don't see him.

Instead, I spot a couple at a table in a dimly lit corner. The guy is young. The ball cap on his head gives that away. The hoodie he's wearing is emblazoned with the logo of a second-rate baseball team. It should be hidden in a box in the back of his closet, not on display when he's obviously on a date.

The blonde facing him has her back to me. Her hair is pinned up in a crooked, messy bun. She's wearing a purple sweater and what looks like black pants. From my vantage point, I can make out the arm of a pair of eyeglasses when she glances to the side.

Is Arietta here? Is that Lowell with her?

"About that drink." The woman who just joined Judd and I taps her fingers on my shoulder. Her gaze blazes a path over the black V-neck sweater I'm wearing before it lands on the front of my jeans. "Make it a double. I have a feeling I'm going to need it if this evening goes the way I hope it will."

It won't.

Any desire I may have had to go home with her is gone.

"I need to take off." Judd's voice draws my attention back to him. "I trust that the two of you will enjoy the rest of your evening."

I'm on my feet as soon as he is.

The brunette standing next to me lets out a frustrated noise. "Are you leaving too?"

"As soon as I place your drink order with the server," I say before I look at Judd. "I'll see you on Monday."

Confused, he raises a hand in the air in a half-wave. "All right, bud."

Shaking my head, I smile. He's been calling me that since we were kids, even though I've told him repeatedly to stop.

As he strides toward the exit, I glance at the woman again. She's pretty. Certainly, my type, and on any other night I'd be curious about her. I'd want to know her name, how she tastes, how her lips feel wrapped around my dick.

"There's someone else, isn't there?" she asks.

There's not, but my assistant sure as hell deserves someone better than a skinny kid dressed like he's going to the ballpark.

"Have a seat." I motion toward the stool Judd was sitting on. "I'll get you that drink. It was good to meet you."

The last line is a lie since I don't know her name and have no interest in finding out what it is.

She silently nods.

That's my cue, so I turn on my heel and head straight for the table where my assistant is wasting her time on a kid who has no idea he's having a drink with a brilliant woman.

"Arietta," I call out her name as I approach.

She doesn't turn around, so I up my pace.

With my heart pounding in my chest for some unknown fucking reason, I reach her. I rest a hand on her shoulder. "Miss Voss."

Her head turns up, and what greets me is a smiling face, but it's not Arietta's.

"Can I help you?" she asks. "Do I know you?"

Hope fills her expression as I drop my hand. "My apologies. I thought you were someone else."

Smiling, she lowers her voice to barely more than a whisper. "I'm sorry I'm not."

I can't say the same. Unexpected relief rushes through me as I realize that I didn't stumble into the middle of Arietta's date. I hope to hell I never do.

Chapter 16

Dominick

After spending the day with my family yesterday, I'm ready to get back to work.

It's been some time since I've participated in a Calvetti family lunch. My grandmother hosts them once every couple of months, and if you're related to her, she wants you there.

I've bowed out a few times because of work, but yesterday I made an appearance.

The food was exceptional, seeing my sisters and cousins was good, and listening to Marti tell stories about when we were all kids was a stroll down memory lane that I didn't mind.

I step off the elevator to see some of my employees clear a path. The whispered, "*good morning, sir*," I hear to my left goes unanswered, as does the cheery "*happy Monday*" that greets me from the right.

I round the corridor that leads to my private office area.

My office door is still closed. On any other morning, Arietta would have unlocked the door and turned on the lights if she arrived before me.

A glance at the watch on my wrist tells me that I'm later than usual, and she's absent when she's contractually obligated to be at her desk.

Her workday begins at nine a.m. sharp, although she's almost always early. The current time is nine-fifteen.

A blonde woman I've never seen before wearing three-inch heels and a red dress approaches me from the direction of the break room. In her hands are two mugs of coffee.

She stops to admire me from head-to-toe. "Are you him?"

I glance to my left and then my right, but unfortunately, I'm the only person standing within her sightline.

"Who are you?" I bark the question out.

"Your new assistant," she chirps.

"Who are you?" I repeat the question because her first answer was wrong.

"I'm the temp," she clarifies. "Your regular girl, Arianna, is out sick, so I was called in."

"Arietta," I correct her. "And who the hell called you in?"

"Jughead."

Since I've called Judd that on occasion, I don't correct that mistake. "What's wrong with Arietta?"

That's rhetorical since I believe I know what ails her.

She didn't finish the assigned task in time and is bowing out under the pretense of an illness to gain my sympathy.

This may very well be the first time that I've proven that Miss Voss is not perfect.

"I heard she has a cold." She shrugs. "I'm Lindsay, by the way."

"You're not needed here, by the way."

The mugs in her hands shake. "I got up early for this gig. I'm supposed to make a cool two hundred for the day, so I'm staying if it's all the same to you."

"It's not the same to me," I say, not knowing for sure if Lindsay and I are still discussing the same thing.

This woman is not Arietta, and if I can't have her, I don't want anyone else.

I hang my head as I contemplate that thought.

I don't want another assistant to fill in for her.

This has nothing to do with anything but work.

"I'm going to sit down behind that." She gestures toward Arietta's pristine desk. "One of these coffees is for you. I added cream and sugar since that's how I take mine. If you need anything else, holler at me, Dom."

Since no one but Judd calls me that, I point in the direction of the elevators. "Leave. You'll be paid for your time."

She places both mugs on Arietta's desk sending coffee splashing over the rim of one.

"Dammit," I bite out. "Just go."

Lindsay has no problem with that. She scoops up a bedazzled red handbag slung over the back of Arietta's chair and storms down the corridor in the direction I just came from.

I fumble in the front pocket of my pants for my keys. When I finally unlock the door to my office, I let out a heavy exhale.

"Why are you hiding from me, Arietta?" I ask under my breath.

"Because you're an asshole?" Judd's voice behind me startles me.

I spin to face him. "Where the hell did you come from?"

"Initially, Philly, but my mom had a dream of headlining on Broadway, so we packed up our meager belongings when I was four-years-old and made our way toward the bright lights of this city."

I fight back a smile. "Don't creep up on me."

He gestures for me to enter my own office. "Let's take this inside."

I gladly do, dropping my keys on my desk. "You called in a temp for me?"

"Yes, and you're welcome, but I passed her in the corridor, and she told me you fired her." He waves a finger at me. "That's not how we make friends, Dominick."

72

"Arietta is sick?" I ask because I should have been the person she called to report that to.

Judd taps a finger against the side of his nose. "She's fighting a pretty bad cold."

"You spoke to her?"

He nods. "I called her early this morning to thank her for reorganizing our digital filing system."

Scrubbing the back of my neck with my hand, I stare at him. "Our filing system? I asked her to input all my client's files into digital format."

"She did that and more." He breezes past me to approach the window. "It's raining again."

I don't want a weather forecast. I want answers to my questions about my assistant. "What do you mean she did that and more?"

"We're a team effort here, Dom." He shoves his hands into the front pockets of his black pants. "We share clients, although you rarely acknowledge that."

I huff out a laugh. "I know how the business works."

"Arietta updated everything, so it's all cross-referenced." He takes a step toward me. "She brought you into this century. We can both access all client files digitally now."

I've relied heavily on handwritten notes in my client's files to keep myself abreast of what's happening with them. It's an old habit that I've hung onto for far too long.

"I don't know how the hell she got all of it done in the three days, but she did." Judd snaps his fingers. "You're damn lucky to have her. Bronwyn is amazing, but the dedication Arietta has for her job is next level."

I glance out the window at the rain. "So, you believe she's genuinely ill?"

"She didn't sound great during our call. I told her to take the day off and tomorrow too if she needs it." He glances at my desk. "I called in a temp because I can't spare Bronwyn this week. I've got that meeting with the Magills today and Gilbert Dunphy tomorrow. I need her by my side for those."

"I'm fine on my own, Judd."

He laughs through his nose. "You? Who the hell will screen your calls?"

Good question, but I'll figure it out.

I don't want to look out of my office and see anyone sitting at Arietta's desk but her.

"I'll leave you to that," he says, chuckling as he walks toward my office door. "Bronwyn will update the Magill file with the details of our meeting this afternoon. If you log into our private server on that computer on your desk, you'll be able to read all about it. It's a novel concept, right?"

"Fuck you," I say with a straight face.

"Love you too, bud." Judd shoots me a smile. "Good luck handling all of this on your own."

Chapter 17

Arietta

I stare out the large living room window at the rain pelting against it. Wrapping my white cardigan tighter around me, I glance at Sinclair. "Grab an umbrella. You're going to need it."

She flashes me a smile as she tugs on the hood of the yellow raincoat she's wearing. "I'll be fine. I'm going to run to the subway stop, and then it's a short sprint to Berk's office when I get uptown."

She points at her feet. "These cute rain boots will keep my feet dry."

They will. They're mine. I've spent plenty of time wearing them when I've taken Dudley for walks during the unexpected showers that surprise New Yorkers during the spring.

"I can leave them here for you if you need to take Duds out."

Dudley barks from where he's snuggled on the corner of the couch.

"I have sneakers," I say before a sneeze escapes. "He looks ready for a nap, so I might curl up next to him and take one too."

"This meeting won't take more than an hour." Sinclair taps her hand on the outside of her laptop bag. "Berk wants to see the progress I've made. He insisted we do it in person, but I know it's because he wants to see that I'm all right. He worries about me. It's a big brother thing."

I wouldn't know about that. I don't have any brothers or sisters.

"I'm glad you finally took a day off." Sinclair sighs. "It's too bad that it took you getting sick for it to happen."

Guilt has kept me from requesting any days off. I know that Mr. Calvetti needs me. I debated whether to accept Mr. Corning's offer for a few sick days when I spoke to him this morning, but he was insistent. He said he didn't want me spreading my germs everywhere at work.

The deep laughter that followed that remark told me he was joking, but I decided to take his advice and stay home. I worked a lot this weekend, so I deserve some time to get over the cold I woke up with this morning.

"I'll stop by the deli around the corner and pick up some chicken soup on my way home," Sinclair offers. "If you think of anything else you need…"

I laugh as her voice trails. "I'll go to the roof and shout, hoping you'll hear me. You need a new phone."

She stomps her foot. "Dammit. I think you're right."

I smile, knowing that soon I'll be able to call and text her whenever I want. After what happened with the email mix-up the other day, I'm extra vigilant. I check the '*to*' field of my messages at least three times before I press send.

"We can look at phones together on my laptop when I get back. I need you to help me decide which model I should get it so I can order it tonight." She zippers up the raincoat as thunder rolls through the air outside. "I better go see Berk before he sends a search party out to look for me."

***

"This is my Aunt Cress." I point at a photograph of my mom and her sister when they were in their teens. "You wouldn't like her. She's allergic to dogs."

Dudley turns his head toward me, but his eyes droop closed again almost immediately.

I turn the page in the photo album that I dug out of a cardboard box in my closet. It wasn't the treasure I was searching for. I wanted to find the poetry book that I'd shoved in my suitcase the day I left Buffalo to move to New York City.

The rain outside reminded me of a gray morning years ago when I woke up not wanting to go to school. I sniffled and coughed my way through an Oscar-worthy performance of a girl with a cold before my mom told me that she knew it was all an act.

I thought she'd send me off to school, but she didn't.

She called my teacher and explained that I was staying home. She didn't make up an elaborate excuse as to why that was. She simply stated that I would be with her, at home, instead of sitting at my desk in the third row learning about fractions and percentages.

We spent that day looking at photo albums, reading poetry, and drinking tea.

Mine was made with more milk than tea and one too many sugar cubes.

It was one of the best days of my life.

I snap the photo album closed and trek my way across the hardwood floors toward my bedroom.

As soon as I'm there, I dump the entire contents of the box on the bed. I rifle through a scrapbook I made in middle school, a drawing that I worked on one summer when I was a kid, and the first pair of eyeglasses I ever got. I was in the third grade and hated wearing them.

I push aside a few framed photographs until my gaze lands on the poetry book I've been looking for.

I sprint back to the living room to hunker down under the warm blanket that's always there regardless of the season.

Just as I drop the poetry book next to the photo album, there's a knock at the door.

It's Sinclair.

She wasn't gone five minutes before I spotted her keys on the foyer table. Since she left almost two hours ago, I don't hesitate at all as I unlock the deadbolt, swing open the door, and outstretch my arms. "I've been waiting forever for you."

Reality hits me like a punch in the face when I realize that I'm not looking at my roommate.

The man in the tailored navy blue suit with the umbrella handle draped over his forearm and what looks like a take-out bag in his hand looks down at me. "Forever is a very long time, Miss Voss."

I watch his gaze wander over my face and my tousled hair until it lands on the front of my shirt. I glance down.

No bra. Dammit. I'm not wearing a bra.

I gather my cardigan around me, trying to shield the outline of my now erect nipples from his view.

"Mr. Calvetti," I whisper. "I wasn't expecting you."

"Clearly," he says in a low tone. "Are you going to invite me in?"

I step aside, and with a shaky hand, I gesture toward the living room. "Please, sir. Come in."

Chapter 18

Dominick

I haven't had this many erections in the presence of a woman in…never.

It wasn't just the sight of Miss Voss with her blonde hair in a messy tangle around her face. Her hardened nipples under her tank top got my attention, but what drove me over the edge, and caused my cock to harden to the point of pain, was her ass.

Tight black yoga pants are the only thing covering my assistant's ass, and what an ass it is.

I drop my gaze from her body because I'm inching toward saying something I'll regret or doing something I'll savor and then regret.

Glancing over her shoulder at me, Arietta motions toward a spot next to a dog shooting me an evil eye. "You can sit there if you like."

I hang my umbrella over the doorknob before I take a seat on a white couch across from the canine.

Arietta lets out a light laugh. "That's Dudley. He won't bite."

Famous last words.

A girl who lived in the same building as my family when I was a kid offered up the chance to pet her dog when we were at the park one Saturday morning. I ended up in the ER with six stitches in my forearm.

Arietta's gaze drops to the bag still in my hand.

I made the unwise choice of stopping by Calvetti's on my way here. I was looking for something to offer Arietta to help chase her cold away so she can get back to work ASAP. My grandmother packed an entire meal as she questioned me about what's wrong with my assistant.

The kicker was when she wanted to know how Arietta's relationship with her Clark Kent lookalike boyfriend is going.

I can only assume that's Lowell and my double assumption is that it hasn't launched yet since I kept her buried in work all weekend, and she's now sick.

I don't need my grandmother to get invested in my assistant's love life.

"I brought soup." I offer the bag to her. "And a few other things."

Seven other things, if I'm going to be precise, which I won't be.

Arietta takes the bag while still holding tightly to the cardigan that she's using to hide her body from me.

I've seen it. Jesus, have I seen it. More times than I care to admit.

I took a second to look at the photo of her in lingerie again as I was getting in the car on my way here.

My driver tried to steal a glance at my phone's screen, so I almost fired the nosy bastard.

"Thank you," she says through a sniffle. "I think in a day or two I'll be good as new."

I hoped that my grandmother's sausage kale soup would have super healing powers. I need Arietta now.

No, I want her back at the office now.

Her presence there makes my life easier.

Still standing in front of me smelling like every good memory I have of the flowers in Sicily, she sighs. "Did you get a chance to check out the new filing system, sir?"

I nod. "I did."

She waits for something I'm not offering. I should tell her she did a remarkable job, but that's for another day. I need to get the hell out of here because I can't stop staring at her.

Just as I'm about to stand, that fucking rooster crows again.

Arietta turns around. "That's my phone."

I'm transfixed as she marches across her apartment on bare feet. Her ass sways with each step.

She cocks a hip when she picks up her phone from the dining table. "Sinclair's in the lobby. She bought some groceries on her way home. I'm going to go down and help her carry everything up. I'll only be gone for a few minutes."

I should be a gentleman and offer to help. Instead, I lean back on the couch, cross my legs and try to hide my raging hard-on. "Fine."

Scooping up a set of keys from the small table in the foyer, she slips a pair of white sneakers on her bare feet. "I'll be right back. Make yourself at home."

As soon as the door shuts behind her, I turn to the small dog staring a path through me. "Keep your distance, doggy."

He tilts his head slightly before he closes his big brown eyes again.

I push to my feet, unsure of what I'm supposed to do.

I know what I want. I want to wander through the apartment, so I can picture Arietta here when she's not at work.

My better judgment takes over as my gaze drops to a photo album on the coffee table in front of me. Next to it is a poetry book.

I pick up the photo album first and thumb my way through a few pages.

I stop at an image of a man and a woman on a beach with a blonde-haired girl. The wind is whipping their hair against their faces.

The child is missing a top front tooth, but that smile is unmistakable.

It's Arietta.

She can't be more than six or seven years old in the photograph. I stare at it, wondering if she's always carried light with her. If the people around her have always benefited from the joy she brings with her into a room.

I snap the album closed and exchange it for the poetry book.

Sitting down on the couch again, I place the book in my lap. It's not a book devoted to a great wordsmith of our time. It's a collection of simplistic rhymes bound together in hardcover form.

I scroll through the table of contents, wondering if Arietta made a contribution, but I come up empty.

Still, I skim through it, scanning the words, taking note of a page that has been haphazardly taped back into place.

I flip to the middle to find a piece of folded paper stuck in the binding.

I pluck it out carefully. I unfold it once and then again so I can read what's written on it in blue ink.

My To-Do List

> *1. Move to NYC! The Big Apple! Gotham! The place I belong!*
> *2. Live in an apartment that's filled with fresh red and pink roses!*
> *3. Dance in the rain. Splash my feet. Sing along to the music!*
> *4. Adopt a dog!*
> *5. Be kissed like heroines in movies are!*
> *6. Fall in love! Deeply. Passionately. Forever.*
> *7. Be proposed to close to the stars.*

> 8.   *Get married in the fall with the leaves
> turning colors.*
> 9.   *Have a baby...or two.*
> 10. *Never stop smiling.*

I read the list again. Not one item on it would match a to-do list of my own. I'm a lifelong New Yorker. Flowers are a fool's investment. They never live beyond a few days. You might as well toss your cash in the trash.

I fucking hate the rain, and my history with dogs will never convince me that I need one as a pet.

The remaining six items would land on my to-don't list.

I fold the paper in half and then again and shove it back into the book exactly where I found it.

Arietta's a dreamer. I'm a doer.

It's only one of the many ways we differ.

I'm twelve years older than her.

I'm her boss.

I turn when I hear a key in the lock of the door. It's time for me to leave. I don't belong here. I belong behind my desk in my office, making my financial dreams come true.

Chapter 19

Arietta

"You weren't kidding when you said your boss is rude and hot." Sinclair's hand dives back into one of the brown paper bags she carted home from the grocery store. "I bet angry sex with him is out of this world."

I bet any sex with him is.

I shake that thought away. "I'm sorry he rushed off like that. At least you got to meet him."

Sinclair turns toward me. Clearing her throat, she lowers her voice. "It's nice to meet you, Miss Morgan. Good day."

I shake my head as I critique her impersonation of my boss. "He didn't add the good day."

Shaking the bunch of carrots in her hand at me, she laughs. "You're right. He didn't."

I shrug. "That's classic Dominick."

She grabs an eggplant from the bag. "He has big dick energy though. Like huge dick energy."

I close my eyes. "Don't talk about his penis."

I feel her fingertip tap the center of my forehead. "You think about it. Don't pretend you have never thought about it, Arietta."

Popping my eyes open, I fight a smile. "He uses that big dick to break hearts."

Sinclair stops unloading the groceries to face me. "It's not his fault women want more after he fucks them. It's a curse. I feel sorry for him."

She exaggerates a frown before she bursts out in laughter.

Rolling my eyes, I point at the bag from Calvetti's. "Let's talk less about him and more about whatever is in there."

She claps her hands together. "Marti made us a feast."

She did. She truly is the sweetest woman in this city.

"Let's put all the food I bought away, and then we'll eat," Sinclair suggests. "We'll save the soup I got you for tomorrow."

I reach to hug her. "Thank you again for that. I had no idea Mr. Calvetti would come here today. I sure as hell didn't expect him to show up with food."

"He came to check you out." She looks me up and down. "I take it your nipples rose to the occasion when you saw him."

I crack a smile. "It's chilly in here."

"Apparently not now." She points at my chest. "He came here because he wanted to see you. Lucky him that he showed up when you're looking more beautiful than ever."

I laugh that off. "My nose is red, and my eyes are watering. I'm a mess."

"You're drop-dead gorgeous." She tips my chin up with her index finger. "There's natural beauty, and then there's you. You have a glow about you. I can't describe it, but I've never met anyone as striking as you."

Tears prick the corners of my eyes. I'm grateful that I can blame it on my cold. "You're too good to me."

"I'm not." She reaches to hug me. "You're as beautiful inside as you are on the outside. If any of that rubs off on me, I'll consider myself lucky."

***

Being the trooper that I am, I took one day off and showed up at work this morning. Mr. Calvetti didn't.

It wasn't until my coffee break that I discovered he was on a flight headed to Boston. Bronwyn clued me into that. Since I had no assigned work for the day, I spent my time helping Mr. Corning and Bronwyn.

I was rewarded with a warm '*thank you*' from Mr. Corning and the chance to leave work an hour earlier than I usually do.

I spent that time wisely.

I went home and had a short nap, took Dudley for a walk, and warmed up the soup Sinclair bought yesterday.

After that, I decided to head out for a little shopping spree. That brought me here.

Yanking on the door to my favorite vintage shop, I'm instantly greeted with the calming smell of vanilla.

Lynn, the owner of Past Over, always burns her handmade vanilla candles on the checkout counter. I've told her at least ten times to sell them. She'd make a mint, but she's always said that old treasures are her passion, not smelly candles.

"Welcome to Past Over," she yells from somewhere near the back of the store. "I'll be right with you."

"It's just me," I call out. "Arietta."

I see her the moment she rounds the corner and treks up an aisle lined with shelves containing hundreds of mismatched dishes. Everything from delicate china teacups to ceramic soup bowls are stacked on top of each other, waiting for the right person to come in to take them home so they can be put to good use again.

Lynn skims a hand over her graying brown hair before she adjusts her wire-rimmed eyeglasses. "Arietta! I've missed you."

It's been a couple of weeks since I've stopped by the store. I'd blame that on work, but I've been spending a lot of time parked on the couch next to Sinclair watching the legal thriller that Leta recommended.

"I'm here now." I laugh. "I brought you something."

I shove a white box tied with pink string at Lynn. "There are two cupcakes in there for you. One is chocolate, and the other is lemon."

Lynn licks her bottom lip. "You know I can't resist a cupcake."

I do know that. I've been coming to Past Over for months. I first stepped into the store late one evening on my way home from work. Lynn was ready to close up shop, but she let me stroll up and down the aisles of treasures while we talked.

Since then, I've been coming back as regularly as I possibly can. I don't just find the best clothing items here, but I've found jewelry, a painting for my bedroom, and books.

"I have something for you too." Lynn sets off toward one of the many wooden bookcases that line the interior walls of the shop. "A gentleman stopped in the other day with a donation. He didn't think I'd want it, but I told him that my very best customer would love it."

If she's talking about me, I know what the donation consisted of. "You have a new book for me?"

"Two," she says, wagging two fingers in the air. "You may need a crane to get them home. They're massive."

I laugh. It's the same joke she always tells when I take home my favorite type of books.

"I'm strong." I flex my bicep under the yellow cardigan I'm wearing. "I can handle it."

She scoops up two large leather-bound books. "You're sure."

An uncontrollable smile blooms on my lips. "I'm very sure."

Bending forward to accommodate the weight of the books in her arms, Lynn laughs. "You're the only girl I know who loves law books this much."

She's never asked me why. I've never offered.

That's one of the many reasons I love Lynn so much.

"How much do I owe you?" I ask as she places them on the worn wooden counter with a thud.

"Are you serious?" She wipes her hand across her forehead. "They're free. Any law books I find will always be free for you. I've been running this store for twenty-five years, and no one but you has ever come in looking for law books."

"Fools," I quip.

That sets her head back in laughter. "Let's split a cupcake, and then I have a new batch of old jewelry to show you."

I settle onto a swivel stool near the checkout counter. "You have yourself a deal."

Chapter 20

Arietta

"Lowell," Lynn repeats his name for a second time. "I like his name, Arietta. He sounds…"

"Kind?" I perk a brow.

"Rich." She laughs.

I have no idea about Lowell's financial situation. It doesn't matter to me because I'm forging my own path in that regard. I don't want to date someone who has no ambition and a zero balance bank account, but it's not a subject we've discussed yet. If things go well on our date tomorrow night, maybe we'll talk about it on our second or third date.

"He seems nice," I offer as I press my fingertip to a few chocolate crumbs on the paper napkin in front of me. I lift my finger to my lips to savor the last taste of the cupcake.

"Is he nicer than your boss?" Lynn scrunches her nose. "Is he still being Dominick Downer?"

That's a nickname I need to add to my list. Smiling, I shrug. "I woke up with a cold yesterday, so I took the day off. He came over with food."

Lynn leans both elbows on the top of the checkout counter. "He came to your apartment?"

Nodding, I smile. "He just showed up. I wasn't expecting him."

Widening her eyes, she tilts her head. "You were decent, weren't you?"

Lynn is old enough to be my grandma. I can't tell her that I accidentally sent Mr. Calvetti a picture of myself in lingerie. I don't think she'd judge me, but why put her in an uncomfortable position?

"I was decent," I half-lie.

I still regret not putting on a bra when I got out of bed yesterday.

"Has he ever come to your apartment before?"

"Never." I glance down at my skirt. "It was strange to see him standing there when I opened the door."

"It means something." Lynn nods her head. "Maybe he was genuinely concerned about you? You're all right now, aren't you?"

"I'm fine," I reassure her with a touch of my hand to her forearm. "I don't think he was concerned. He's not like that."

"So he stopped by to make sure you weren't playing sick to score a free day off?" she asks matter-of-factly.

I thought of that too, but he could have done that without bringing half of Calvetti's menu items with him.

"I don't know," I say softly. "Maybe I'll never know what motivated him to come over."

We both turn when the bell over the door to the shop rings.

A blonde-haired woman, around Lynn's age, enters. "Hello again."

Recognition floats over Lynn's expression as she returns the woman's smile with a grin of her own. "It's good to see you."

The woman tugs on the belt of the light blue trench coat she's wearing. "I'm here to browse. Don't mind me."

Slipping off my stool, I skim my hand over my skirt. "I should too. I need to get home soon."

"Go look around." Lynn points toward the jewelry area. "I just put out some new pieces. I think you'll fall in love with a few."

She's likely right. I have two jewelry boxes filled with vintage pieces I've picked up over the years. I've always been drawn to secondhand things. I see beauty in the tarnished silver or worn edges that not everyone can. To me, they are a part of someone's story from the past. I always try and imagine who owned those things before me.

It's the same with clothing. Why buy new when gorgeous items are sitting in this shop for me?

Straightening the collar of the white blouse I'm wearing, I start toward the jewelry area when the sound of fingernails dragging down a chalkboard stops me in my tracks.

I close my eyes.

My heart thumps an extra beat knowing that Mr. Calvetti has sent me a message.

I tug my phone out of my purse and open the email app.

Subject : Boston

Miss Voss,

I need a reservation for dinner at 8 p.m. tonight at the best restaurant in this city.

Book that and forward me the details.

Note: The reservation is for two.

Signed,
Dominick Calvetti

"What the…" I say under my breath.

Mr. Calvetti usually books his own reservations for dinner, especially when he's out of town. This has to be another test.

"Did I hear fingernails on a chalkboard?" The woman in the blue trench coat approaches from the left. "It sent goose bumps straight up my back."

I wince. "It's my phone. That's the notification I set for when my boss emails me."

Laughter rolls out of her. Her blue eyes widen. "You're serious?"

Nodding, I fight a smile. "I am."

Her gaze wanders my face. "He must be something else."

"You have no idea. " I sigh. "He wants me to make a reservation for two at the best restaurant in Boston for eight o'clock."

I glance at my watch. Great. I have just over an hour to do that.

Opening the browser on my phone, I whisper. "I don't know where to start."

"You'll want to book him a table at Axel Boston." The woman standing next to me rests a hand on her hip. "Their New York restaurants are divine, but there is something special about their location in Boston."

I smile at her. "I hope they can fit him in."

Her ruby red lips part. "My nephew is the executive pastry chef there. He'll get you in. Call and tell them Elvis's aunt needs a table for a friend."

"Elvis's aunt?"

She nods. "They'll know."

"Thank you," I say as relief rushes through me. "You're a lifesaver."

"It's nothing." She taps my forearm. "You can return the favor by telling me where you got that beautiful brooch."

My hand leaps to the blue and white rhinestone wreath brooch pinned to my cardigan. "I got it here. I bought it last winter."

She leans closer. "It's remarkable. It reminds me so much of one my grandmother had. My uncle misplaced it after her death. I've been searching for a similar one since."

I reach up and unhook the brooch. "You can have it."

Her gaze leaps up to my face. "What?"

I carefully place it in her hand. To me, it's been a pretty accessory I bought for ten dollars, but the tears forming in her eyes tell me it's priceless to her. "Please take it as a thank you for helping me with the restaurant."

Her bottom lip quivers as she cradles the brooch close to her chest. "I don't know what to say. Thank you."

"You're welcome." I glance down at my phone again. "I better call the restaurant to book a table for my boss. I don't want him to get hangry."

"You should do that now," she says, pointing at my phone. "Don't forget to mention Elvis."

Nodding, I pull up the website for Axel Boston in the browser and click on the icon to connect the call.

"Good evening." A man's voice greets me after just one ring. "How can I help you?"

"Elvis's aunt needs a table for a friend at eight tonight," I repeat everything the woman next to me said.

"Of course, " he says happily. "Under what name would you like the reservation?"

"Calvetti." I give the woman next to me a thumbs-up and a smile. "The reservation is for Dominick Calvetti and a plus one."

"He's booked in. We will see Mr. Calvetti and his guest at eight."

I hang up and turn to the woman who just saved my night. "Thank you so much!"

A soft smile settles on her lips. "There's no need to thank me. You're the one who gave me a priceless gift tonight. You're a very special young woman. One in a million I'd say."

"Arietta!" Lynn calls from where she's standing near a rack of dresses. "I think I just found the perfect dress for you to wear on your date with Lowell tomorrow night."

The woman in the trench coat glances at Lynn before her gaze settles on me. "It sounds like a special occasion."

My mouth curves, feeling slightly embarrassed. "It's just a first date."

She studies my face. "That is special. First dates can lead to lifetimes together."

I glance down at her left hand to the sight of a simple gold band on her wedding ring finger.

"I should go see what Lynn found for me," I say, wishing I had more time to talk with her. "You helped me more than you know. Please enjoy the rest of your evening."

"I will." She looks past me to where Lynn is standing before her gaze settles back on me. "Enjoy your date tomorrow night. I hope it's the first of many."

I hope for that too, or at least I think I do.

Chapter 21

Dominick

"Dominick, you must have some pull to get us a table at this place last minute."

I'm as impressed as my dinner guest that Arietta was able to secure a table at Axel Boston this late in the game. She had barely an hour to get the job done, and she, once again, surpassed every one of my expectations.

Since I'm sitting across from my cousin, I see no reason to take credit for something that was my assistant's doing. "Arietta has the pull. She booked our table."

Rocco Jones shoves a hand through his brown hair. "We'll have to toast to her tonight."

"After we toast to you." I gesture to the silver band on his ring finger. The three black diamonds that adorn the band are unique and hard to miss. "I still can't believe you're married and having a baby."

Rocco is just another person in my life taking on the role of a parent. Bella became a mom when her daughter Luisa was born. Judd's about to have another child, and Rocco's wife is pregnant with their son. They plan to name him Bryant.

His smile beams. "I never thought this would be my life."

It's good to see him like this. We're close in age and grew up as friends. His talent playing professional poker took him in one direction. My goal of making money took me in another.

Since he's retired from playing for cash, he's an angel investor. It's how he met his wife, Dexie.

When the server approaches, Rocco takes control, ordering us each a glass of his vodka. He's a partner in Rizon Vodka. I have a lifetime supply if I want it. When I was in Sicily, Rocco sent me a crate of the stuff.

This dinner is my way of paying him back for that. We flew to Boston together from New York this morning. Rocco wanted me to tag along to check out a business opportunity that he's considering. The fact that he values my opinion matters, so I couldn't say no.

"Thanks again for letting us use your villa for our honeymoon," Rocco says as the server takes his leave. "Dexie loves Italy as much as we do."

I like it. I enjoy being there because of the escape it provided from my hectic life in Manhattan, but I don't love it. It's a home facing the Mediterranean Sea where the problems of the world slip away under the crushing sound of the waves hitting the beach.

I adjust my tie as I lean back in my chair.

Rocco huffs out a laugh. "Don't you get tired of the day-to-day grind, Dominick? You look uncomfortable as hell in that suit."

His style has never matched mine. Rocco conducts business in jeans and T-shirts most of the time. When he wants to step it up a notch, he'll pull a sweater and a pair of black pants from the back of his closet.

"Rich people expect you to look a certain way when you're handling their money."

The server returns with two glasses filled with vodka and soda water. A lime wedge sits on the rim of Rocco's glass. He knows I always pass on the citrus. That's why he ordered mine without.

I was with Rocco the first time I got drunk. I was fifteen. He was sixteen. He snuck a bottle of his dad's orange liqueur out of the house. We sat in a park in Queens drinking it on a Saturday night.

I couldn't get out of bed on Sunday morning.

Rocco took the blame for it all, telling my folks he blackmailed me into drinking it by threatening to expose my crush on a girl at school. There was no girl. There was just a decent kid looking out for his cousin.

I envied Rocco at one time for being born first. He was gifted with the name of our grandfather. He's Rocco Calvetti's namesake, but I take pride in the fact that Marti has told me that I'm just like our grandfather. The man worked hard every day of his life. He was driven. He never gave up on anything.

"You handle my money." Rocco lifts his glass in the air. "I don't care what the fuck you wear, as long as you do a good job."

Laughing, I tap my glass to his. "Here's to keeping you filthy rich."

"Speaking of that," he begins before he huffs out a laugh. "I realized the other day that I owe you ten grand."

Since I collect my commission off the top of Rocco's investments, he's not talking business. We've played poker in the past, but I've never held a winning hand against him.

Stumped, I shake my head. "For what?"

He leans forward to tap his finger in the center of the table. "For that Vernon Greenwalt wager we made when I was…I want to say twenty, maybe twenty-one. Whoever made a million first had to give the other ten thousand of it. I know you got there before I did."

Recognition hits me instantly. "I fucking forgot about that bet."

"How?" He laughs. "You read everything you could find about Vern. If I remember correctly, you once said that you were going to follow his footsteps to your fortune. It worked out for you."

Vernon Greenwalt is one of the richest men on the planet. I first read about him in a piece in Forbes, along with a dozen other self-made billionaires. I showed the article to Rocco when we met at Calvetti's for lunch one day.

Greenwalt came from humble beginnings and amassed a fortune in the auto industry. My goal when I started college was to get established enough that he'd consider me as his wealth advisor. I've never gotten close enough to him to shake his hand, but I haven't given up trying.

He's next in line behind my father as my idol. I studied the steps Greenwalt took to find success, and I mirrored them right down to making my job my number one priority.

"I always pay my debts, so I'll get that to you in the next week," Rocco offers.

"No." I hold up a hand to wave that idea away. "Put it into that trust you set up for baby Bryant."

"You're sure?" He smiles. "You don't need to do that, Dominick."

"I'm sure."

"Thank you." Dropping his gaze to the menu in front of him, Rocco clears his throat. "Is there anything new to report in your life?"

He's as bad at fishing for information about my personal life as our grandmother is. "No."

That draws his head back up. "That sounded like a hard no."

"I work," I pause. "A hell of a lot. I don't have time for anything else."

"So you're celibate now?" He cocks a brow. "I'm a betting man, and even I would never have placed a wager on you giving that up."

I laugh. "I'm not celibate."

It's starting to feel as though I am. The last time I fucked was in Virginia.

"There is a lot to be said for falling in love." He runs a finger over his wedding band. "I never thought I'd take the plunge, but when Dexie stormed into my life, that was it for me. I was gone."

I stare at the ring. "I told Judd the other day that marriage and kids aren't for everyone, so I'm telling you the same now."

He leans forward, resting his forearm on the table. "Don't shut down the possibility, Dominick. You never know who might be waiting around the corner for you. If someone had told me I'd fall for a pink-haired purse designer, I would have laughed in their face."

I take a drink, mulling over his words.

"If you feel something for someone, see where it goes." He taps his fingers on the table. "Love doesn't always show up in the form you expect it to. Be open to it."

The server arrives to take our dinner orders, giving me the break from this conversation that I was craving.

I look to the left at a bank of windows as Rocco questions the server about what he recommends.

My gaze catches on a man and woman standing outside the restaurant. As the rain that battered Manhattan starts to fall over Boston, he takes her in his arms and twirls her around.

They dance together, oblivious to everyone who is shuffling past them in their haste to find shelter from the sudden storm.

"Dominick."

The sound of my name breaks my trance. I glance at my cousin before I look at the server. "I'll have whatever he's having."

As soon as he's taken off in the direction of the kitchen, Rocco lifts his glass again. "Let's toast to whoever you were thinking about just now."

Arietta.

I lift my glass to his again.

"Here's to my cousin's secret crush." Rocco chuckles. "Whoever she may be."

Chapter 22

Arietta

I take in a deep breath as the sun beats down on my face. I've missed it. The rain that has soaked Manhattan for the past few days finally moved north.

I'm relieved and excited.

Tonight is my date with Lowell.

We chatted briefly on the app this morning. Lowell suggested we both think about where we want to have dinner tonight. We'll reconnect on the app at lunch so that he can firm up a reservation.

I admit I was mildly disappointed that he hadn't taken the bull by the horns and done that already.

My favorite restaurant in Manhattan is Calvetti's. I can't suggest that as the destination for our first date. Marti would tell Dominick all about it. He wouldn't care, but I want to keep my personal life out of the office.

I walk through the lobby of the building that houses the offices of Modica Wealth Management.

The day I came for an interview, I was impressed with the polished marble floor and the reception desk crafted from imported wood. It was the first time I'd ever stepped foot in a building like this in New York City. Now, it feels like my second home.

I stroll to the bank of elevators, all the while planning out my outfit for the evening.

I'll wear the black lace dress that Lynn showed me last night. I fell in love with it immediately. I'm going to cinch it at the waist with a thick pink ribbon.

My gaze drops to the shoes of the people standing near me waiting to board the elevator. A pair of bright red heels stands out, but that's not my style. Tonight, I'm wearing black strappy sandals with low heels. I brought them with me from Buffalo. When I modeled the dress for Sinclair, she dug the shoes out of my closet, insisting they were perfect for my date.

I'm going for a classic, sophisticated look, and I think with the vintage silver necklace and earrings I picked out of my jewelry box, I'll nail it.

Once the elevator dings its arrival, I crowd into the car with the others who are on their way to earn a living.

Just as the doors start to close, a hand reaches around to stop them in place. "Hold the elevator."

I'd know that deep voice anywhere.

Mr. Calvetti and I have never arrived at work at precisely the same time.

I assumed he'd be in Boston, taking his time getting out of bed this morning.

I sigh, realizing that I'll likely have to screen calls from yet another woman who fell under his spell after having sex with him.

As the doors slide back open, he comes into view.

Dressed all in black save for a silver tie, he looks like the devil personified.

My heart races to the point that I fear my cheeks are going to flush pink.

He's not Lowell. Stop staring.

I silently chant that to myself as he boards the lift, turning his back to me.

As the elevator creeps its way up, people take their leave, rushing out toward their offices.

The crowd thins, and yet, Mr. Calvetti never turns around.

It's only when we are nearing our floor that he clears his throat. He doesn't turn around. There's no acknowledgment that he knows I'm standing behind him before he says in a clipped tone, "I'd like my coffee in…"

"Ten minutes," I finish his sentence. "I'll get that for you, sir."

The two people still on this ride with us make small talk as Mr. Calvetti shifts slightly so he can glance over his shoulder at me. He rakes me from head-to-toe taking in the powder blue dress I'm wearing under a red blazer.

"Thank you, Miss Voss."

As he turns back to face the elevator doors, a smile blooms on my lips. "You're welcome."

***

I've packed more into this workday than I thought I would, and I still have two hours to go before I'm off the clock.

I returned close to three dozen emails. I spoke to four potential clients and five clients that Mr. Calvetti has had for years. I also arranged several important meetings for him later this week while I reorganized the top drawer of my desk.

The best part of my day so far is that I haven't had to lie to any women about passing along messages to my boss.

Since I made the executive decision that I needed an extra boost of caffeine to get me through the next sixty minutes, I snuck back to the break room to grab a mug of coffee and a chocolate bar from the vending machine.

This will tide me over until I meet Lowell at a seafood restaurant in Times Square tonight. It was a joint decision we made when we chatted on the app during my lunch break.

As soon as I reach my desk, the phone starts ringing.

I check which line is calling. I pick up the call, thankful that it's coming from the reception desk in the lobby and not Mr. Calvetti's office.

I don't want him to assign me anything that will keep me here past six tonight. I need time to get ready for my date.

"Hi. This is Arietta," I say into the receiver.

"Arietta, it's Bonnie at reception. There's a woman here who'd like to see Mr. Calvetti."

This was bound to happen. Although Modica Wealth Management's website doesn't list the floor our offices are on, it does list the building's address. I knew a woman would show up eventually looking for The Dick.

Drawing in a deep breath, I level my tone. "Bonnie, please tell her that Mr. Calvetti is busy at the moment. If she'd like to call and leave a message, I'll be happy to help her."

"Hold please," Bonnie directs me.

The soft sound of jazz music floats over the line as Bonnie passes my message to one of my boss's former lovers.

The music fades as the call reconnects. "She says he'll want to see her."

Of course she's saying that. He probably whispered sweet nothings in her ear while he was drilling his cock into her. Or maybe he's a dirty talker.

I close my eyes, willing that thought to go away.

"Her name is…" Bonnie's voice fades.

It doesn't matter what her name is. Mr. Calvetti will not want to see her. He'd probably sneak out one of the windows in his office and crawl down the exterior of the building to avoid seeing any woman he's fucked.

Picturing that in my mind's eye, I hold in a laugh.

"Clarice Blanchard."

I press the receiver closer to my ear. "Repeat that please, Bonnie."

With my heart pounding in my chest, she does. "It's Clarice Blanchard. She doesn't have an appointment with Mr. Calvetti, but she's wondering if he has time to see her now."

"Yes," I say without hesitation. "Send her up."

Chapter 23

Dominick

Arietta's clothing may be as ill-fitting as ever today, but it's charming. The entire outfit makes no sense, yet on her, it's a ray of sunshine.

A ray of sunshine?

What the actual fuck is wrong with me?

I'd attribute it to jetlag, but the flight from Boston to New York City is too short to have any lasting impact on me.

A knock at my door steals my thoughts from my assistant's wardrobe choices.

"Come in," I call out since Judd is on the other side of the door.

I've been waiting for him for well over an hour. We're scheduled to meet to talk about the next step we need to take to get face time with Clarice Blanchard. That has to happen soon if we want to stay in the running to handle her fortune.

My door flies open. "Mr. Calvetti. Oh, sir. Oh my god."

I dart to my feet when I get a glimpse of the expression on Arietta's face. It's a mix of confusion and horror. "What is it?"

She jerks a thumb over her shoulder. "She's here, sir. Did you know she was coming?"

Fill-in-the-blank is a game I've never conquered, so I roll my hand in the air looking for another clue. "Who?"

I suspect it's a woman I've bedded recently. This has happened in the past. It was before Arietta's time when a woman dressed in nothing but a black trench coat and sky high heels showed up on this floor.

She tossed the coat aside and strolled completely nude up the corridor that leads to my office.

She deserved a standing ovation for her courage but a failing grade on the execution. She tripped before she reached the threshold of my office and broke her wrist.

I took her to the hospital to have it set in a cast before I took her home.

Nothing happened between us that night, or ever again, for that matter. She didn't just suffer an injury. She was dealt a blow to her ego.

I was honest on the drive to the hospital when I repeated what I'd told her two nights prior. I wasn't interested in more. I would never be interested in more with her or anyone else.

"Her," Arietta stresses the word. "It's her, sir."

Buttoning my suit jacket, I glance at Arietta again. "You're going to need to be more specific."

Her gaze travels my face. "Clarice Blanchard is here. She's on her way up right now to see you."

Jesus Christ.

"Here? Now?" I repeat for fear that I'm not hearing her correctly.

"Arietta's gaze darts over her shoulder. "She'll be here any second."

I should call Judd to join me in greeting Clarice, but if she's looking for me, I'll handle this with all the skill I've earned over the years.

"Do you need me to do anything?" Arietta asks before she exhales. "Should I do something?"

"Take a deep breath," I instruct her in a soft tone. "We've got this. I've got this."

She nods. "I know you do, sir. You always do."

That's debatable.

My gaze drifts past Arietta to the woman walking down the corridor toward us. Clarice Blanchard is a master of staying out of public view. I've never seen an image of her, yet she's exactly as I've pictured her.

Her blonde hair is cut into a stylish bob. Her eyes are laser focused on me. As she nears, her blood red lips part into a soft smile. "There you are."

Damn right. Here I am.

My gaze drifts back to Arietta's face as her brow furrows. "What the…"

She turns before she can finish the question.

Clarice's smile widens even more. "Arietta!"

"It's you?" Arietta asks with obvious surprise in her tone. "You're her?"

Clarice bundles my assistant into her arms as if they are old friends. Laughing, she glances at me. "I'm her."

What the ever-loving fuck is happening?

Arietta pulls back from the embrace. "I'm sorry. I had no idea."

"I know, and that's why I'm here." Clarice finally looks at me. "Your assistant is the reason I'm here, Mr. Calvetti."

Taken aback, I look to Arietta, hoping for an explanation, but her back is still to me.

"I've looked over your proposal." Clarice lifts her chin. "You're smart. I see promise here but let me make one thing crystal clear to you."

Arietta finally turns to face me. I'm not surprised to see a wide smile as her brows perk.

"If I sign with your firm, Arietta is my contact person. She's to attend every meeting, and I only want her calling and emailing me. Is that understood?"

No, but do I have a fucking choice in this?

I look directly into Clarice's eyes. "Understood."

She turns her attention back to Arietta. "I've booked a table for you and Lowell for dinner at Axel Tribeca tonight. Everything is covered."

Arietta's hands leap to her chest. "Really? Thank you so much! Did Elvis arrange that?"

Fucking Lowell. And Elvis? Elvis Presley? What the hell?

I feel like I've been transported to another universe where nothing makes any goddamn sense. In what reality is my assistant besties with my most desired client?

"He did. He made the call to book you the best table in the house." Clarice's hand taps a brooch pinned to the collar of her black dress. It looks identical to one that I've seen Arietta wearing. "I told you first dates should be special."

"You're not doing this because of the brooch, are you?" Arietta's voice softens. "You don't need to do that, Mrs. Blanchard."

"It's Clarice," she corrects Arietta. "And it's my pleasure."

I need to step off this merry-go-round of confusion. The best way to do that is to ground myself in what I know. That's wealth and how to manage it. "Clarice, do you have a moment to discuss the proposal I sent last week?"

With a lift of her gaze to my face, her lips thin. "It's Mrs. Blanchard to you, and you have thirty minutes, Mr. Calvetti. I suggest you make the most of it."

Chapter 24

Arietta

I stare across the table at my date. With a sense of relief and excitement, I clear my throat. "I'm so glad you were open to coming to Axel with me."

Lowell's blue eyes squint behind his glasses as he gazes around the restaurant. "I've never been. I can't believe you have a friend who covered the cost of our dinner at this place."

I smile at the assumption that Clarice Blanchard is my friend. We're barely acquaintances. She told me that after hearing me book the table at Axel Boston, she realized that I work for Dominick.

With any luck, she'll be a Modica client in the next few days. Mr. Calvetti met with her in the conference room with Mr. Corning at his side. I sat at the far end of the table taking notes.

Whenever I glanced up, Clarice's gaze was pinned to my face. Before she left the office, she told Mr. Calvetti that she'd been in touch '*soon.*' Then she turned to me and promised that she'd call me tomorrow to see how my date with Lowell went.

The scowl on The Dick's face when I looked back at him was evident.

Once Clarice was on the elevator, I explained to him that I'd met her last night at Past Over. I left out the details about how I wasn't raving about what a stellar boss he is.

He was surprised that I randomly ran into her in a vintage store.

I am too.

Mr. Corning was the one who thanked me for being so nice to Mrs. Blanchard that it brought her to the office. He said if she signs with the firm that I'll get a bonus.

That's when Mr. Calvetti left the conference room.

I nod. "She's a very kind person."

"So are you." Lowell adjusts his blue tie.

He's dressed impeccably in a gray suit and white button-down shirt.

When I met him outside the restaurant, he complimented me on my dress. I took that as the first sign that the date will be a success. The second came when he held the door open for me.

"I'm glad you finally agreed to meet me in person, Arietta." Lowell grins. "Your pictures don't do you justice. You're beautiful."

I should tell him he's handsome because he is.

It's not the kind of breath-stealing handsome that Mr. Calvetti is. Lowell is attractive in a low-key way. His black hair is cut short on the sides but flops over his forehead. His nose is sharp, and his lips are thin.

He has a boy next door air about him, although he's five years older than me, so he's definitely a man, not a boy.

"Thank you," I respond. "You're very good-looking."

His smile brightens. "You just made my night."

The server approaches to ask for our drink orders. I expect Lowell to order a bottle of wine, but he defers to me. "It's the pretty lady's choice tonight. I want her to pick her favorite."

I don't have a favorite wine. I usually sip a glass of the house red at Calvetti's when Sinclair and I go there. Sometimes Marti brings us a bottle to share.

I point a finger at the menu under the list of red wines, even though I have no idea what I'm ordering. "This one, please."

The server smiles. "Excellent choice."

I hope it is. It was one of the least expensive bottles listed. I appreciate the fact that Clarice is paying for this dinner, so I don't want to take advantage by indulging in anything I wouldn't be able to afford on my own.

As he leaves the table, Lowell turns his attention back to me. "I thought we would talk about work tonight, but I think we should focus on what you like to do when you're not at the office."

I run my fingertip up the bridge of my nose. It's a habitual move I do countless times a day to push my eyeglasses up. I drop my finger when I remember I put my contact lenses in before I left the apartment.

"You're looking for these, aren't you?" Lowell touches the frame of his glasses. "I didn't realize you wore contacts."

The corners of my lips quirk up. "I don't wear them often."

I won't add that I usually only wear them for special occasions or when I'm exercising. I've never worn them to the office. At first, that was because staring at my laptop all day caused eye irritation. I have eye drops for that now, so my excuse is that they are part of my signature look at work.

I know that my co-workers call me Little Librarian and Geeky Grandma. I don't mind since I'm the person most of them come to when they need advice on a work matter.

Leaning closer, Lowell lowers his voice. "We chatted on the app about some very personal things, Arietta. I just want to say that I feel honored that you trusted me with that."

I gaze into his eyes. I never intended to tell Lowell about my experiences with intimacy. It just happened late one night when we started talking about our first times. None of my sexual encounters so far have been memorable since I've never had an orgasm with a man before.

"I'm not going to push you for anything," he goes on. "I feel a connection to you that I've never felt with a woman before, so I want you to know that sitting this close to you right now is making me a little crazy. I'll wait though. I'll wait as long as it takes."

I'm not as naïve as I look. I know that Lowell may be laying the charm on thick to get me into bed. Time will be the test as to whether that's the case or not.

"Thank you, Lowell."

"Let's enjoy tonight." He leans back in his chair. "I'm excited to get to know you better."

The sound of an incoming email from Mr. Calvetti turns Lowell's head to the left and then the right. "Did you just hear fingernails dragging over a chalkboard? Tell me I'm not crazy. You heard it too, right?"

Laughing, I slide my phone out of the beaded clutch I bought at Past Over last month. "I just got an email from my boss."

Lowell joins in with a chuckle. "I take it he's a jerk?"

I avoid answering the question by the quick and very effective trick of diversion. "I think it's regarding an important client. I need to look at it."

Lowell mumbles something to himself about needing to check his messages too.

As he does that, I skim my fingertip over my phone's screen to open the email.

Subject: Today

Miss Voss,

I was remiss in not thanking you today.

The kindness that you displayed to Mrs. Blanchard was instrumental in securing our meeting with her this afternoon.

As Mr. Corning stated, when Mrs. Blanchard signs with our firm, you'll be compensated for your role in that accordingly.

My apologies if this email is interrupting your date with Lowlife.

Signed,
Dominick Calvetti

I stare at the email. *Lowlife?*
Squinting, I read it again before I hit reply.

Subject: Re: Today

Mr. Calvetti,

You're welcome.

As for my date's name – it's Lowell, not Lowlife.

Arietta

Before I can slip my phone back into the clutch, another email from Mr. Calvetti arrives.
Lowell's head pops up. He taps the face of his watch. "You should tell your boss you're off the clock."
I sigh. "Give me one more minute, and I'm all yours."
Lowell wiggles his dark brows. "How can I say no to that?"
Dropping my gaze, I open the unread email from Dominick that just arrived.

Subject: Re: Re: Today

Miss Voss,

It seems the spell check in my email program auto-corrected his name.

By the way, how is your evening going?

Signed,
Dominick Calvetti

I should ignore the question, but I don't. Instead, I hit reply.

Subject: Re: Re: Re: Today

Fine.

I press send. It's one of my boss's favorite responses to my questions, so I'm giving him a little taste of his own medicine.

As the server approaches to take our dinner orders, the sound of fingernails running down a chalkboard fills the air again.

Lowell laughs. "I thought my boss was a hard ass."

I try not to think about Mr. Calvetti's ass, so I smile.

Lowell starts a conversation with the server as I drop my gaze to my phone's screen.

Subject: Re: Re: Re: Re: Today

I'm sorry to hear that.

Maybe Lowlife isn't the guy for you.

Signed,
Dominick Calvetti

How dare he? He doesn't know anything about Lowell, and there's no way in hell that auto-correct is at fault again.

I curse under my breath when my phone sounds again with an incoming email. I put it on vibrate as I open the message.

Subject: Tomorrow

I'll see you in the morning, Miss Voss.

I need you at the office at 5 a.m., so make it an early night.

Signed,
Dominick Calvetti

Five? In the morning? What the ever-loving crazy is that?

"Are you ready to order, Arietta?" Lowell asks.

Sliding my phone back into my clutch, I look up at him and the server. "I'm ready."

I won't fall victim to Mr. Calvetti's latest test. If he's expecting me to respond to ask why I need to be at the office so goddamn early, he'll be disappointed.

I'll show up at four-thirty just to spite him.

I order my dinner, silently calculating in my head how long it will take me to eat it, have dessert, and get home and into bed so I can get at least a few hours of sleep.

Fortunately, I only live a few blocks from here.

"Arietta," Lowell says my name before he reaches across the table to cover my hand with his. "I hope we can do this again tomorrow night. Maybe at the seafood restaurant we planned on going to tonight?"

I'll be dead tired by this time tomorrow, but the soft smile on his face and the dimple in his left cheek sways me to agree to his proposition. "I'd like that."

He squeezes my hand gently. "It's a date. I have a feeling I'm going to dream about you tonight."

I'm going to have a nightmare tonight about my boss. It's already started.

Chapter 25

Dominick

In my effort to sabotage Miss Voss's date with Lowlife, I screwed myself.

Why the hell did I order her to the office at five a.m.?

When I sent the email, I chuckled, thinking that she'd end the date and rush home to bed to get her eight hours in.

She didn't.

How the fuck do I know that?

Because I'm the asshole who decided it was in my best interest to continue standing near the entrance to Axel Tribeca after Miss Voss put her phone back into the clutch purse on the table.

Yes, I'm that guy.

I went to get take-out at the same restaurant where Arietta was dining with Lowell. I convinced myself it was because I was craving the pan-seared salmon and the 'medley of fresh vegetables,' which turned out to be thinly sliced red peppers and green beans.

I fucking hate green beans.

As I waited for my food, I watched her. Lowlife's back was to me, but I could see Arietta. I saw the expression on her face as she read my emails, and then Lowlife reached for her hand.

The smile that sat on her bee-stung lips after that was pure torture.

I grabbed my take-out, took off, and handed the bag of expensive food to a guy on the street corner asking for spare change.

Then I went home. I tossed and turned for hours before I finally fell asleep.

I'm exhausted and irritated.

Why the fuck do I care if she holds hands with a man? She's available. She should be dating.

I exit the elevator on the floor that houses the offices to my company.

The lights are on.

That means Miss Voss beat me at my own game. She's here early.

I shouldn't be surprised. She's always early, right, kind, thoughtful, patient, and has soft gray eyes that reflect wisdom far beyond her years.

I shove a hand through my hair as I round the corner toward my office.

She bolts to her feet. Her hands fall to the waistband of the skirt she's wearing. It's patterned with red and blue butterflies. The white blouse she has on is buttoned to her neck.

Her hair is piled on top of her head in a bun that sits a little too far to the left.

She's so fucking beautiful.

"Mr. Calvetti," she calls out to me in her sweet voice. "How are you today, sir?"

"Fine," I say. "And you?"

The look of surprise on her face is one for the records books. I've never asked her that, and it shows in her expression. "I'm very well, sir. Thank you for asking."

Thank you for existing.

I need to get a fucking grip, so I fall back on my routine with a slight twist because I need caffeine immediately. "I'd like my coffee now."

The fact that I didn't say ten minutes from now doesn't faze her. Instead, she points a finger toward my office. "It's on your desk."

I glance in that direction. Next to the coffee is a bagel, toasted how I like with poached egg whites sitting atop one half of it.

"I know you usually workout first and then eat, but I thought since we're diving headfirst into work early, you might need something to satisfy your craving."

I glance at her. Eating her would satisfy my craving.

"If you'd prefer to have it later, I can get you one then," she goes on. "Your schedule doesn't indicate anything before nine."

That's because I had to scramble to come up with a reason for ordering her down here this early. I couldn't tell her it's because I didn't want Lowell's dick anywhere near her last night, but that would fall well beyond the scope of what I'm willing to share.

There's no need to tell Arietta I'm… *what the fuck am I?*

Am I protective of her? Am I attracted to her? Am I looking for a chance to bury my face between her thighs?

Scrubbing a hand over the back of my neck, I exhale harshly. "I have a phone meeting with a client in Sicily in thirty minutes. Alessia Sagese. I want you to pull up her file on the computer for me."

She looks at me like I've lost my mind. "You want me to open a file on the computer for you? That's why I had to come in early?"

I wait for her to say more, but a smile slides onto her lips.

Damn, she's good.

She's holding her anger in like a champ.

"Yes," I answer succinctly. "I'm still getting acquainted with the new filing system."

She rounds her desk and types something into her laptop. "Once you open your computer, the information will pop up on your screen."

"Just like that?" I question like I have no idea how to click open a client's file.

"Just like that," she repeats with a snap of her fingers. "It's like magic."

I fight like hell to hold back a smile. "I'm all set."

I start past her desk on the way to my office.

"Sir?" she asks from behind me. "What would you like me to do during your call?"

Good question.

I turn to face her. Her glasses slip down the bridge of her nose. With a push of her fingertip, they slide right back up.

"Prepare all the documents for Mrs. Blanchard to sign."

It's premature, but Arietta has already secured this deal. I saw it yesterday when Clarice hugged her goodbye and promised to call her today to find out how her date with Lowlife went. Lowell. Fucking Lowell.

"You believe she'll sign with the firm?" she questions with a lift of her brow.

Nodding, I step closer to her. "I do, and it's thanks to you, Arietta."

She doesn't push back on the compliment. Instead, she straightens her shoulders. "I'm glad I could help. She's making the right choice. You're the best in the business."

The temptation to ask about her date is strong, but that's showing too much of my hand. I have to play this close to the vest until whatever the fuck I'm feeling for my assistant fades away.

It *will* fade away. It has to.

Chapter 26

Arietta

"You look like you're about to fall asleep in your salad."

I glance down at the wilted lettuce and overripe slices of tomato in front of me before I set my gaze on Bronwyn. She has a cheeseburger in her hand. "What?"

"You zoned out." She waves the burger in the air, causing a slice of red onion to tumble to the top of the table. "Are you tired?"

Nodding my head, I pick up my fork and try to spear a piece of too-soft cucumber from what's left of the salad I had last night. I took the leftovers so I could bring them for lunch today.

Lowell carried the container for me when he walked me home. He didn't move in for a good night kiss as we stood in the lobby of my apartment building. He did give me a soft peck on the cheek.

It wasn't good. It wasn't bad. It just was.

"I had to come in early today," I confess as I push the salad container a few inches away from me. "I only got a few hours of sleep."

Bronwyn places the burger on its wrapper before she goes for a fry. Sliding it in a puddle of ketchup that's next to the burger, she takes a bite. "Why did you have to come in early?"

Because The Dick was being a dick.

Since we're not the only two people in the break room, I keep my answer PG rated. "Mr. Calvetti needed to make a call to Italy."

Chewing the last bite of the fry, she giggles. "What was your part in that? Holding his hand through it?"

I should laugh too, but I've wondered too many times what it would feel like to hold his hand or to feel his hands on me. They're large. They look soft.

"Wake up, sleepyhead." Bronwyn taps my wrist with her fingers. "Why did you have to come in early if he had to make a call?"

I shrug. "You know how he is."

She picks up another fry. Using it to draw a line through the center of the blob of ketchup, she smiles. "I know he must be grateful to you for connecting him with Mrs. Blanchard."

"He is," I admit as I pop the plastic top back on my salad container. "He emailed me during my date last night to thank me for that."

She stops mid-chew. "Your date?"

I didn't lead into this conversation on purpose, but I won't turn away from it. I know Bronwyn is curious, and sooner or later she's bound to ask about my date. "I went out with Lowell last night."

"Lowell," she repeats his name. "He sounds…"

"Smart?"

Shaking her head, she leans closer to me. "Wealthy. You're not dating a client, are you?"

I know the rules.

A personal relationship with a client is a big no-no for any employee of Modica. The only exceptions to the rule are Mr. Calvetti, Mr. Corning, and Mr. Lawton. The clients they know personally are all family members.

"He's not a client." I steal a fry and dot the end with ketchup. "We met on that dating app I was telling you about."

"Was last night your first date?"

I nod while I chew.

"Well, tell me." Her face brightens as she smiles. "Did he look like his pictures? Will there be a second date?"

"Yes, and tonight."

"Tonight?" She questions with surprise in her tone. "That's fast."

It is. It's too fast. I should have told Lowell tomorrow would be better. I don't know if I can stay awake until seven. That's when he's scheduled to pick me up at my place.

"I'll cover for you if you want to take a nap." She laughs. "You can do it in Judd's office. He's out for the afternoon, and that couch in his office is way too comfortable."

I raise a brow. "What?"

"I caught him asleep on it once, so he told me if I didn't tell Dominick he was sleeping on the job, I could take a nap whenever I want."

It's tempting, but Mr. Calvetti is expecting me back at my desk in fifteen minutes.

"I'll sneak in a short nap when I get home," I say, hopeful that The Dick will leave early today so I can do the same.

"Rest up because tonight might be the night." Bronwyn winks.

I inch forward on my chair, feeling the chafe of the lace against my core as I move.

I didn't wear my pretty pink lace bra and panty set for Lowell yesterday. He won't see it tonight. I have it on because I like knowing that under my clothing, hidden from everyone's view, I'm wearing something that makes me feel beautiful in my own special way.

Scooping the salad container in my hand, I push to stand. "I'm going to trash this and get back to my desk."

"I expect a full report on tonight's antics on my desk by nine a.m. tomorrow," she says in a low tone meant to mimic Dominick's voice. She still can't nail the gruffness. "Do everything I would do…and more."

I laugh at that, not knowing what she's done or would do. "I'll talk to you later."

"You can bank on it."

***

An hour later, I have a cup of coffee in front of me and multiple spreadsheets open on my computer.

All of the numbers are running together in a jumbled maze in my mind.

I take another large sip of the hot coffee, hoping the caffeine will jolt me awake enough that I can finish my work.

Mr. Calvetti is still behind his desk. His gaze has been stuck on his laptop screen since I got back from my lunch break. Either he's looking at something fascinating, or he can sleep with his eyes open.

My desk phone rings, sending a jolt through me.

I pick up the receiver. "Good afternoon. This is Arietta."

"Arietta." Bonnie's soft voice carries over the line. "Clarice Blanchard is on her way up. She insisted on surprising you, but I'd thought I'd give you and Mr. Calvetti a two-minute warning."

I glance into my boss's office. He's already on his feet, headed in my direction.

"Thank you," I say with whatever cheer I can muster. "I appreciate the heads-up."

By the time I hang up the phone, Mr. Calvetti is next to me. I don't look in his direction because *cock-a-doodle-do-me,* the bulge in his pants is always there, and since I first noticed it, I have to fight not to stare at it.

"What's going on, Arietta?"

"Clarice is on her way up."

He rounds my desk, so he's standing across from me. I finally drag my gaze up to his face. Damn. Dominick Calvetti with a little stubble on his jaw is freaking hotter than my coffee.

"This is it." He scrubs a hand over the stubble in the mesmerizing way only ridiculously gorgeous guys can pull off. "She's going to sign with us."

From his lips to her ears.

I hope he's right. I could use the '*compensation*' Mr. Corning promised I'd receive if Clarice officially becomes a Modica client.

Snapping my laptop closed, I push back from my desk. I glance down the corridor when I hear the elevator ding its arrival on our floor.

Clarice pops into view a few seconds later, dressed in the same blue trench coat she was wearing the night we met. She's paired it with black slacks and a white scarf around her neck. The brooch is pinned to that.

"Arietta!" she calls out my name with a wave of her hand in the air. "How are you?"

I steal a glance at my boss. He's watching me. I'd say he's waiting with bated breath for my answer, but his expression doesn't match up with that. He wants me to skip past the pleasantries, so he can find out if Clarice is ready to take the plunge to become his number one client.

"I'm well," I say as she approaches my desk. "How are you today?"

Her gaze flits over my face before it lands on Dominick. "You probably think I'm here to sign with your firm."

"I hope that's the case," he says quietly.

"My lawyer looked over the contract, and…" Her voice trails as she turns to me. "We'll get to that momentarily. First, Arietta is going to tell me all about her date last night."

Sweet torture is not Dominick Calvetti's forte. I can tell by the tic in his jaw as he waits for me to recount my date with Lowell.

"It was fun," I answer honestly. "The food was incredible."

"And Lowell?" She leans in closer. "How was he?"

"A gentleman," I say with a smile.

The Dick clears his throat, likely because that's a foreign concept to him.

"When's the next date?" Clarice toys with the brooch.

"Tonight," I say, even though I've considered postponing it to a night when I don't feel like I'm stuck in a patch of fog, unable to see or think clearly.

"That's a great sign." She looks me over. "What a lucky man this Lowell is. Don't you agree, Dominick?"

We both turn toward my boss. He clears his throat again. "Arietta is indeed something."

Something? Is that a half-compliment or a full-on insult?

I can't tell.

It wouldn't kill him to toss some kindness in my direction now and again.

Clarice nods in agreement. "She's something special. That's why I've decided to sign with your firm, as long as you agree to my stipulations about Arietta being my point of contact."

I turn to Mr. Calvetti, and the air catches in my lungs. I stare with my mouth ajar.

He's smiling. He's actually smiling with his perfectly straight white teeth in view and the corners of his eyes squinting upwards.

"Agreed." He extends a hand to Clarice.

She takes it for a brief shake. "My lawyer will send the amended contract over for your perusal. We'll meet again soon to sign."

He nods with that drop-dead gorgeous smile still on his face.

I look down because it's striking something inside of me. Something I should feel for Lowell, not my boss.

"I have a meeting," Clarice announces. "Blocks from here, in twenty minutes, but you know traffic."

I don't. I know walking, the bus schedule, and the subway with its sticky seats and men with untoward glances.

"Arietta will see you to the lobby," Dominick offers. "She's on her way home for the day."

I am?

The question gets caught in my throat behind a lump of confusion. He's letting me leave early? I can walk out of here in the middle of the afternoon without a solid excuse?

I don't waste time trying to figure out my boss's motivation.

As I scoop up my purse, I glance at him. "What time do you need me here tomorrow, sir?"

His gaze slowly travels over my face, landing on my lips. With a hint of a smile, he leans closer to me. "Nine a.m. will be fine, Arietta. I'll see you then."

Chapter 27

Dominick

There is no way in hell that this plan I'm putting into action is a good idea. It's a fraction better than the plan I initially cooked up while Arietta was talking to Clarice this afternoon.

I listened as my assistant spoke about her second date with the lowlife Lowell. Jealousy hit me with the force of a freight train.

If she's seeing this guy two nights in a row, surely there's something there.

I decided on the spot that I'd send Arietta home early so I could go to a bar for a drink and a much-needed distraction.

That distraction being a fuck with a stranger who isn't named Arietta and doesn't resemble her in the least.

I found a woman with dark hair, green eyes, and a promise that she could swallow my cock in a way I'd never experienced before.

Since my dick has always been open for any new adventure with a woman, I paid for our drinks and suggested we take our party for two to the hotel down the street.

We didn't make it into the lobby before I spotted a petite blonde wearing a purple dress, red ballet flats, and eyeglasses getting out of a taxi.

That was it.

My dick mistook her for Arietta, and any interest I had in the cock-swallowing brunette evaporated.

I bid her farewell before I had a chance to book a room.

I've moved onto Plan B.

I'm in the lobby of my assistant's apartment building, hoping like hell that I've beat Lowlife here.

If I get upstairs and he's got her in bed, I'll toss him out the window.

I stroll across the lobby, noting the smile on the doorman's face. He waves a hand in greeting even though we've never met. That's the sign of a good man. He'll make an effort to be friendly to a stranger regardless of whether it benefits him or not.

Once I reach the bank of elevators, I push a finger into the call button, again and again. I'm eager to see my assistant. When she opens her apartment door to find me standing there with a bouquet of pink and red roses, I hope to hell I'll figure something out that will halt her date in its tracks.

The sound of whistling turns me around.

Fuck me.

Lowell is on the approach with a trio of withering daises in his hand.

Amateur.

"Hey," he calls out to me in a nasal tone. "It looks like we both have hot dates lined up."

My stomach churns as I respond. "Your date is going to be disappointed if that's all you've got."

His gaze drops to the almost-dead flowers in his palm before it shifts to the fresh bouquet in mine. "Like the flowers really matter."

He steps on the elevator first when the doors slide open. He jabs a finger into the button labeled 20 before he perks his left brow. "Where are you headed, dude?"

"Same floor," I bite out.

He leans back on his heel. "I'm on my way to see a cute one. Even her name is sweet. Arietta."

My fist clenches around the flowers as I silently stare at him.

"I'm getting laid tonight." He elbows me as he rakes a hand through his hair. "I can taste it already."

My eye catches on the gold band wrapped around his ring finger. With my teeth clenched together, I step closer to him. "You're fucking married."

Chuckling, he shakes his head. "Thanks for the reminder."

He slips the ring from his finger, depositing it in the front pocket of his pants. Daisy petals fall to the floor with the movement. He drops the rotting stems. "It looks like these are a lost cause."

The elevator creeps upward, so I turn to face him. "So are you, asshole."

He turns to look at me. "Calm down, dude. The wife is too busy spending my money to care where I put my dick."

Jesus.

I slap my palm against the red emergency button on the panel bringing the elevator to a sudden stop.

He stumbles forward. "What the fuck is your problem?"

I'm on him before he realizes what's happening. My left hand still holds tightly to the bouquet as I fist the lapel of his cheap suit jacket with my right hand. In one fluid movement, I've backed him up to the wall.

"Did Lauren send you to follow me? She's going to take the kids, isn't she? I'm going to lose my boys over this."

A wife? Kids? He is a lowlife through and through.

"Stay the hell away from Arietta." I stare into his eyes. "Do not contact her again. Do not try and see her, or I will hunt you down."

He nods his head so hard it looks like it's about to fly off his pencil-thin neck. "I won't. Please don't hurt me. Jesus Christ, please, don't hit me."

I inch back when a male voice fills the elevator. "Is anyone in there? We're going to get you out as soon as possible."

130

I punch the red button again, sending the elevator up toward the floor where Arietta is waiting for this worthless piece of shit. "As soon as I step off, you're headed back to the lobby. Once you're there, get the hell away from here as fast as you can."

Still nodding, he wipes away the sweat that has gathered over his upper lip. "You'll never see me again. Arietta won't either."

I brace myself when the elevator doors slide open. I wanted to halt her date, but not like this. Now, I have to be the one to tell Arietta that the man she was about to spend the night with is a goddamn liar.

Chapter 28

Arietta

I take one last look at myself in the mirror.

I'm wearing a pink dress that I bought months ago at Past Over. It's sleeveless with a fitted bodice and a skirt that falls just above my knee.

Before Sinclair left to have dinner with Berk and his daughter, Stevie, she helped me pull my hair into a high ponytail. My makeup was also her handiwork, even though I argued that I could handle it on my own.

She did a fantastic job though. My eye makeup is a mix of pink shadows, and black liner finished with a coat of mascara. The lipstick I have on is a shade lighter than my dress.

I slide my glasses back on when I hear a faint knock at the apartment door.

After one last look in the mirror, I head out of my bedroom.

Inviting Lowell here to pick me up wasn't a strategic move. He offered to stop here so we could take an Uber together to the restaurant. It will save us both a little money. Since I started living in this city, I've realized that every extra dime counts.

Another knock at the door lures a playful bark from Dudley. He leaps off my bed and heads toward the foyer at breakneck speed.

I chase after him, giggling as he slips on the hardwood before he finds his balance again.

We reach the door at almost the same time.

I swing it open.

"Lowell," I say to the solid chest of a man who is at least six inches taller than my date.

Blinking my eyes in confusion, I follow the man's chest with my gaze until I reach his lips and then his dark eyes.

"Mr. Calvetti?" I whisper his name, not sure if I'm seeing what I'm seeing.

With mussed hair, and his jaw freshly shaven, my boss looks down at me. "Arietta."

I glance past him to where the elevator is at the end of the corridor. "I wasn't expecting you."

"You were expecting Lowlife," he says matter-of-factly.

"Lowell," I correct him because it's not funny anymore.

I don't feel any loyalty to Lowell. I don't have to defend him, but since The Dick has never met him, he doesn't have a right to judge him.

"May I come in?" he asks in a low tone.

My gaze drops to the bouquet of pink and red roses in his hand. The stems are tied neatly together with a white ribbon.

I step aside, curious about why he stopped here when he's obviously on his way to a date. I always wondered what he dresses like outside of the office.

He's wearing dark gray pants, a black V-neck sweater, and very nice black wingtip shoes.

My heart thunders inside my chest as he brushes past me.

Why did he have to come here right before Lowell is set to arrive? I can't be thinking about my ridiculously hot boss while I'm eating shrimp and imitation crab with a guy who kissed me on the cheek in a way that didn't fan any flames inside of me.

Right now, I feel like I'm standing in the center of a roaring inferno.

Shutting the door, I turn to face him. "How can I help you, sir?"

He rakes me from head-to-toe slowly, his gaze catching on the gold heart necklace I'm wearing. "You look lovely, Arietta."

I'm taken aback by the compliment. He looks more handsome than a man should ever look, but I keep that to myself. He knows it. Men like him are well aware of how every head turns when they walk into a room.

"I have a date," I blurt out even though he overheard me telling Clarice that this afternoon. "He's going to be here any minute."

His gaze drops to the bouquet he's holding. "These are for you. I wanted to thank you again for introducing me to Mrs. Blanchard."

With a shaky hand, I take them. I've never seen such a beautiful arrangement of roses. There are at least two dozen of them, each perfect in shape. "Thank you, sir."

His gaze flits to the door before it settles back on my face. "We need to talk. It's important, Arietta."

Since he's never given me flowers before, I can only assume that he's going to rescind the offer to compensate me for Clarice signing with Modica.

I knew I should have gotten it in writing and had his signature notarized.

The flowers are lovely, but they're not an ironclad legal agreement.

I don't have time to do this now. This is a discussion we can have tomorrow morning after I've gathered my thoughts so I can present a compelling argument as to why I am entitled to what Judd promised.

"I'm having dinner with Lowell tonight," I explain in an even tone. "I think any conversation concerning a work issue should take place at the office."

His brow furrows. "This isn't a work issue."

134

It takes a second for that to sink in. I bring the flowers to my nose and inhale. The scent is sweet, enveloping. Taking a breath, I exhale. "Why are you here?"

"Lowell."

Hearing my date's name coming from Mr. Calvetti surprises me. "Lowell? What about him?"

"Maybe you should take a seat, Arietta." With a broad sweep of his hand in the air, he points at the couch.

I glance over to see Dudley napping. "No, I'm fine."

Dominick rubs a hand over his chin. "I'm sorry I have to be the one to tell you this."

I brace myself because those words are rarely followed by anything but bad news.

"Tell me what?" I ask, still standing in place.

Since he doesn't know Lowell, the worst it can be is that Lowell called the office to cancel our date. I should feel a twinge of sadness at the prospect of that, but I don't.

Dominick steps toward me. "Lowell is married. He has children."

The flowers tumble from my hand. Mr. Calvetti surges forward to grab them the moment they hit the floor. I glance down to see him on one knee, looking up at me.

He abruptly straightens until he's standing in front of me. He's so close I can feel the heat from his body.

"That's not right," I say slowly, looking up at him. "He's never been married. He doesn't have kids."

"We arrived in the lobby at the same time. We rode the elevator up together," he explains in a soft tone.

"That wasn't Lowell," I say to convince myself that I didn't misjudge him. "It wasn't him."

"He was headed to the twentieth floor. Your name came up, Arietta." He rubs his forehead. "It was Lowell. He's married."

Speechless, I stare at him.

Exhaling harshly, he goes on, "I spotted his wedding ring. He slipped it off."

My gaze drops to my feet. "He had a ring?"

Anger fuels the fisting of my hands in front of me. He lied. He fucking lied to me for weeks. I told him things. Personal and private things that I thought I was sharing with a single guy.

"He dropped it into his pocket before I pushed him against the wall."

My head snaps up. "You what?"

"Lowlife bragged about cheating. He mentioned his boys." Dominick's tone is calm, controlled. "I told him to get lost. He'll never contact you again."

As relieved as I am by that, I'm shocked that he did that for me.

"You're too good for him." He places the flowers in my hand again. "You deserve better than a cheating asshole, Arietta."

Cheating.

Lowell was cheating on his wife.

We never slept together or kissed for that matter, but I shared secrets with him. Those secrets weren't meant for a married man with children.

"I had no idea," I confess with a tremor in my voice. "When I looked him up on social media, everything was set to private."

Mr. Calvetti is a rapt audience, stuck on my every word.

"He told me he'd abandoned those pages years ago." I look away from Dominick's intense gaze. "His Facebook profile was a picture of him holding an infant. He said it was his nephew."

But it was likely his son, one of them since Dominick mentioned *sons*.

Tears prick the corners of my eyes. I'm not emotional from my loss since the connection I felt to Lowell was still burgeoning. It may have fizzled out after tonight.

My sorrow is for his wife.

I don't know her, but I feel guilt for having dinner with her husband and spending all those hours on the app talking to him.

"He was scared shitless that I was trailing him for his wife." Dominick crosses his arms. "He accused me of being a spy. He was panicked over the prospect of losing his sons over this."

I wipe a tear before it can fall down my cheek. "I feel bad for her. Every woman deserves honesty from her partner."

Silently Dominick stares into my eyes.

I break the gaze again when I glance down at the bouquet in my hands. "Thank you again for the flowers, sir, and for telling me about Lowlife."

The corners of his lips edge up. "You're welcome. You should put the flowers in water before we leave."

Narrowing my eyes, I ask the obvious question. "Where are we going?"

"The one place that will make you forget about Lowlife."

Being this close to him has virtually erased Lowell from my mind. "Where is that?"

"Calvetti's. You haven't eaten. I'm starving, so let's go." He flashes me a mega-watt smile just like the one I saw this afternoon.

Flowers, a dinner invitation, and a heart-stopping smile.

This may feel like a date, but it's not. It's a pity plate of pasta.

I'll take it since the man I was supposed to be with tonight is a cheating, no-good bastard. Besides, it will give me time to craft a message to Lowell in my mind. I have every intention of sending him a 'you're-a-fucking-jerk' message before I block him on the app.

Once I've done that, I'm contacting the legal department of the company that owns the app. Their guarantee that they screen every potential client means I'll get back the twenty dollars I spent when I signed up for their service.

"It will give us a chance to discuss how we'll handle correspondence with Clarice moving forward." He slides right back into boss mode as the smile slips from his lips. "I'm confident that you can handle it, Arietta, but it's important that we're on the same page when she reaches out to you."

Sure, boss.

Tell me my date is a married cheater, and then effortlessly shift the conversation to work.

Since Sinclair is at Berk's for dinner, and I have nothing to look forward to but watching TV with Dudley until she gets home, I nod. "Okay."

This evening isn't going the way I thought it would, but now I know Lowell Wellington is a waste of my time, and I have Mr. Calvetti to thank for that.

The least I can do is spend an hour or two with him while he tells me what I should and shouldn't say to Clarice Blanchard. Little does he know that I'm following my instinct when it comes to Clarice. It worked when I met her, so it's bound to work going forward.

Chapter 29

Dominick

The short white cardigan that Arietta put on over her dress is enough to ward off the wind that picked up while I was in her apartment. She pushes a wayward strand of hair back from her cheek as she glances at me.

Jesus, every single fucking time I look at her, I see pure beauty.

I've never known a woman who can capture attention with just a smile.

Arietta is doing it now.

She grinned at a couple pushing a toddler in a stroller as we exited the lobby of her apartment building. They both stopped to wave to her.

From the bits and pieces of the conversation she's having with them, they've never seen her before today. The woman wanted to know where Arietta got the dress she's wearing.

I missed the answer as I called the driver I often use to pick us up. He told me he was on Judd duty tonight, so I fired him.

Thankfully, he's been with Modica long enough not to take me seriously.

As I debate whether to flag down a taxi or order an Uber, Arietta steps in place next to me.

"Our Uber will be here in a couple of minutes, sir."

I glance over to see the couple she was speaking with walking away. "You ordered a car?"

"Yes," she says with a nod. "I did it when we were in the elevator on our way down. I told you. You don't remember?"

No. Not at all. That likely has everything to do with the fact that I was staring at her. Her body in that dress is out of this world, but the way she was biting her bottom lip as she typed into her phone was hypnotic.

I didn't realize the elevator made it to the lobby before she stepped out.

I drag a hand through my hair. "How long have you lived here?"

It's a generic question. It's random enough that my cock will calm the fuck down. There's nothing sensual about living accommodations.

"Before I moved to New York, I arranged to live in Midtown in a three-bedroom apartment with five other people." She shakes her head. "It was dirt cheap, and I thought I'd make new friends."

Lifting a brow, I ask the question she's waiting for. "It didn't work out?"

Rolling her eyes, she lets out a laugh. "There was no apartment, and the five other people were one scam artist with a bogus ad on Craigslist. He took my deposit, and when I went to the building, no one knew anything about it."

Damn, that's a cold welcome to the city.

"Asshole," I spit out.

Her eyes brighten. "It all worked out. I rented a room at an airport hotel, and a week later, I met the woman who owns the apartment I live in now. She's Sinclair's sister-in-law. She gave me a cut on the rent as long as I took care of the cleaning and cooking."

She's lucky. Most stories like hers end with the scam victim fleeing back to wherever they came from.

"I'm glad it worked out, although that's a tough blow about the security deposit."

Glancing down at her phone, she takes a step toward the curb. "It did all work out. I contacted him again when he posted another ad a month later. I used a different name and told him I could only pay in cash, so we agreed to meet up at a diner."

This woman has steel balls. It takes courage to do that.

"What happened?"

She gestures to an approaching black SUV. "There's our ride. I told him that he was guilty of committing wire fraud. Since it's a misdemeanor, he faced up to a year in jail, and I was prepared to present my evidence to the prosecutor's office that afternoon."

I hold back a chuckle as the car stops next to us. "You had evidence?"

She steps back as I swing open the back passenger door. "He used his real first name in our correspondence. That's all I had. I sent the money to a bank account that my bank couldn't trace."

Arietta slides onto the back seat. "He was younger than me. When I brought up fraud, he broke out in a sweat."

I get in next to her. "It sounds like you gambled and won."

"I got my money back that day in cash." She smiles. "That's all I wanted."

She's incredibly fortunate. That meeting could have ended much worse.

"If he would have looked like a mobster, I would have walked out of the diner." She laughs as the driver pulls into traffic. "But he looked like my first boyfriend. Clean-cut, well-dressed, geeky."

She's describing Lowlife to a tee.

"Is that your type, Arietta?"

Her gray eyes scan my face. "Nerdy guys or dorky assholes?"

I don't answer because I suspect that's a rhetorical question.

"I need to swear off men like that." She glances out of the window of the car. "I haven't had good luck with those types of men."

I drop my gaze to her legs and the skin in view just above her knees. It has to be soft. It must taste like heaven. I follow the skirt of her dress with my gaze, wondering what she's wearing underneath it.

"I'd ask what your type is, sir, but personal questions are still prohibited, right?"

I catch the hint of a smile that plays on her full lips.

"I don't have a type, Arietta."

She cocks a perfectly arched blonde brow. "Really?"

I lean closer until the scent of her perfume hits me. "Really."

She lets out the tiniest sound, almost a moan, before she shifts her gaze back to the window of the car. "You should go through Central Park. It's faster."

The driver glances in the rearview mirror and smiles. "Your wish is my command, Miss."

I toss him a *back-the-hell-off* look when he shifts his gaze to me.

This may not be a date, but she's mine tonight.

I plan on spending the next several hours in the company of Miss Voss in a place I know I'll be forced to behave myself.

Chapter 30

Dominick

"Is your new boyfriend meeting you here for dinner?" My grandmother asks Arietta as soon as we walk into the restaurant. She looks me over from head-to-toe. "What are you doing here?"

"Talk about brutal," I say, raising a hand to the center of my chest. "It's good to see you too, Marti."

She's had the nickname forever. I still slip a grandma or granny in from time-to-time, but for the most part, she's Marti to all of her grandchildren.

Laughing, she perches on her tiptoes to plant a kiss on my cheek and a soft slap on the other. I know that move. It's the *I-love-you-but-smarten-the-hell-up* move.

"Lowell and I aren't going to see each other again," Arietta confesses. "He wasn't honest with me."

Marti crosses her arms over her chest. "He's a weasel, is he?"

Arietta nods. "A big one."

"He can go straight to hell," Marti swears for maybe the third time in her life.

I straighten and toss her a look. "Language, Marti."

She shakes a fist at me. "You're trouble tonight. Why are you really here? Do you have a date? Am I finally going to meet a woman you like?"

Arietta and I lock eyes before she breaks the gaze. "Mr. Calvetti is having dinner with me tonight."

Marti glances at Arietta before she turns to me. The way her eyebrows are dancing around, I know what's bouncing around in her head. I shoot her a look to stop her from blurting out something that will embarrass the hell out of Arietta.

"Mr. Calvetti?" She questions. "Why is she calling you that? It's the evening. You're on a date."

"No," I say in unison with my assistant.

Arietta takes over with laughter bubbling out of her. "This is so not a date, Marti. Why would I be on a date with Mr. Calvetti?"

I don't find this nearly as amusing as she does.

"Dominick is a nice boy." Shaking her head, Marti taps the center of my chest with her index finger. "All right, he's a smart boy, and he does well for himself at work. You know that, Arietta."

What kind of backhanded compliment was that?

I look at my grandmother. "What?"

"Mr. Calvetti is a nice man," Arietta interjects. "He saved me tonight."

Marti's gaze darts to me. "You saved her?"

Glancing up at me, Arietta smiles. "He saved me from making a huge mistake. I'm indebted to him."

I know exactly how I want to be repaid. It starts with those lips of hers. I want them on mine.

"He keeps his kindness hidden." Marti wraps an arm around my waist, and I take her in a side-hug. "My grandson has a big heart."

"I'm ready to eat," I interrupt before my grandmother says more. "Arietta and I will have spaghetti."

Marti points to a table in the corner. "Go and sit. I'll bring two bowls of the penne with vodka sauce. I made it myself."

I motion for Arietta to lead the way. She does, giving me a dick-aching view of her ass as it sways with each step she takes.

144

***

Arietta spends fifteen minutes picking her way through the pasta before she takes a first bite. I can tell something is off. I doubt it's the food. It's as delicious as ever. The wine is superb. She's downed half of what's in her glass in between checking her phone.

Watching her stare at her phone screen, I take a swallow of wine from my glass. "Is everything all right?"

Her gaze darts up to meet mine. "My roommate is asking about Lowell."

Of course she is. Arietta was set to go out with the scum of the earth before I derailed that. "Have you told her he's…"

"A fucking asshole?"

My gaze drops to her lips. *Fucking.* The way she says the word with a bite stirs my cock again.

"Yes," I answer succinctly.

She finishes what's left of her wine. "He's the worst of the worst."

Since I can't argue with that, I remain silent.

With one forearm on the table, she leans closer to me. "I made such a big mistake with him."

I know she's not talking about a fuck because Lowlife made it crystal clear that he hadn't rounded first base with her.

Even though I sense she won't confide in me, I press. "What mistake, Arietta?"

She steals a glance at Marti standing near the kitchen, watching us with an eagle eye. "I shouldn't say. It's too embarrassing."

I pry because my fucking curiosity is driving this. "What's too embarrassing?"

Her gaze drops to the table. "It's so personal."

"Dominick?"

I close my eyes briefly. It's not possible that I'm hearing my mother's voice right now. She's in Italy. I sent her and my dad there for a vacation. They're not due back in New York until the day after tomorrow.

"Your mom is here, and your dad too," Arietta exclaims before she's out of her chair headed in their direction.

What the hell is happening? How does she know who they are?

I push to stand as I see my mom gather my assistant in her arms, but my ass drops right back down when my father greets her.

It's a hug, the same bear hug he gives me, but then I see something that catches my breath in my throat.

Arietta raises her hands in the air and uses sign language to communicate with my father: *I got the postcard you sent, and you got a tan. How was the trip?*

Each movement of her hands is measured and precise.

My dad signs back at a slower pace than his usual: *Good. Beautiful. Has my son been behaving himself?*

I catch my dad's eye, and he waves to me. He follows it with a thumbs-up, our special signal that everything is right in his world. It's the world in which he's never heard his wife's voice, the laughter of his children, or anything else.

Arietta glances in my direction with a smile before she signs to my dad: *He's the best. He's just like his father.*

That's the greatest compliment I've ever received. It's unwarranted. It's rooted in her limited knowledge of the man that I am, but I take it. I absorb it because one day, before I leave this earth, I hope to be a quarter of the man my father, Louis Calvetti, is.

Chapter 31

Arietta

Watching Mr. Calvetti interact with his parents tonight was a glimpse into his soul. Greed slipped to the side and made space for kindness, at least for a few hours.

My boss hugged his mom and dad before he yanked two chairs from another table so they could join us. I watched as he used sign language with ease. He even helped me when I was unsure of a word.

We're outside of the restaurant now. I've ordered an Uber for one. Mr. Calvetti is planning on seeing his parents to their apartment on the Upper West Side before he goes home or wherever he'll end up tonight.

He glances back at Calvetti's. "I didn't expect my folks to be back this soon."

I could tell he was surprised when they showed up. The shocked expression on his face when he realized that I know sign language was more pronounced.

"Your mom said they missed everyone so much they booked an earlier flight home," I remind him. "They stayed at your villa in Sicily?"

"They did."

"I'm sure it's beautiful there," I say quietly.

"I had no idea you knew American Sign Language, Arietta." He shoves a hand into the front pocket of his pants. "That wasn't listed on your resume."

"I didn't know it when I started working at Modica," I confess. "I don't know it all that well now. Your dad is still teaching me."

His gaze flits over my face. "My father is teaching you?"

I've never considered my friendship with Louis Calvetti as crossing a boundary until now. Did I overstep when I asked him to teach me sign language? I never gave any thought to whether that would upset my boss or not.

I straighten my shoulders. "Yes. He brought me lunch one day when you were in Italy, and I wanted to thank him using sign language. I wrote a note asking him to show me, and he did."

His gaze darts to the windows of the restaurant and beyond that to where his parents are still seated at the table with Marti.

"He'd come back a few times a week and spend my lunch break with me," I go on in a rush, "he didn't always bring the food. Sometimes I got him two of the hotdogs he likes from the food cart around the corner from the office. His favorite is the cheeseburgers at a deli called Crispy Biscuit. He's always happiest when I have one waiting for him with chili fries."

Mr. Calvetti's brow furrows. "This went on the entire time I was in Italy?"

"Yes," I answer honestly, taking it a step further. "I hope it starts again now that he's back from his trip."

Since he's silently contemplating what I'm saying, I continue my confession. "Your mom invited me for dinner twice. I went. Their home is beautiful."

Having dinner with his parents was a treat that I always looked forward to.

"My mother invited you for dinner?" he asks quietly. "You've been to their apartment?"

I spot the white sedan that is picking me up approaching. "I have, sir. It was lovely."

He glances over his shoulder to where I'm looking. "Is that your Uber?"

"Yes," I say, moving closer to the curb. "Thank you for dinner and for everything you did tonight."

He steps onto the street to open the back passenger door of the car for me. When he turns to look at me, I see a soft smile on his lips. "You're very welcome, Arietta."

Feeling relieved that I didn't screw everything up by spending time with his parents, I return the smile with one of my own.

He reaches out his hand to help me get into the car. I take it as I step off the curb. "I'll see you in the morning, Mr. Calvetti."

His hand closes around mine. With a brush of his thumb against my palm, he leans close to me. It's so close that I can feel his breath rush over my cheek. "It's Dominick. Call me Dominick, Arietta."

I glance into his eyes as I repeat his name back to him. "Dominick."

"Just like that." He smiles. "I enjoyed this evening."

"Me too," I whisper as I slide onto the seat of the car. When he shuts the door, I suck in a deep breath. "Me too, Dominick."

***

"Back up." Sinclair stares at me. "Are you saying The Dick has a heart?"

I laugh.

She curls her fingers on both hands together to form the shape of a heart. "Does it beat inside that sexy, broad chest?"

I move around her to drop my cardigan and purse on the couch. "I'm saying he may not be the biggest dick around."

"No." She shakes her head. "He may very well have the biggest dick around. You don't know. I saw the bulge in his pants when he was here the other day."

She bounces to her tiptoes and cups her hands around her mouth. "Cock-a-doodle-do-me, the man is packing something impressive in his boxers."

"You should have seen him tonight." I fan a hand in front of my face. "He was wearing a black sweater and gray pants. His hair was mussed. It was like he took a shower and didn't bother with it after that. He looked like he stepped out of the pages of a magazine."

"You left out the part about how the pants fit perfectly, accentuating what's inside of them."

Laughing, I settle down next to Dudley. He crawls into my lap. "Seeing him with his family was great, but it's when he told me to call him Dominick that I saw him differently."

"Wait. What?" Sinclair falls into a chair across from me. "You've been talking to me since you left the restaurant. Why is this the first time I'm hearing that he asked you to call him Dominick?"

Running a hand over Dudley's head, I sigh. "That's because you spent the first ten minutes of our phone conversation ranting about Lowell."

She did. I called her as soon as my Uber rounded the corner, headed away from Calvetti's. Sinclair wanted to know how it was going with Lowell. I filled her in. She then proceeded to call him every name in the book and a few she just thought up.

By the time I was in the elevator on my way up to our apartment, she finally let me get a word in about Mr. Calvetti. That's when I explained that we spent time with his parents, and I got to see another side of him.

"I sense a love connection." She picks a piece of lint from her jeans. "My heart is telling me that you just had your first date with your future husband."

I toss my head back in laughter. "You're not serious?"

"Dead serious." Her facial expression matches her tone.

"I'll bet you that he'll be having sex with someone else tonight."

Sinclair purses her lips. "I'll up that and bet you that he has not fucked anyone since he saw the picture of you in lingerie."

"He can't go without sex for that long."

"A man will wait for the woman he wants." She points a finger at me. "He really wants you, and don't try and tell me that the picture you accidentally sent him was low quality. None of the pictures you take are low quality. He got a good look at everything you're hiding under your clothes."

"This is silly." I manage a half-laugh. "He's going to take his parents home, and then he'll find a woman to spend the night with."

Sinclair pushes to her feet. "I'm taking Duds out for a walk, and then I need to write. Email The Dick in an hour; an hour-and-a-half tops. Thank him again for kicking Lowell out of your life. I bet you a week of cooking dinner, he'll reply right away."

Sinclair isn't the best cook, but I could use the break from the kitchen, so I jut out my hand. "It's a bet."

She shakes it before she kisses the top of it. "This is the beginning of something amazing for you, Arietta. I'm right. You're wrong, so start meal planning now."

I bring our joined hands together so I can kiss the top of hers before I drop it. "I'm right. I know I am."

I say the words even though my heart is hoping I'm dead wrong.

Chapter 32

Dominick

I toss my phone and keys on a small table that sits in the foyer of my apartment. The sound when they hit the wood punctuates the silence. I live on the top floor in what many would refer to as a penthouse.

It's spacious, tastefully decorated, and affords me views of Central Park that can steal the breath of even the most jaded New Yorker.

It was the thirtieth apartment that I'd toured in a month. Something about it hit a spot inside of me. I wouldn't call it love, but I could see success when I walked through the door.

It resembled the place I envisioned I'd live in when I read all of those financial magazines in college. In the Forbes article that featured Vernon Greenwalt, there was a picture of him at his ten thousand square foot summerhouse in Nantucket. Another billionaire in the article, Wheaton Comsort Jr., was photographed on his yacht in the French Riviera.

This apartment is a symbol of my achievements. It's an empty, quiet symbol. My villa in Italy is the same.

I move to the windows as I tug the sweater I've been wearing all night over my head. I toe out of my shoes, rid myself of my socks and drop my pants before I reach the glass.

No one can see in, although it wouldn't matter if they could.

I stand in my boxer briefs and stare out into the vastness of Central Park and the city it centers.

I glance over my shoulder when I hear my phone chime signaling the arrival of an email. I should ignore it since I've ignored every other notification from my phone all evening.

But, it's late. It's too late for anyone to be worried about money except my clients that live across the Atlantic.

I stalk back to my phone and scoop it up.

I skim my fingers over the screen to open my email app.

The ten alerts that sounded during the evening are all emails from clients. I know what they want. It's a slice of my time tomorrow.

I'll get to them in the morning, but the most recent email can't wait.

That one is from Arietta.

I read the subject line and click open the message.

Subject: Thank You

Dear Dominick,

Thank you again for what you did tonight.

If you hadn't figured out that Lowell was the lowest of the lowlifes, I might have made a very big mistake.

You saved me.

If there's anything I can do to repay you for that, please let me know.

Arietta

You can repay me by riding my cock or sitting on my face.

Hell, at this point I'll take a kiss as repayment because I'm infatuated with my assistant.

I suck in a deep breath before I hit reply.

Subject: Re: Thank You

Dear Arietta,

You're welcome.

There's no need to repay me, as I'm the one in your debt.

Not only did you introduce me to Mrs. Blanchard, but you also found my dad a copy of that book that's been out of print forever. What's the title again?

Dominick

I hit send.

Strategy is an integral part of every form of communication.

After Arietta left the restaurant tonight, I ordered an Uber to pick up my parents and me. My mom insisted I go up to their apartment, so I went. As soon as I was inside, my dad shoved a book in my hands with a tattered dust jacket.

Ruins of Roses.

It was written a century ago by an author I've never heard of. The print run was small, but my father searched and searched for a copy for years. His interest in the story was stoked by a lone review he read online that coined the work 'a stunningly overlooked piece of rare literary beauty in the form of a fairytale for the ages'.

I've tried to find a copy for years. Bella has too. My mom stopped at every vendor on the street selling used books. We always came up empty.

Arietta didn't. She found a copy that was signed by the author.

She gave it to my dad during one of their *cheeseburger and chili fries with a side of sign language lessons* lunches.

It touched him.

I witnessed that tonight when his smile beamed as he held that book.

My phone chimes, so I drop my gaze and read the incoming email from my assistant that I was expecting.

I knew she'd write back immediately with the name of the book.

I would prefer face-to-face contact with her tonight, but I'll take what I can get.

Subject: Re: Re: Thank You

Dear Dominick,

Ruins of Roses.

That's the name of the book.

Speaking of roses, I put the ones you brought me on my nightstand before I got into bed.

That way I can smell them in my dreams.

Thank you again.

Arietta

She's in bed.

Jesus. What the fuck is she wearing or not wearing?

Does she sleep on her back or side?

I shake away all of that and move to my leather sofa. Taking a seat, I lean back and stare at my phone.

It almost falls from my hand when it starts ringing.

Arietta.

She's calling me.

Clearing my throat, I reach down and graze a hand over my rock hard cock. I need to get a grip.

I answer on the second ring. "Hello."

"Mr. Calvetti," she whispers. "I mean Dominick."

I smile at the sound of her voice. I've always found it sweet and soft. Now, I find it sexy as hell.

"Arietta," I say her name in a low tone.

"I have to tell you something." She lets out a soft exhale. "It couldn't wait until morning."

Jesus. Is this happening? Is she about to tell me she wants me to come over?

"Tell me," I bite out a bit too sharply.

Silence greets me. Then a noise. It's too faint to gauge precisely what it is, but if forced to, I'd place it midway between a moan and a whimper.

Is she touching herself?

I reach down and dive a hand under the waistband of my boxer briefs. I stroke myself, one long, slow stroke before I squeeze the crown of my cock. A bead of pre-cum escapes.

I'm primed for this.

I've never wanted a woman more.

XOXO   Deborah Bladon

"Arietta?" I say her name softly, but there's nothing gentle in my tone. It's not tender. It's filled with the same need that I feel.

Need. Yes, I goddamn feel it, and it's fucking intoxicating.

There's a rustling sound on her end. "It's good news. Clarice is coming in tomorrow to sign the contract with Modica. She sent me an email just a few moments ago."

My hand stops on my dick mid-stroke. "What?"

She lets out another noise. This one is unmistakably a soft chuckle. "Stop it. You're tickling me."

My cock softens instantly.

She's in bed, with the flowers I gave her on the nightstand next to her, and some guy who is in no way worthy of her by her side.

How the fuck did I not see this coming?

"You're obviously not alone." My voice is laced with frustration. "I'll speak with you in the morning, Arietta."

"What?" she asks through a stuttered laugh. "No. Oh no. It's just Dudley. He's trying to lick my neck."

I shake my head. Now, I'm jealous of a goddamn dog.

"I'll arrange for Clarice to come by in the afternoon if that works for you?"

"Sure. Yes." I close my eyes and rest my head back.

"You have a free hour starting at four," she points out. "I didn't want to fall asleep without telling you. I know how important this is to you."

Suddenly, it doesn't seem that important anymore.

"I'll see you in the morning, sir...I mean, Dominick." Her breathy voice carries over the line. "Goodnight."

Before I have a chance to respond, she ends the call.

I toss my phone on the couch next to me and head straight for the bathroom. One long, cold shower awaits.

Chapter 33

Arietta

Trying to sleep after talking to Dominick on the phone late at night was a waste of time.

I took a shower instead. It was cold. It didn't help.

His voice sounded extra raspy and deep when we were talking. I was relieved when he responded to my email, even though it means I'm on dinner duty for the next week.

I could have easily told him in an email that Clarice agreed to sign the contract, but I was desperate to hear his voice. I also wanted extra confirmation that he was alone.

I'm ninety-nine percent sure he was.

Before we ended the call, I wanted to tell him that our non-date was the best non-date or date I've ever had, even though his parents crashed it.

I was able to see a side of him that I didn't know existed.

I heard him laugh.

I saw him smile again and again.

And I got to hold his hand when he helped me get into the Uber. I don't know if the wine caused the jolt of electricity I felt at his touch. I couldn't tell. I was too wrapped up in the realization that his hands are large, his skin is soft, and his eyes are specked with the smallest flecks of gold.

"Daydreamer!" Sinclair calls out from outside my bedroom door. "You need to get to work, young lady."

For the first time since I started working at Modica, I'm taking my time getting ready today. I spent most of that in a warm shower. I used the expensive Matiz body wash Sinclair got for her birthday from her brothers. I snuck just a little because it makes my skin so smooth.

Once I finished toweling off, I chose an outfit from my closet. I'm wearing a red dress with a black blazer. I cinched the dress at the waist with a macramé belt and pinned a faux diamond brooch to the blazer's lapel. My hair is on top of my head. I tried to center it in a bun, but it's crooked and too far to the right. I doubt anyone will notice. Today is all about Clarice and the signing of the contract.

"I'm coming," I say in a voice loud enough that she can hear me over Dudley's barking.

He snuck out of my room when I went to shower. I'm hoping Sinclair has taken him out for his morning walk.

I head toward my bedroom door. Swinging it open, I find my roommate on the other side in a pink T-shirt and jeans with her hair braided to the side.

She leans to the right to look around me. "Is The Dick in there?"

Startled, I bark out a nervous laugh. "No. Why? Where did that question come from?"

Narrowing her eyes, she straightens. "It came from that hopeful place inside of me that wishes one of us would get fucked into tomorrow soon. Since I have no one on my radar, you're going to have to take one from The Dick for the team."

I push past her. "You must have someone on your radar."

I hear her footsteps behind me. "There's no one. I've done the one night stand thing. It's not for me. I need a connection or at least a good meal before I hop into bed. You had both last night with Dominick."

I did.

I spin around to face her. "I spoke to him on the phone late last night."

Studying me, she tilts her head. "Is that your polite way of saying you had phone sex with your boss?"

"No."

"You wanted to," she states confidently. "I mean, who wouldn't? I bet he's a world-class dirty talker."

I stare at her. "Sinclair."

"Miss Voss," she says in an attempt at a deep voice. It's no better than her last impression of Dominick. "Drop your clothes. Get on my desk. I have something I want to show you. It's big. It has energy, and it's my…"

"Stop," I interrupt her with a laugh. "You're ridiculous."

Her hands fly up to my shoulders. Holding them, she stares into my eyes. "I'm excited for you. He likes you. I think he wants to ravish you. He didn't take you to his grandmother's restaurant because he felt sorry for you because of what happened with Lowell. He took you because he wanted to be with you last night. Why the hell do you think he brought you that gorgeous bouquet of roses?"

"Those were a thank you," I point out. "A client is signing with Modica today, and I introduced her to Dominick."

"He could have thanked you at work today. He came here to see you. I believe he came here to stop your date with Lowell."

That's not possible. It was a coincidence that he arrived in the lobby at the same time as Lowlife.

She raises both hands in the air. "I have one more thing to say, and then I promise I'll drop it."

"Forever?" I ask skeptically.

"For an hour," she answers.

Laughing, I glance at my watch. "Make it quick. I need to get to work."

With one hand holding mine, she softens her voice. "You're more beautiful and kind and everything than you realize. Dominick sees that. He came here dressed like a GQ model because he wants you. He took you to dinner because he's falling for you. He told you to call him Dominick because he needs you, and he was alone when you emailed him last night because no one is you but you, Arietta."

My hand shakes slightly. "Do you really think that?"

"I know that," she says in a whisper. "Trust me. You're on the verge of something incredible and some mind-blowing sex."

I take her in my arms for an embrace. "I can't be late for work."

Pulling back, she straightens the lapels of my jacket. "Go get 'em. For the record, I'm talking about The Dick, not some client with billions."

"Since I can now call you, I'll do that at lunch."

"Unless you're busy." She steps next to me to nudge me in the side with her elbow. "We're at the point where a good fuck trumps our friendship."

I nudge her back. "You're the best roommate I've ever had."

"I won't tell, Maren," she promises. "Get out of here."

I rush down the hallway to grab my purse. "I'll talk to you later."

"Say hi to your future husband for me," she calls after me. "Ask him if he has a cousin I can crush on."

Chapter 34

Arietta

"I know your big secret, Arietta."

I turn and face Bronwyn. She can't know. The only two people in Manhattan who know my big secret are Maren and Sinclair. Neither of them would share it with anyone. They both promised me that when I told them what brought me to New York City from Buffalo.

I smile, trying to hide the anxiety that I suddenly feel. "What secret? That I steal peppermints from the bowl you have on your desk? That's not a secret."

Her hand dives into the pocket of her black pants. "Open your hand."

I do, and seconds later a half dozen pink foil-wrapped peppermints land in my palm.

I let out a soft laugh. "Thank you."

"I was talking about that vintage store you go to." She tugs on the bottom hem of the red peplum sweater she's wearing. "I wandered in there last night, and when I told the owner where I work, she mentioned you. You've been keeping Past Over all to yourself."

Silently, I let out a sigh of relief that she's discovered that secret, which isn't a secret at all. Whenever one of my co-workers has asked me where I buy my clothes, I tell them. I've always thought they asked as a joke. It never bothered me. I've always had a preference for vintage clothing.

"You bought that sweater there, didn't you?" I look it over. It fits her body to a tee.

Her hands drop to her hips. "You know it. It's the most flattering thing I own now."

"It looks great on you," I say honestly. "Did you get anything else while you were there?"

"Just the sweater." She looks me over. "We should meet up after work and head over there together."

On any other day, I'd agree to that in a heartbeat, but I plan to buy everything I need to make a celebratory steak dinner complete with champagne cocktails for Sinclair and me.

Once Clarice signs the contract with Modica, I'm hoping to learn more about the compensation I'll receive for introducing her to Dominick.

If it's substantial it could change the course of my life.

I have a set plan for where I want to be when I'm twenty-five and thirty-five. A big bonus could get me to those goals sooner.

"I need to get back to my desk." Bronwyn fills up the coffee mug she brought into the break room. "I can't believe that today is finally the day!"

It's all anyone in the office has been talking about all morning. Everyone, except Dominick. He hasn't arrived yet, and it's nearing ten.

I'm trying not to let my mind wander to where he might be.

I plant a smile on my lips. "Is Judd excited?"

"That's an understatement." She rolls her eyes. "I think he had five cups of coffee before he came to work."

Judd can't handle caffeine. His energy level spikes after just one cup.

"At least Clarice isn't coming in until later this afternoon." I top up the coffee in my mug. "By then, Judd won't be bouncing off the walls, and my boss will be here."

She glances at the clock on the wall. "Dominick's not here yet?"

"No." I shake my head. "Not yet."

A slow smile slides over her lips. "He must have celebrated early. I can't say I'm surprised."

I don't say anything. I can tell she's taking joy in gossiping, so I let her run with it.

As I expected, she leans closer to me. "This was before your time here, but the day Brooks Middlestat signed with Modica, Dominick didn't get in until just after noon."

I dump a sugar packet in my coffee and grab a stir stick, even though I never add sugar to my coffee.

Bronwyn giggles. "Judd asked me to call Dominick at eleven that morning to find out where the hell he was. A woman answered. She could barely talk, and the noises she was making...well, I'm pretty sure Dominick was..."

"I get it," I interrupt. "I'm sure he'll be here before Clarice arrives to sign the contract."

Her gaze wanders over my shoulder toward the entrance to the break room. "Speak of the devil. Judging by the size of that smile on his face, he had a great time last night."

Instead of glancing in that direction, I turn to face Dominick.

Wearing a three-piece light gray suit and a black shirt and tie, he raises a hand in greeting when our eyes meet, and I know instantly, that gorgeous, toe-curling smile on his lips is just for me.

Chapter 35

Dominick

Every man on this planet who isn't staring at Arietta Voss right now is missing out. Her gaze is set to my face, but I caught her checking me out.

I chose this suit, shirt, and tie today because the last time I came to work dressed like this, Miss Voss, tripped her way into my office because she couldn't tear her eyes away from me.

The same is true now, but it's not the custom fit of the suit that has her attention. It's my face, or more precisely, my smile.

I'd fight the urge to smile at her, but that's a battle I can't win.

"Mr. Calvetti," Bronwyn calls out. "Today's the day!"

Indeed it is.

Today is the day I ask my executive assistant to have dinner with me.

It takes a smattering of applause rippling through the break room for me to realize she's referring to Clarice Blanchard signing with Modica. That's monumental, but having Arietta in my apartment while I cook dinner for her is the life-altering event I'm looking forward to the most.

It will be a first for me.

My home is my sacred sanctuary. Only my close friends and family have been there. If Arietta accepts my invitation, she'll be dining there with me tonight.

"How's Judd?" I ask because I know him.

By now, he'll be on his sixth or seventh coffee of the day as he focuses on what could go wrong between now and the moment Clarice arrives.

The same thing happened years ago. It was the day we signed Brooks on as a client. I'd spent the night before with a woman and in my rush to get out of her place I had forgotten my phone next to her bed.

From what Judd told me, she answered when Bronwyn called, believing I was the one calling her from Modica's office. She masturbated her way through an awkward greeting with Bronwyn before she hung up on her.

I stopped by her place on my way home that night to get my phone.

She held it hostage, clutching it next to her naked tits. The price was another night together. I opted to purchase a new phone twenty minutes later at a store close to my apartment.

Control is something I've always craved, but I'm losing it now, and I don't give a fuck.

Arietta is taking it bit-by-bit, and I don't know if she even realizes it.

"Mr. Corning has had a lot of coffee." Bronwyn raises her mug in the air. "I'm sure he'd appreciate it if you stopped by his office."

I shift my gaze from her back to Arietta. "I have something I want to take care of first."

Arietta's brows perk. "Do you need me, sir?"

For the first time in my life, I'm ready to admit I need something. I need her. "Yes."

That one word is all it takes to lure Arietta in my direction. She takes steady, measured steps as she approaches where I'm standing. She breezes past me and leads the way as we walk down the corridor toward her desk.

***

"I had breakfast with my father this morning," I explain to Arietta as she shuts my office door. "I always have breakfast with him before I sign a new client to the firm. It's tradition."

The celebratory breakfast meetings with my dad began when I signed my first client. As the business grew, I shifted the meetings to those days when I was securing a client with a net worth of more than one hundred thousand dollars. That became a million, then five. Now, it sits above one hundred million.

"Traditions are important," she says. "How is he?"

Considering the fact that she just saw him last night, I answer with a smile. "He's good."

He's better than good. He was happy that he'd made it back to Manhattan before Clarice signed on the dotted line so we wouldn't miss our time together this morning. My father may not know any details about my clients or their wealth, but that has little bearing on how excited he is whenever I reach a milestone.

"He's very proud of you," Arietta's fingers slip over the silver bracelet on her wrist. "He tells me that all the time."

As I step even closer to her, she retreats by just as much.

I stop in place when her ass hits the door of my office. I want to pin her there and kiss her, touch her, fuck her.

With a brush of her tongue over her bottom lip, she exhales. "I should respond to emails or make calls."

I bite back a smile as I close in on her. "Which emails? What calls?"

Her eyes glide up my body until they lock on mine. "Work ones."

I shove both hands in the front pockets of my pants to stop myself from touching her. I'm going to do this right. She deserves that. She deserves everything from a man, from me.

"Those work emails and calls can wait, Arietta."

167

She shakes her head. "They can't. You like them responded to promptly, sir."

I edge closer. "Dominick."

Her hand reaches up to adjust the frame of her glasses. "Yes, Dominick. You like if I answer emails quickly."

Nodding, I agree. "I do, but I'd like something else more."

Her breath hitches. In a strangled whisper, she manages one word. "What?"

Staring straight into her gray eyes, the corners of my lips edge up into a smile. "Celebrate with me tonight."

Her gaze searches my face. "You want to celebrate with me?"

"I would be honored if you allowed me to cook dinner for you tonight," I say softly. "At my apartment. I can send a car to pick you up at seven."

I watch as she pieces together everything I just said. Her brow furrows before her face brightens in a smile. "Who else will be there?"

With my lips almost touching hers, I take a deep breath. "Just us, Arietta. I want to spend the evening with you, alone, at my apartment having dinner."

I want more. Fuck, do I want more, but I have no grasp of what she wants or needs from me.

She looks directly into my eyes. I swear she can see my soul on display for her.

I'm infatuated. I don't know how to hide it anymore. I don't want to because this feels too damn good.

I watch as she swallows hard. Her lips move, but nothing comes out.

Wanting to save her the vulnerability of asking the question I know is perched on her lips, I answer it for her. "I'm asking you on a date, Arietta. I want to cook for you."

Her index finger skims a path over her bottom lip. I want to take it as an invitation to kiss her, but I'll wait.

"I'd like that," she finally answers. "I'd really like that."

A knock at my office door puts a halt to our conversation, but I'm satisfied. I got what I wanted, and that's time with Arietta away from here.

She turns and opens the door without a word to me.

Just as I suspected, Judd is waiting on the other side with two mugs of coffee in his hands. "Good of you to finally drag your ass to the office, bud. Today's a big day for us."

I reach for one of the mugs and motion for him to come in as Arietta takes her leave. Today is indeed a big day for Modica, but I'm most looking forward to tonight.

Chapter 36

Arietta

I didn't tell anyone that I'm on my way to Dominick's apartment.

When Sinclair called me earlier today to invite me out for lunch, I told her I was too busy with work. It wasn't a lie. There was prep that needed to be done before we met with Clarice.

Sinclair said she understood before she told me she was going to spend the evening with her niece since Berk has a dinner meeting.

Maren reached out today via text to ask if I wanted to meet up soon for movie night with Sinclair. I told her I would, but I left it at that.

I didn't mention my date with my boss to either of my friends. I didn't want to answer questions or have them critique the dress I chose from my closet. I couldn't stand the idea of them making a big deal out of something that I'm not sure is a big deal yet.

I suck in a deep breath as the driver rounds the corner to Central Park West.

Dominick didn't offer his address to me, but the driver knows exactly where we're heading.

He glances in the rearview mirror at me as we slow. "We're almost there."

I skim a hand over the skirt of the black dress I'm wearing. It's one of the few pieces in my wardrobe that fits me perfectly.

I've paired it with black heels and my favorite gold necklace.

My hair is down and in soft waves.

My nervous fingers fumbled with my contact lenses before I put them back in the case and slid my glasses on.

I look out the window of the car as the driver stops close to the curb. I wait, knowing he'll come around to open the door and help me out of the car.

My gaze catches on the people coming out of the pre-war brick building. The architecture is breathtaking. I can't imagine what the views must be like from the windows that face the park.

As my stomach flips and then flops, I glance to the left. My heart stutters in my chest.

Wearing gray pants and a white sweater, I see Dominick standing near the entrance to the building. He rakes a hand through his hair just as the driver swings open the car door.

Before he can get a hand inside to help me, Dominick is there.

He reaches out to me. "Arietta. I'm so glad you're here."

I place my hand in his, relishing in the warmth and strength of his touch. I step out of the car and into the personal world of my boss.

I know that everything between us will change tonight, and without any trepidation, I hold his hand as he leads me into the building he calls home.

***

I take in the beauty of Dominick's home as he pours us each a glass of wine. The floor plan is open and welcoming. Even though I'm across the room from the windows, I can tell that the view is indeed breathtaking.

Unlike his office, Dominick's apartment is filled with warmth and charm.

The furniture consists of mostly large pieces. The cracks in the dark brown leather on the arm of the sofa that sits in the center of the room speaks of comfort.

There's a fireplace surrounded by weathered bricks and a wall displaying framed photographs of people and places.

"I took most of those," he comments as he nears me.

I take the wineglass he offers after I place my clutch on the foyer table. "You took those pictures?"

I gaze at them, taking in the masterful composition and lighting. My father takes pictures for a living, but his portfolio features one thing. He's a school photographer. The best days of my childhood spent in the classroom were when my dad would show up with his camera, lights, and diffusers to take pictures of my classmates and me. He'd made everyone laugh with his dad jokes, and I'd beam with pride, knowing I'd get to hear them again at dinner that night.

He gestures toward them. "It's a hobby."

Tearing my eyes away from his, I study the pictures. I step closer to look at one of Marti, at the restaurant, with her hands in the pockets of her apron and her head falling back in laughter. "You're really good. I'm not an expert, but I know beauty when I see it."

"So do I."

I turn to find him staring at me. I want to pinch myself to see if this is real. How am I standing next to Dominick, drinking wine and looking at his private photo collection?

"Clarice adores you," he says before he takes a sip of wine. "After we signed the contract today, she told me you reminded her of herself when she was young."

That's a compliment I don't take lightly. "She said that?"

"In the elevator," he confirms. "I got the whole story of what happened the night you met."

I knew that would eventually come out, so I smile. "How could I not give her my brooch? She helped me get you and your date a reservation in Boston, and the brooch reminded her of one her grandmother had."

"For the record," he says, leaning closer to me. "I had dinner in Boston with my cousin Rocco, and I was referring to this..."

He sets his wine glass down on the coffee table before he reaches into his pocket to slide out his phone. His fingers move deftly over the screen.

The silence is broken by the sound of fingernails racing down a chalkboard.

I take another sip of wine when I realize Clarice must have mentioned that I have my notifications for his incoming emails set to that horrific sound. "Uh oh."

His deep laughter fills the room. "What is that I hear? I think you have a new email, Arietta."

I rarely blush, but there's no way I can ward it off. I'm busted.

"Should I read it now?"

"Right now." His eyes linger on my lips. "Give me your wine."

I take one last gulp before I hand over the glass to him. "I can explain about the fingernails on the chalkboard."

He sets my glass next to his on the table. "Read the email."

I set off back toward the foyer. It takes seconds for me to open the clutch and retrieve my phone. By then, he's next to me.

I look up and into his eyes. "I set up that incoming email notification sound a long time ago."

He taps his finger on the corner of my phone. "The email, Arietta."

Nodding, I drop my attention to my phone.

I smile when I see the subject line of the email he just sent.

Subject: Tonight

Dearest Arietta,

Your presence here tonight is the best part of a truly memorable day.

Thank you for accepting my invitation.

Signed,

THE DICK

XOXO

I laugh. I can't help it. "I'm sorry about the nickname."

His gaze travels over my face. "I'm not."

"But, you're not as…"

"Bad as you thought I was?" he interrupts as he takes my phone and drops it back on the table.

Nodding, I answer softly. "Yes."

His eyes search my face, stopping at my lips. "Don't jump to that conclusion just yet, Arietta. The night is still young."

Chapter 37

Arietta

I watch him from behind as he places all of the dishes into the sink. He cooked the most delicious dinner. I ate every bite of the perfectly seasoned chicken breast and roasted vegetables.

He assured me that even though it looked rustic that the taste would be memorable. He was right.

"Where did you learn how to cook?" I ask from where I'm seated on the sofa.

"Marti taught me," he calls back. "Every Calvetti has to learn how to cook something. I started with lasagna. I've honed my skills in the kitchen since then."

My gaze wanders back to the wall of photographs. Is there anything he can't do?

I dart to my feet to get a closer look at an image of Dominick and his father. They are both dressed in baseball shirts. On the top of Dominick's head is a baseball cap. Strands of dark hair are peeking out from under it.

"Did you used to play baseball?"

That turns him around. "I did."

I glance at him. The smile that was on his face is gone. I chased it away with that question. I focus on another image in the hope that I can lure it back. I'd trade sleep for a week to see it again.

"Is that your niece?" My fingertips trail over the corner of a silver frame.

"Luisa," he comments as he nears me.

I know her name from talking to his sister. Bella stops by the office regularly to see her older brother. If he's in a meeting, she'll pull up a chair next to my desk, and we'll talk about everything from books to her love story.

I smile at the image of the baby. "She's beautiful."

He stands so close to me that I can feel the brush of his sweater against my bare arm. "She's a handful."

I take comfort in seeing the corners of his lips edge up again as he talks about his niece.

"Babies generally are," I counter.

"Are they?" he grins. "I'm not a dad, so I have no idea."

"I'm not a mom, so I have as much knowledge as you do when it comes to kids."

Silence sits between us as I shift my gaze from the pictures to the bank of windows. "Your home is gorgeous, and that view is everything."

"So is this one."

His hand edges closer to mine as I turn back to look at him.

"You're a beautiful woman, Arietta."

I won't discount the compliment by giggling or feigning disbelief. "Thank you."

I sigh when his hand closes around mine.

"I realize that I'm your boss." He lowers his voice. "That could make for a possible complication, but I believe we can handle it."

I assume that the '*it*' he's referring to is sex.

I glance around his apartment as if I've just woken up in an unfamiliar place. Maybe I have. He asked me here tonight to have sex with me. Why did I think this was more? My romantic heart wanted it to be, but I know him.

He fucks and flees.

In our case, it will be fuck and fire since I work for him.

Regretfully, I tug my hand free of his. "I shouldn't have come, sir. I'm not that… I've never had a one-night stand. I can't."

I keep fumbling through an explanation about why I'm about to bolt. "My job…it's the most important thing to me…it's a crucial step in my life plan, and I can't mess it up. I won't mess it up."

Just as I turn toward the foyer, his hands encircle my waist, halting me in place. "Arietta, stop."

I have no choice but to do as he asks. He's more than a foot taller than me and at the very least a hundred pounds heavier.

I hang my head in sorrow or regret, maybe a little of both.

With a touch of his finger to my chin, he edges my head up. "Don't run away. I'm not good at this."

"At what?" I ask, searching his face for an answer.

Closing his eyes, he rests his forehead against mine. "It's not obvious?"

"No," I spit out. "I'm lost, but let me make this clear. If you asked me here to have sex with you tonight, I can't. I know you cut women out of your life after you sleep with them, which means I'll probably lose my job. I have to choose it over you even though you're hot as hell, and I want to fuck you."

My hand jumps to my mouth when I realize I said that aloud.

Before I can say another word, he takes my hand in his and presses his lips to mine in a slow, lush kiss. His other hand moves to my neck to angle me just right before he slips his tongue over my bottom lip. I let him into my mouth and my heart and every part inside of me that is aching for him.

He groans out my name as the kiss breaks.

"I have been dying to do that for weeks," he says before he kisses me again. "Goddamn weeks, Arietta."

I've been waiting my entire life to be kissed like that.

"I want to fuck you," he whispers. "So damn much."

I take a measured breath, trying to will my heart to stop hammering inside my chest. "Me too."

"I don't want to screw this up," he admits as he drags a hand through his hair. "You have my word this will not cost you your job."

The words of a wanting man aren't the bricks I need to build my career on. I have to end this date so that I can think. I need to think. "Kiss me goodnight, Dominick."

With a hand on my back, he twirls me in place before he kisses me just like the kisses I've seen in the movies.

It steals my breath. It's everything I've always wanted, but it comes at a price I'm not sure I'm willing to pay.

Chapter 38

Dominick

The offer to take Arietta home on Friday night never left my lips. I let her go after I called for the driver to swing back around and pick her up.

Once I got his text message telling me he was waiting at the curb, I walked her down.

There wasn't another kiss goodnight. Before I opened the car's back passenger door, she thanked me for dinner with a light brush of her fingers over my chin.

It was enough for me.

I don't know how the hell it was, but it satiated me enough that I got back upstairs and into a shower. I didn't jerk off. I stood under the warm water and held my hands close to my chest until the water temperature cooled.

I spent much of the weekend working. I carved out a few hours yesterday to visit Bella and her family in Brooklyn.

I'm at the office now waiting for Arietta to arrive.

"You look happy," Judd says from my open office door. "I take it you had a good weekend."

"The best."

He steps into my office. "That's a bold statement. What's her name?"

I ignore that because it's none of his fucking business. "How's Judith?"

"The classic Dominick ignore and defer move." He crosses his arms over his chest. "I'll let it go for now, but if you're finally doing more than screwing a woman, I'd like to be the first to know."

I chuckle. "You won't be, and I asked about your beautiful wife."

"She's the sunshine to my rain." He points at the window. "There's a thirty percent chance we're going to get a late day storm. That three thousand dollar suit you're wearing won't survive it. I hope you brought an umbrella."

I gesture to the three umbrellas hanging from the coat rack in the corner of my office. "I'm covered."

"You're early," he points out. "You beat Arietta today. That's a rarity."

"She'll be here soon," I say before I drop my gaze to a file folder in front of me.

He steps closer. "What's that?"

I tap my finger to the front of the folder. "Our next conquest."

Shaking his head, he steps back. "You're chasing whoever that is on your own. I'm bowing out. I'm taking paternity leave."

"Paternity leave?" I repeat.

"We added it to the standard employee contract eight months ago." He darts a finger into the center of his chest. "You signed off on adding to my contract too."

Leaning back in my chair, I narrow my eyes. "Let me guess. This all occurred right around the time you found out your wife was pregnant for the fourth time."

He shrugs. "That's pure coincidence."

"Can I count on you hanging around until the day she gives birth?"

"No promises." He holds up his hands. "If my wife needs me before our princess is born, you're going to have to keep this place running on your own."

I've done it before. I'll do it again. This business has always been as much a part of me as my skin and bones are. The drive to make it bigger and better has swallowed everything else in my life.

Until now.

I glance past Judd as I see a mess of orange and yellow headed in my direction. The sunburst on the dress that carries over the shoulder may be designed to brighten someone's day, but it's the woman wearing it that has brought light into my life.

I push to stand. "Arietta is here."

Judd glances over his shoulder. "I have to say, Dominick, she's an original. I wasn't sure of her when you promoted her, but I like her."

So do I. I like her a lot.

***

I watch Arietta as I impatiently wait for her to finish her conversation with Judd. He brought up the impending birth of his daughter, and Arietta listened intently as he spoke about what it means to him that he's on the cusp of being a girl-dad.

That conversation has shifted to the clouds gathering in the sky. Judd is talking weather. He doesn't use it to fill in the uncomfortable blanks in conversations. He'll carry an hours-long discussion about cumulus clouds and heat waves.

I clear my throat. "As fascinating as this is, Judd, we need to work."

He shoots me a look that tells me to fuck off, but his words convey a different message. "Sure thing, bud. I've got a few things to take care of."

By my calculations, he has more than a dozen things that need his immediate attention, including a preliminary meeting with a prospective client in five minutes. "I'll touch base with you before lunch."

"If you buy me lunch, you have yourself a deal."

I hold in a laugh. "Calvetti's at one."

Setting off toward the corridor that leads to his office, he calls back. "I'll be there."

"I'll get your coffee in ten minutes," Arietta says quietly with her gaze pinned to the floor. "I checked your schedule for the day and noticed that you have free time between eleven and eleven fifteen. I'm wondering if I could have a word with you then."

I step aside to give her a clear line to enter my office. "We'll talk now."

She glances at the watch on her wrist. "You have a phone meeting in fifteen minutes. You need this time to prepare."

That's what I've always told her before my meetings. I used the '*I need time to prepare*' line to grant me time alone to edit the photographs I take or text one of my sisters. I've always viewed it as the calm before the storm.

"My office, Arietta," I insist as I gesture toward the door.

She reaches into the large purse that is still slung over her shoulder. With a tug, she yanks out a file folder. "I'm ready."

I search her face for some clue as to what she's hiding in the folder, but all I get is a half-grin from her.

"Lead the way." I point at my desk, wondering what the hell is about to happen.

Chapter 39

Arietta

I've rehearsed this in my mind for hours, but I'm still nervous.

When I left Dominick's apartment on Friday night, I went home. I took Dudley for a walk and cuddled with him while watching an episode of the legal thriller that Leta recommended.

I don't remember any of it. The only things I've been able to focus on have been the way Dominick kissed me and the promise he made about my job.

I need this job if I want to keep my life plan on course.

That's why I spent time this weekend working on something that will guarantee my job security even if things don't work out between my boss and me.

I don't expect them to.

I've witnessed firsthand through emails and phone calls how cold he can be to women he's slept with.

My better judgment is telling me to end whatever is happening between us now, but I want him. I want to be with him, even if it's just for one night.

"What do you have there?" he asks as he moves to stand next to me.

He hasn't ordered me to sit in one of the chairs that face his desk, and he hasn't taken a seat either, so I stand on shaking legs and look up at him. "The other night was really nice. I had a good time."

Easing into this is the best approach, or at least I hope it is.

"I did too." His gaze volleys between the file and my face. "I hope we can have dinner together soon."

"I'm free all of this week unless my boss forces me to work late."

A ghost of a smile passes over his lips. "I heard he's a dick."

Shaking my head, I chuckle. "He's The Dick."

His teeth tug on the corner of his bottom lip, and every thought in my head disappears save for the one where he's doing that to my lip, or my thigh, or my clit.

I've never had good oral sex.

My first boyfriend didn't know what he was doing. I'm very sure Dominick could teach a master class on how to eat pussy.

Since I want to experience that, I need to explain what I'm holding in my hand. I breathe deep, trying to calm my racing heart. "I have something to show you."

His gaze rakes over my body, stopping just above my breasts. "Show me."

I raise the file folder, so it's in his line of sight. "It's this."

"Did you write me a poem?" he asks with the hint of a smirk on his sexy lips.

Where the hell did that question come from?

Leaning back on my heel, I shake my head. "Why would I write a poem?"

His eyes search mine. "I assumed you like poetry. There was a book of poems on your coffee table the day I stopped by to bring you soup. It belongs to you, doesn't it?"

Real concern etches his brow as he waits for me to answer.

"It's my book," I acknowledge with a sharp nod of my head.

The tightness in his jaw disappears. "Good. I'm glad to know that."

I have no idea why, but I smile through my confusion. I push the folder toward him. "Read it."

He hesitates briefly before he takes it from me. With a lingering look at the closed file, he clears his throat. "I'm not accepting your resignation, Arietta."

I won't bow out if I belong somewhere. I do good work for Modica, and I earned this position and the benefits it brings, including my generous salary.

If he wants to sleep with me, it has to come with rules.

"It's not that." I point at the folder. "It's a contract."

His gaze lands on my face. "For which client?"

I see the surprise in his expression. I know the rules about privacy. No client's file is ever to leave the office, and a Modica employee is not permitted to share client data with anyone outside the organization.

We are even assigned security colors. It's a phrase coined by Mr. Corning. I'm an orange. Bronwyn is too. Judd, Dominick, and Daniel Lawton, the third owner of Modica, are all assigned red.

"For me," I say quietly. "And for you."

He flips the cover of the file folder open and scans the first page of the contract I worked on this weekend. It details my job as it is now, including my salary and benefits package.

It also highlights the main points of the employment contract I signed when I was hired as Dominick's assistant.

He skims that with his gaze darting to me every few seconds.

As he flips over to the second page, my stomach knots.

I stand silently while he reads each paragraph of the agreement I want him to sign. It guarantees that if our relationship changes and it becomes uncomfortable for me to work with him, I'll be reassigned to another position with the same annual salary and benefits. I can't be terminated for any reason other than those already specified in the original employment contract.

In simple terms, if Dominick wants to fuck me and forget me, I'll still have a job guaranteed through the end of my original contract. That's not for another two years.

He exhales harshly before he looks into my eyes. "When did you have this drawn up?"

I can't read what he's feeling, so I stand my ground and answer honestly. "I drew it up over the weekend."

The corners of his lips curve up. "You wrote this?"

"Yes," I say. "I think it's fair, and it protects us both."

I want him to feel assured that I won't lodge a complaint against him with Human Resources if we fall apart after we fuck. I'm going into this with my eyes wide open. I know the chance of this being long-term is very slim.

He opens the folder again and flips to the second page. "This is tighter than some of our clients' contracts, Arietta. It's more in-depth. You know the law."

"I read law books." I laugh it off. "It's a hobby of mine."

"Poetry and law books," he mutters. "It's no wonder you're a genius."

I smile. He must know how high my IQ is.

"Why are you not in law school?"

The answer to that is too complicated to summarize in just a few words. I search for something witty to say, but I come up empty.

He glances at the contract again. "Get me a pen. I'll sign it."

I raise a hand to stop him as he steps toward his desk. "You can take your time to read it over. I don't need you to sign it this minute."

"I want to sign it this minute. I want you in my bed as soon as possible."

The roughness in his voice hits me. The desire in his gaze takes me a step closer to him. "Are you asking me on another date?"

He reaches forward to run his hand down my cheek. "If I weren't committed to this dinner meeting with Judd and the Cunninghams tonight, I'd take you home with me."

"You'd cook for me again?"

"We'd order in." His eyes lock on mine. "The next time I have you at my apartment, my focus will be solely on you."

I can't wait.

He taps the file folder against his palm. "I'm impressed that you're looking out for yourself, but I need you to know that I would never do anything to jeopardize your position here."

I believe him, but I don't trust myself.

How can I sit behind my desk and look at him for hours each day if things between us come undone?

I'm falling in love with my boss. I feel it, and there's nothing I can do to stop it.

Chapter 40

Dominick

I underestimated my executive assistant. I knew that she'd have serious reservations about engaging in a relationship with me outside of the office. What I didn't realize was that she'd take measures to protect her job.

It's smart.

I've traveled down this road before. I swear I'd never do it again.

It was with Judd's former assistant.

Her name escapes me, but her body was the escape I needed when it felt as though the world was closing in on me.

I'd invested everything, including the futures of my two closest friends, in a business I wasn't sure would launch.

Every night I'd leave the office uncertain if the clients I chased during the day would ever call me back. Judd's assistant saw the stress I was under, and she took me under her spell.

It was good while it lasted until she decided that a few random, blurry pictures she'd taken with her cell phone would give her the leverage she needed to cut a deal with me.

She wanted ten percent of my shares in the company in exchange for a promise from her that she'd keep the photographs private.

I didn't give a shit if she posted the pictures in Times Square.

I was nude.

I called her bluff. She went to Judd, and he worked out a severance deal with her.

That was the only time I let a woman I work with catch my attention, until now.

"I said the meeting went well, didn't it?" Judd nudges my shoulder with his. "Are you in some big money trance?"

I laugh at that. It's the phrase he used to throw at me when we were kids, and I'd get my weekly allowance from my folks. It was just a few dollars but, at the time, it felt like a fortune. I always did the same thing with it.

Two thirds of it went into a shoebox under my bed. I blew the other third on candy and comic books. By the time I was ten, I was delivering newspapers with my father following close behind. That turned into two afterschool jobs in high school.

By then, almost all the money I earned, I saved.

"The Cunninghams are good people," I comment as we wait for the light to cross the street.

We just left the restaurant after spending a few hours with two of our favorite clients celebrating their thirty-fifth wedding anniversary.

"My dream is for Judith and me to make it as far as they have." He tugs his suit jacket closer around his body. "It's windy tonight. It's coming at us from the southwest."

"You two will make it," I assure him because I'm starting to understand what has kept him and Judith fighting for their marriage. "What's the forecast for tomorrow?"

He looks up at the darkened sky. "Sunny and fifty-five degrees. There's a slim chance of showers late in the day and a bigger chance that my best friend is falling in love."

The light changes, but neither of us moves. "Which best friend is falling in love?"

"The one who took Marti's insults at lunch today with a smile."

"My grandmother teases me, and I take it like the Calvetti that I am, " I point out. "So you're obviously referring to someone else."

"He's the same guy that brought flowers to the Cunninghams and arranged a video call with their daughter from Denmark." He gestures for me to follow him across the street. "He's also had a smile on his face for days. What's she like, Dominick?"

"One-of-a-kind," I answer as we hit the sidewalk. "There's something about her that just makes my world better. I can't explain it."

"That's not just the sex talking?" He laughs. "Good sex can mess with a man's head."

I tap him on the elbow as we continue walking up Fifth Avenue. "We haven't gotten there yet. We've kissed, and that was something, Judd. Jesus, that kiss."

He stops mid-step and yanks on the sleeve of my suit jacket to stop me in place. "You haven't fucked this woman you're falling for? How the hell is that possible?"

"I need her to know that she's important to me," I say aloud for the first time. "I need her to feel I'm there for more than a fuck."

He taps my cheek with his palm. "I'm feeling this. This could be your Judith, bud."

I swat his hand away. "Don't go there. This is a one-step-at-a-time deal. There's no rush to get anywhere."

"Do you answer when she calls you?"

Laughing, I nod.

"Fuck. Dominick Calvetti has gone and fallen in love right before my eyes." He narrows his gaze. "Hold onto her because I like this version of you. You deserve to be happy."

"It's not love," I say even though I'm not sure what I'm feeling for Arietta. "It's like."

"It's a hard like, but without the hard dick." He shrugs. "I need to meet this mythical creature. She's kept you at bay while making you smile. This woman is something else."

"You have no idea." I slap him on the back. "I'm heading back to the office. You're on your way home."

"Is that a question?" He laughs. "It sounded more like an order than a question."

"Go home." I point toward the building he calls home with his family. "Kiss your kids for me and tell Judith she's a lucky woman."

He sets off before he turns back to face me. "Marry this woman, Dom. I don't know how the fuck she did it, but she made you see that the best parts of life are beyond the job."

That hits me hard. I turn to walk away, realizing that he's right. There is life beyond the job, and for the first time in my life, I can picture it.

Chapter 41

Arietta

I slide a blanket over my bare legs. I've been fighting to stay awake for the past hour. I did a yoga workout, and just as I was about to take my contact lenses out, Dudley whined to go out. By the time we got back inside, I had no energy left, so I plopped down on the couch.

I promised Sinclair I'd wait up for her. She's on a blind date set up by one of her college friends.

He wanted to take her to dinner, but she countered with an offer to meet for a drink at the bar down the street from our apartment.

I told her to send me a text message if she decides to bring him home.

She lightly punched me in the arm and reminded me that she doesn't do one-night stands.

I look to where Dudley is passed out in the chair across from the couch. He's called it a night. I'm tempted to as well, but since I promised Sinclair I'd wait up, I can take a nap here before she gets home. That way, I'll still get my eight hours in before I have to get up and go to work.

The sound of fingernails on a chalkboard cut through my fantasy about napping.

Almost every night Dominick sends me an email with tasks he wants to be completed the next day. I was anticipating this.

I pick up my phone from the coffee table and open my email app.

His email sits atop a slew of emails from clients that I need to respond to first thing tomorrow.

I click open his email immediately when I read the subject line.

Subject: Contract Amendment

Arietta,

I've made an amendment to our contract.

It seems as though you missed an important detail.

Dominick

XOXO

Even though my stomach is knotting at the idea that he's altered the contract I gave him, I smile at the XOXO at the bottom of the email.

I hit reply because I'm curious about the changes, and I know that I won't be able to sleep until I find out what I overlooked.

Subject: Re: Contract Amendment

Dominick,

What amendment?

Arietta xoxo

I stare at my phone's screen, waiting for his reply. When ten minutes pass, I close my eyes and lean my head back. At just that moment, I hear the sound of his incoming email.

Subject: Re: Re: Contract Amendment

Arietta,

As an addition to the last page, I want this added:

Paragraph 6(a): Arietta Voss will not date, kiss, or fuck another man for the duration of this contract.

Dominick

XOXO

My heart hammers inside my chest. Is he saying we're exclusive? We haven't even slept together, and he wants me all to himself.
If that's true, it has to work both ways.
I hit reply.

Subject: Re: Re: Re: Contract Amendment

Dominick,

I'll add it if you agree to the addition of this clause:

Paragraph 6(b): Dominick Calvetti will not date, kiss, or fuck another woman for the duration of this contract.

Arietta xoxo

I want him to say yes. I want this contract to last forever.
I hit send.
A knock at the apartment door sends my gaze in that direction. I can't believe Sinclair forgot her keys again. I need to pin them to her sleeve the next time she leaves here.

Feeling bereft at the prospect of having to juggle this email exchange with Dominick with listening to my roommate tell me about her blind date, I sprint across the cool hardwood floors on my bare feet.

I debate grabbing a robe from my room, but Sinclair has seen me in less than a tank top and panties.

With my gaze still pinned to the screen of my phone, I swing open the door.

"Agreed," Dominick spits out. "I agree to your amendment. Get me a goddamn pen."

I stare at him. Dressed to kill in a dark blue suit and silk tie, he looks incredible.

"You're here?" I question.

His gaze rakes me over. "A pen, Arietta. Give me a pen."

I glance down at my body. I should run to find something to cover up, but I don't. I step to the side and let him in.

He moves fast, dropping the file folder in his hand on the foyer table, along with his phone. "Tell me you're alone."

Speechless, I nod.

"Tell me you're ready for this." His hands clench at his sides. "Tell me I can touch you, Arietta. My hands are burning with need. Look at you. Jesus, just look at you."

Trembling, I rake both hands through my messy hair. "I'm ready."

Nothing registers but the feeling of his lips against mine as he pulls me close for a heated kiss. His hands are on me, cradling my neck and my back. I can smell his cologne. The groan that escapes from deep inside of him spurs me on.

My hands jump to his shoulders. "Dominick."

"You're so fucking beautiful," he says with his lips pressed to the skin of my neck. "I haven't stopped thinking about you since we kissed."

He spins me quickly, pushing my back against the door.

I take control of the kiss, using my fingers in his hair to guide him. I tilt his head, parting his lips with my tongue.

His hand drops to my waist before it slides to my thigh. "No other men, Arietta. I don't want you to fuck anyone else."

"You can't either." I moan as his fingers glide closer to my core. "Please say you won't touch another woman."

"No one," he bites out as his teeth run along the shell of my ear. "Compares to you. Compares to this."

His fingertips dive under the lace of my panties. I shudder when I feel the first touch of his skin against my core.

"So smooth." He groans. "So wet."

I close my eyes against the rush of desire. "For you."

The sensation when his fingers glide over my clit almost drops me to my knees. He tightens his grip on me, parting my legs with his knee. "I can't wait. I can't wait to make you come."

His lips take mine for a deep kiss as he circles my clit softly at first and then harder. Each draw of his finger over the tender nub lures me closer and closer to the edge.

"Look at me."

I open my eyes, scared that the vulnerability I feel inside will shine through for him to see. He doesn't know what he's doing to me.

Sliding one finger into me, he growls. "I'm so fucking hard."

I'm so fucking close.

I've never felt this before. I've never had an orgasm with a man.

My back bows as I clench down on his finger. A sound escapes me that's rough and filled with raw desire.

A sharp "oh," falls from my lips when he slides another finger over my clit.

"You're close." His voice is deep and laced with pure need.

The pleasure grips me from the inside out. Lighting up every nerve ending, every broken piece of me that's wondered and waited and wished for this, for a man who isn't in a rush to take what he needs from me.

With a gasp, I orgasm. I shudder through it, closing my eyes to savor this moment.

His stuttered breath is the only thing I hear as he thrums a finger against my clit, slowing his movements with each passing second.

Exhaustion hits me suddenly and completely. I reach out to blindly grasp onto him, fisting the lapels of his suit jacket in my hands.

"That was incredible," he whispers so close to my ear I can feel his breath skirt over my skin. "You're incredible."

I inch open one eye to see his gorgeous face. His lips are red and swollen from our kisses. His skin is flushed.

I want to thank him, but I don't. I stare into his eyes, hoping he knows the gift he just gave me.

"Get me a fucking pen, Arietta." He smiles as he slides his fingers over his bottom lip. "I had one taste, and all I want is more."

Chapter 42

Dominick

I scrawl my signature on the line marked '*Dominick Calvetti.*'

Arietta grabs the pen from me and does the same over the line marked with her name. Since this is the second copy we've signed, it's official.

My dick belongs to her.

My heart does too.

Maybe that is the high of watching her orgasm talking, but I feel something I've never felt for a woman before.

She puts one copy back in the file folder and slides it across the dining table toward me. "Thank you for signing this."

I know it's important to her. If another woman had demanded a contract before I took her to bed, I would have walked away.

I can't do that with Arietta.

For the first time in my life, I feel like I'm exactly where I need to be.

She tugs on the bottom of her tank top. "My roommate will be home soon."

The urge to ask her to come home with me is there, but I resist. I may not have gotten off tonight, but she did. That's all that matters to me.

"Are you kicking me out?"

Her gaze flits across my face. She's trying to read me. "Do you need to go?"

"That's not an answer to my question." I toy with her, keeping my face stoic.

"I'm not kicking you out." Her bare foot taps against the hardwood floor. "I am going to put on a pair of jeans before Sinclair gets home."

I glance at her toned legs before my gaze settles on the small triangle of lace between them. "My loss."

A small bubble of laughter escapes her. "You'll see all this again."

"And more?" I perk both brows.

Her hands drop to the bottom of her tank top. In one fluid motion, it's up and over her head.

My jaw must come unhinged as I stare at her ample tits. The pink nipples are tight and furled into points. Her name leaves me in a breathless rush. "Arietta."

She leans closer, giving me a hint of that perfume she wears. "There's more."

Stealing a glance at her apartment door, I manage to spit out two words wrapped in a strangled groan. "Show me."

Her hands move at a snail's pace as she slides the lace panties down to reveal her mound. Standing before me, completely naked, I see beauty radiating through her confidence as she drops her hands to her hips.

I step toward her, wanting more, needing more of her tonight.

She takes off in a sprint down the hallway with me on her heel, my gaze transfixed on her ass and her smile whenever she glances back at me.

I catch up to her, taking her in my arms from behind.

I grind against her. My erection feels like a fucking steel rod in my pants. "Where's your bedroom?"

She spins in my arms until she's facing me. Her hands leap to my cheeks. A slow, deep kiss follows, melting me from the inside out.

I glide a hand down her smooth back and the curve of her ass. I hold her there. Staring into her eyes, I know I won't walk out of this apartment tonight as the same man that walked in.

I'm losing myself to her. Every touch of her skin against mine and every time she looks into my eyes only adds another layer to what I'm feeling.

If this is the beginning of love, I want all-in.

"Turn to your left," she whispers.

I glance in that direction to find a closed door. "That's it?"

She pulls away from our embrace. Leaning against the doorframe, she smiles. "You can't enter without a condom."

I stare a slow path over her perfect body. "I don't have one on me, but let me counter that with an offer I think you might like."

Her smile dips into a frown. "You don't have a condom?"

I dive a hand into one pocket of my pants and pull it out to show her my empty palm. "I didn't know that I'd need one tonight, Arietta. I came here to sign the contract. That was all I wanted."

"You want more now," she states as her hand trails down her flat stomach. "Tell me about the offer."

I lean forward and lower my voice even though we are the only two people here. "I want my mouth on you in the next thirty seconds."

Her gaze drops as her fingers scatter a hurried path over her flesh to her core. "Here?"

There's innocence in the slight tremor of her hand.

I reach forward and cup my hand over hers. The heat from her pussy sends a pulsing need through me. Pushing her fingers into her folds, I bite a path over her neck toward her ear. "I'm going to eat this until you beg me to stop."

"Fuck," escapes her lips in a hushed tone.

I stand there in the brightly lit hallway with my hand guiding hers. Her eyes close as I push harder, bringing her close to the edge again.

"On second thought, I won't stop when you beg me to. I won't stop until I've had my fill." I plant kisses along her shoulder. "That will take a very, very long time."

"Now?" she asks softly. "Please do it now."

I don't need to hear more.

Our hands part before she reaches for the door's handle. I follow her in, slamming it shut behind us with a kick of my shoe.

Chapter 43

Arietta

Bronwyn was right. Chocolate can't match this. Nothing can.

My eyelids flutter shut as Dominick's tongue glides over my cleft. The long-drawn-out groan that accompanies it shoots straight to my core.

"I can't…" I begin before everything gets lost behind a moan.

He glances up at me with his lips pressed to the top of my mound. "You can't what?"

I can't believe this is happening to me.

"I can't believe you're here," I whisper. "In my bedroom."

His tongue moves roughly over my folds. "Believe it. I'm here."

He's here, still dressed in his suit and tie while he buries his face in my pussy.

I cry out when he inches the tip of his tongue over my swollen clit.

"You taste so sweet." He laps at me. "I could stay right here forever."

I close my eyes against the assault of emotions that invade me. Hope, fear, pain, and something that feels too intense to describe.

His hands slide over my hips to pin me down.

The gentle touch that's been there since he helped me onto my bed is gone in an instant.

The growl that escapes him flows through me as he sucks on my clit.

I whimper beneath him, wanting to feel everything but terrified that it's all too much.

"Breathe," he whispers into the dimly lit room. "Breathe and feel."

My hands fall to his hair. I grip it tightly as my hips buck in rhythm to the strokes of his tongue.

He spears it into me, sending a shot of pleasure through me. I grind against his mouth, not caring what I look like, only caring about what I feel.

I sense the orgasm as it approaches. I arch my back, trying to get as close to him as I can. I ride his face. Holding him there as the pulses drag through me, each more powerful than the last.

Nothing escapes me but his name. "Dominick."

I fall from the high in shaking tremors.

Before I can catch a breath, he flips me over, dragging me in place until I'm on my knees.

I try to retreat, embarrassed by the position. I've never been exposed in this way to any man before.

"Christ, you are so fucking beautiful," he growls as his teeth catch the flesh of my ass. "You need to come again. Give that to me."

I let go. I trust. I hand my vulnerability to him along with my heart as I inch my body back until I feel his mouth take possession of me again.

***

Twenty minutes later, I'm satiated and unable to move. I've wrapped myself around him on my bed. He's still fully dressed, smelling like that expensive cologne he wears and me.

After I came a second time, he flipped me onto my back and crawled over me. He kissed me. It was deep and decadent and flavored with him and me.

I saw something flash in his eyes when he broke the kiss.

It might have been satisfaction, but it felt deeper than that.

I should offer to take him in my mouth. I don't know to bring that up, so I rehearse what to say in my head as I glide my hand down his chest.

Just as I reach his belt, his hand grabs mine, stopping it. "You're not blowing me tonight."

My head pops up so I can look at him. "Why not?"

He kisses me softly. "Tonight was for you."

The words are so tender that my heart aches.

He stares into my eyes in a way that touches my soul. "I've never known someone like you. Why didn't I see that before? It's taken me so long to see it."

"You see it now," I offer as I run my fingers over his bottom lip.

He catches one with his teeth. I watch as he kisses it almost immediately.

"I never want to hurt you, Arietta."

"Then don't," I whisper in a plea I try to disguise as a lighthearted quip.

He hesitates before he responds. "I'll do everything in my power not to."

I rest my hand on his chest. "You're a good man."

I see the dip in the corner of his lips. "I want to be that."

My gaze drops. I want him to be that too.

I'm startled by the sound of footsteps in the hallway. Dominick leisurely glances in that direction. "Your roommate must be home."

A knock at my bedroom door confirms his assumption.

"Arietta?" Sinclair calls from the hallway. "Were you dancing naked in the living room again? You left your underwear there."

Dominick cocks a brow in a silent query.

I laugh softly. "It happened once. I was home alone. I forgot to pick up my clothes."

He moves to press a kiss to my mouth. "I want a private nude dance."

I slap him playfully on his chest. "Only if you join me."

"The Dick doesn't dance naked."

I let out a laugh. "He doesn't? Does he dance at all?"

"Arietta!" Sinclair pounds on the door. "I know you're awake. I can hear you moving around. Come out so I can tell you what a joke my date was."

Dominick slides to his feet before he offers his hand to me. "Your roommate is persistent."

I stand, glancing around for something to put on. "You have no idea."

Reaching for my short silk robe, I gather it around me. Dominick takes over, tying it tightly at the waist.

"I'll go first," he announces. "That'll give you a chance to see the look on her face."

I playfully swat his chest. "You don't want to hide in the closet until she falls asleep?"

"What fun is that?" He leans down. "Goodnight, Arietta."

I reach up to capture another kiss, a soft one. "Goodnight, Dominick."

He turns and swings open the door.

The phone in Sinclair's hand crashes to the ground. "Oh, shit."

Dominick gazes at the cracked screen. "Oh, shit is right."

I laugh. "You remember Dominick, don't you?"

Before Sinclair can reach her phone, Dominick is bending down to pick it up. He hands it to her carefully. "It'll survive. It looks like all you need is a new screen. I know a place in Greenwich Village that will fix it tomorrow. Get my number from Arietta, and I'll set that up for you."

Her gaze volleys between him and me. "He's nice."

He steals a glance at me before he brushes past her. "Arietta will tell you that The Dick isn't all bad."

Her eyes widen like saucers. "He knows?" Her attempt at whispering is an epic fail.

"Oh, he knows." He turns to look back at me. "I'll see you in the morning, Arietta. Sleep well."

"You too," I call out as he disappears from view.

A few barks from Dudley are followed by the sound of the apartment door clicking shut.

"You fucked The Dick!" Sinclair screams. "Holy hell, Arietta! Tell me all about it."

I breeze past her on my way to the dining room to pick up my clothes. I spot the file folder sitting right where I left it. Judging by her reaction to finding him in my room, she didn't read our sex contract.

"Was it phenomenal?" She laughs. "What a ridiculous question. It was beyond phenomenal, right?"

I won't spill details. I don't want to. What happened tonight was special; too special to turn into gossip. "It was everything."

The tremor in my voice is enough to send the message to her that I need this for myself.

She gathers me into her arms. "Did you see the way he looks at you? I think he's falling in love."

I cling to her as I hold onto that hope. I want him to be because I'm already in a free fall, and there's no saving my heart from this.

Chapter 44

Dominick

I have no fucking idea how I'm still sitting in this chair.

Arietta arrived at my apartment an hour ago looking like the angel she is. She's wearing a white sweater and ripped jeans. On her feet were sneakers that she kicked off as soon as she stepped over the threshold and into my home.

I ordered food in so that I could take advantage of every second I have with her tonight.

I polished off the sandwich and fries that were in front of me, but she's taking her time eating each fry as if it's something to be savored bite by every tiny bite.

My day was spent being tortured as I watched her sitting at her desk while I made call after call to potential clients. Asking her to meet me here tonight was supposed to be a reprieve from that.

I want her in my bed before daybreak, but at the pace she's nibbling on those fries, we'll be here until next week.

With a sigh, she drops the fry in her hand to look across the table at me. "You won't hurt me tonight, will you?"

I'm on my feet and kneeling next to her before she can catch her next breath. I slide a hand over the back of her neck. "No. Never."

Her gaze darts to the front of my jeans. "I can tell that you're not like the other men I've been with. They weren't as large…"

I kiss her to shut her the hell up. I don't want to know about those men.

When our lips part, she darts a hand to cup my cheek. "You'll be gentle with me?"

I reassure her with another kiss. This one is softer and meant to convey how much I cherish this moment with her and the trust she's placing in me.

"I promise that I'll be gentle," I whisper against her mouth. "If you're not ready tonight, we'll wait."

"I'm ready," she says in a rush. "I'm so ready."

I push to my feet and reach out a hand to her. "Come with me, Arietta."

Her hand slides into mine as she stands. "I'll never forget tonight."

I lean down and kiss her softly. "I won't either, beautiful."

***

I wanted to bury my face in her pussy, but my self-control was pushed to the breaking point as I watched her undress.

I offered to help, but she ordered me to sit on the bed as she slowly removed every bit of her clothing.

When it came time for me to strip, I did it in record time.

We're on my bed now, next to one another. My cock is in her fist. With slow, hesitant movements, I fear she's trying to kill me with need.

"Arietta," I breathe out her name in a hiss. "You're going to make me come."

"Like this?" she perks a brow. "You can come from my hand?"

I can come from smelling her perfume from across the room. She has no fucking idea what she does to me.

"Like this. "I reach down to circle her hand with mine. I even her strokes, increasing the pace, guiding her to jerk me off.

Her eyes widen. "Holy fuck."

I stare at her, watching as her expression shifts from wonder to want. Then it stops. She stills.

My cock aches. "Arietta."

"Condom," she purrs. "Put one on."

I roll over, quickly grabbing one of the foil packets I left on my nightstand. I rip it open violently, shaking as I sheath my dick.

This isn't my first fucking time. I need to calm down.

I'm on top of her then. My fingers skim over her cleft. She's wet. She's soaked with need, so I slide the tip of my cock along her seam until I'm there. I push in.

An uncontrolled hiss escapes me because she's so fucking tight.

Her whimpers spur me on. I plunge deeper in a slow, steady move that sets her teeth into the skin of my shoulder.

"Arietta," I whisper her name as I cling to her.

"More," she answers with a lick of her tongue over my neck. "Please."

I cry out in pleasure as I fuck her with a need I didn't know existed. Each stroke into her is relentless, driven by something I've never felt before.

She comes quickly, unexpectedly, and with a moan that's so deep that it fuels me more. I thrust through her orgasm, chasing her into another until I come with a heady call of her name that vibrates through every part of me.

Chapter 45

Arietta

I put on my glasses so I can stare at him.

His body is magnificent, but that's not what I can't take my eyes off as he rests. It's his face. With his eyes closed and his breathing steady, he looks peaceful.

All of the intensity that's usually there in his gaze and voice is silenced like this.

"You're staring at me," he says with his eyes still closed.

I pat his chest. "How can I not? You're perfect."

He trails one hand over his rock hard stomach. "I'm not perfect."

"You're close."

His right eye pops open. "I'm far from it. You, on the other hand."

"I'm as imperfect as a person can be." I rest my head on his chest.

He shifts us until we're on our sides facing each other. "That's not how I see it."

"How do you see it?"

He leans closer to press his lips to my forehead. "I see a young woman who has it all together, and she's only twenty-two."

That's so far from reality that I almost let out a laugh. "What were you like when you were twenty-two?"

His eyes squint slightly. "Not like you."

"That's a non-answer," I point out with a press of my lips to his mouth. "Tell me about twenty-two-year-old you."

His hand cradles my chin. "He thought he knew everything, but he didn't know a thing."

"Your dad would call bullshit on that."

He perks both brows. "Bullshit? What's that supposed to mean?"

"He told me you were driven and determined when you graduated college." Dominick rolls onto his back, his hand raking his hair. "He did? He told you that?"

"Louis has told me a lot."

That perks his brows. "Like what?"

I inch closer to him, running a finger down his bicep. "That you once tried singing lessons, but the teacher asked you to drop out."

He huffs out a laugh. "Thanks a hell of a lot, dad, for keeping that secret."

"He said he wrote a note to the teacher telling her that you're the best singer he's never heard."

His hands jump to cover his eyes as he shakes his head. "That's fucking hilarious. My father is brilliant."

I crawl over him, pressing my breasts into his chest. "Just like his son is."

He peeks at me from beneath his fingers. "Neither of us is as smart as you."

"Compliments deserve to be rewarded." I inch back slowly on his body, running my pussy over his stomach and groin.

He lets out a loan groan. "What's my reward?"

I move again until I'm seated on his thighs. I take his cock into my hands, stroking it the way he showed me. "I want to taste you."

His lips part. "Arietta."

"Just please know that I've never wanted anyone like this." I stare in wonder at the drop of pre-cum that's beaded on the lush crown. "That I've never felt like this before."

He edges up so his hand can capture my chin. "This is all new to me too."

I sigh. "I know it's not."

His hand darts to the center of his chest. "It's new. This feels new to me. All of it does."

I close my eyes and soak in those words and the overwhelming need to pleasure this man.

I move back, lean down, and lower my lips over the head of his cock, scooping up the pre-cum on the tip of my tongue.

He jerks under me, his hand trailing over my hair. "Like that. Just like that."

I take more of him, inch-by-inch, sucking, licking, moaning, and needing him to feel everything that I've felt under his touch.

Chapter 46

Dominick

I gather her clothing from the floor of my bedroom, taking a moment to hold her sweater close to my face to smell her perfume.

I would have gone for her panties, but her scent is still there lingering on my lips. I ate her to an orgasm hours after she swallowed my release.

I stared at her as she refused to stop when I told her I was about to come.

She persisted, stroking me with her tongue in a way that left me craving more. I want more. I'm never going to get enough of her.

She comes marching into my darkened bedroom, naked, with her hair a messy tangle around her face and her arms outstretched in front of her, grasping at the air. The soft light trailing in behind her from the hallway halos her body, showcasing all of her lush curves.

She squints at me. "Dominick?"

I hold in a laugh. "Arietta?"

"I can't find my glasses."

They're on the nightstand, but I'm not about to tell her that. Her face is adorable like this, with her nose scrunched up and her brows furrowed together. "Do you remember where you left them?"

She chuckles. "I can barely remember my name after what you did to me."

I step closer and reach out to guide her to me. "You did a few things to me too."

Her gaze travels over my body, although I have no fucking idea what she can see without her glasses on. "Did you like it?"

I run a finger over her chin. "I fucking loved it."

I fucking love you.

I hold those words inside because it's too soon. It's too much. It's too goddamn everything.

"You're not going to fuck and flee, are you?" She reaches for what I suspect is my chin, but her hand lands on my nose.

I slide it down to my lips. I plant a kiss on her palm. "I'm not going anywhere."

She leans closer to me, her eyes still searching. "Can I tell you a secret?"

I want to know every secret she's ever kept inside of her. "Tell me."

Her voice comes out in a strangled whisper. "You're the first man I've ever had an orgasm with."

That hits me hard. I hate that she's been with other men, but it kills me inside that they didn't take care of her.

"Selfish assholes," I mutter.

"There were only two," she confesses. "They were back home. I never slept with anyone in New York. I'm so glad I didn't have sex with Lowell."

That bastard didn't deserve a minute of her time.

"I told him that I wasn't very experienced." Her tone is soft. Vulnerability blankets the words. "He knew that I'd never come with a man before."

Regret courses through me. He was boasting in the elevator about taking her to bed, knowing full well that it would mean more to her than a random fuck. I should have throat punched him when I had the chance.

I cup her face in my hands, desperately wanting her to stop talking about other men; men who couldn't satisfy her and one who didn't respect her or the woman he made his marriage vows to.

"Thank you for trusting me with your secret, Arietta."

Now, trust me with your heart.

She falls into my chest, so I wrap my arms around her, cradling her against me, relishing in the feeling of her naked body.

"I like you," she says quietly. "Like a lot."

I'm the goddamn luckiest man on this earth.

"I like you a lot too."

She presses her lips to my chest for a kiss. "I need to go home."

"Stay," I insist. "Spend the night."

She gazes up and into the darkness that surrounds us. "I need to sleep a little and then get ready for work. My boss is a dick."

Laughter consumes me. "What the hell?"

"You live up to the nickname," she says with her hand gliding down my body. "You really are The Dick."

"Grant me one more chance to prove that to you before you leave." I cup my hand over hers so she can feel how hard I am for her through my boxer briefs. "One last fuck before you take off."

She spins around, taking me with her. I have to gather her up into my arms because she's about to plant us both on our asses on the floor just inches from the bed.

I toss her on her back in the center of the bed. "I'm getting a condom, and then I want you on top of me."

"Your wish is my pleasure, sir." She leans back, opening her legs. "Just don't break me in two."

I won't. I can't. I will hurt myself before I ever cause her any discomfort.

I slide off the boxer briefs, grab the condom package, and sheath myself while watching her every move. When she rolls to her side, I crawl onto the bed, flip her on her stomach and glide my tongue over her cleft.

"I'm supposed to be on top," she protests in the middle of a slow moan.

"You will be," I promise. "I want this first."

215

I want it always. I want all of this forever, even if I don't deserve any of it or her.

***

An hour later, I watch as she slides her feet into her sneakers. "I hate that you're leaving, Arietta."

She insisted on going home alone even though it's nearing three. Sending her out in the dead of night to ride the subway wasn't going to happen. I called Modica's driver and woke him up with the promise of a bonus if he got his ass in gear and had the car down here in fifteen minutes.

He's due to arrive in five.

"It's the best thing." She runs a tongue over her bottom lip.

Christ. She's so fucking beautiful.

I push that thought away because there's something I need to say before she walks out my apartment door. Something I didn't have the self-control to say earlier because my need for her swallowed everything in its path.

I reach forward to cradle her face in my hands. "I want you to know how much tonight meant to me."

"To me too," she says softly. "And last night too."

If I had known that she'd never gotten off with a man before, I would have taken my time. I sure as hell wouldn't have pushed her against a door to ride my hand to her release.

"I feel like I've been missing out. I had no idea sex could feel this good." Her head shakes, causing her glasses to inch down her nose.

Before she can slide them back into place, I do it for her by grabbing the frame and adjusting them.

She rewards me with a smile. "Thank you."

A faint chime fills the air from the phone in the pocket of my jeans. I don't have to look at it to know. The damn driver can wait. I'm not ready to let her go yet.

Arietta glances at my face when the phone chimes again. "He's here, isn't he? I should go. I want to check in on Sinclair and Dudley, and then I need some sleep."

I nod. "I'll walk you down."

"I can get there on my own." She perches on her tiptoes to press a kiss to my mouth. "This was the best night of my life, Dominick."

I grab her arms to hold her in place so I can deepen the kiss. "Mine too."

"I'll see you in the morning, boss."

"In the morning, beautiful," I whisper before I take another kiss. "Sleep well."

"You too." She pats my chest. "Dream about me?"

I'll do everything in my power to make that happen every night for the rest of my life.

I open the apartment door. "Goodnight, Arietta."

"Goodnight," she says in barely more than a whisper before she walks away.

Chapter 47

Arietta

"I'm looking for Dominick."

I glance up from my computer at the sound of an unfamiliar man's voice. He's older, around the same age as Louis Calvetti, I think, but he's dressed much differently than Dominick's dad usually is.

This man is wearing an expensive suit and tie. His gray hair is cut with precision. He's very well put together on the outside, but something is going on inside of him.

A layer of sweat is peppering his forehead, and he's fidgeting from one foot to the other.

"He's at a breakfast meeting." I glance at the clock in the corner of my laptop screen. "I don't expect him back for at least another two hours. Can I help you?"

"What's your name?"

"Arietta," I answer without hesitation.

"Brooks Middlestat." He shoves a hand at me.

I take it. Shaking it firmly, I recognize his name from our client records and from Bronwyn's story about the day he signed with Modica. "It's nice to meet you, sir."

That draws a smile to his lips. "I really need to speak with Dominick. He usually answers whenever I call his cell, but he's not picking up."

He silenced it because he's having breakfast with a potential new client worth almost as much as Clarice. Orson Borgon called Dominick at the break of dawn and told him he had thirty minutes to get to a restaurant on the Upper East Side if he wanted a shot at managing his portfolio.

Dominick called me on his way to the meeting. As rushed as he was, he was calm and in control. He told me what a great time he had last night with me before he even mentioned the meeting.

"I'm sorry, sir, but he can't be disturbed." I push back to stand. "Is there anything I can help you with?"

He looks me over, taking in the green plaid dress and white cardigan I'm wearing. "I don't think so. His cousin, Nash, isn't around either. I usually turn to him when Dominick is busy."

"Can I get you anything?" I offer. "The coffee in the break room isn't fantastic, but there's a café down the street that I really like."

He takes a step closer to my desk. "Has Dominick told you about our lunch meetings?"

I try and piece together exactly what he means. There is more going on here than a man who wants to see his wealth manager.

"The urge is strong right now," he goes on, "I'm dying to play a hand."

I nod because I've heard those words before. It's not verbatim what my dad said, but the message behind them was the same.

Addiction.

My dad bet on the horses at the racetrack a few miles from our house. He did that weekly until I was fourteen, and he hit rock bottom.

Brooks isn't there yet.

"Why don't we go and get that cup of coffee?" I open my desk drawer to yank out my purse. "I think we have a lot in common."

"You're…you…gamble…" he stutters out a question I can tell he doesn't have the strength to ask.

Rounding my desk, I set my hand on his forearm. "My dad."

His eyes catch mine. "You understand, don't you?"

I understand what it's like to watch someone you love struggle in a way that leaves you feeling powerless to help.

I nod. "I understand."

"Dominick takes me to meetings," he confesses in a low tone. "He waits outside for me."

I bow my head to try and find my composure.

There's so much about Dominick I don't know.

"I can do that too," I assure him. "You're not alone. I'm here to help."

He wraps my arm around his. "Your father must be very proud of you, Arietta."

"He is," I say as we start our walk toward the elevator. "But I'm more proud of him."

***

Dominick beat me back to the office.

I can tell by the look on his face that his meeting with Mr. Borgon went well.

He's standing in the doorway to his office. His gray suit coat is buttoned, and his hands are in the front pocket of his pants.

He's sexy-as-hell as he watches me stalk toward him with a coffee for him in one of my hands and a law book tucked under my arm.

I made a quick stop at Past Over on my lunch break.

Lynn had a new book for me. She also told me that she'd have a new shipment of old dresses later in the week.

I approach Dominick with a smile on my face. "You're back."

"You're beautiful," she says quietly. "You're also unbelievably kind, Arietta."

He must have spoken to Brooks.

After I rode the subway with him to a community center where a meeting was being held, I waited outside at a park across the street. I sat on a bench and called my dad to tell him how much I loved him.

Our conversation ended when Brooks emerged from the meeting. I gave him my cell number and told him to call me in the future if he can't reach Dominick.

He hugged me and thanked me for everything I'd done for him.

I wanted to thank him because he helped me see a side of the man I'm falling in love with that I didn't know existed until today.

I shove the cup of coffee into his hands. "I was glad to help."

He sets the coffee on the corner of my desk. "You did more than help. Brooks was pretty damn emotional when he called me. He told me you went above and beyond."

"He told me you have been doing that for years."

His gaze locks on mine. "He's an old friend of my dad's."

I take a measured step closer to him. "You're a good person, Dominick Calvetti."

"Not as good as you."

"It's not a competition," I say. "We can both be good."

His lips turn up into a grin. "We were both good last night."

I lower my voice to almost a whisper. "I can strive to be even better tonight."

"You're making me regret a decision I made earlier." His gaze travels over my body. "I'm leaving town in two hours."

Disappointment halts my excitement about climbing back into his bed tonight. "You don't have a trip booked."

"I do now." He exhales on a sigh. "Orson Borgon wants me to accompany him on his business trip to Philadelphia. He wants more time to talk things over. I suspect this is a test I need to pass before he signs with Modica."

I'm not surprised.

Clients have made Dominick jump through hoops for them in the past.

"It's just for one night?" I ask hopefully.

"He mentioned the possibility of introducing me to his wife and kids. That means a detour to Miami after Philadelphia." He rakes a hand through his hair. "I'm in if that happens, but I don't have a timeline. I can't say for certain when I'll be back."

I can't fault him for any of this. The commission on the Borgon portfolio would be huge.

"I understand, " I say with a stilted smile.

"Of course you do." He cups my chin with his hand. "I, on the other hand, don't understand how I'm going to stand not touching you for more than a few hours."

"Just imagine our reunion when you get back." I sigh.

"You'll spend the night with me when I'm back."

I love that it's not a question. It's an assumption.

"I will," I agree.

"I'll use all of my charm to get him to sign as soon as possible. " He lifts his hand to run a finger over my bottom lip.

"You're charming?"

His head falls back in laughter. "That will cost you, Arietta."

"I sure as hell hope so," I say before I nip at his fingertip. "I can't wait for you to get back to Manhattan."

"Me either, beautiful. Me either."

Chapter 48

Arietta

I glance to where Sinclair is seated on the couch. Her fingers are flying over the screen of her phone. "Who are you texting?"

Her head pops up. "Not a guy I want to sleep with."

I let out a little laugh. "Why not?"

She drops the phone in her lap. "I have a new project coming up. My brother is giving me all the details."

I don't bother asking what those are because she can't tell me.

Her work is as much a mystery to me as her romantic history. All I do know is that she's had more lovers than I have, and there hasn't been a man in her life since she moved in with me.

I finish plating the dinner I prepared. It's a couple of quinoa bowls filled with all of the vegetables I found in our fridge. I roasted those, added a honey mustard dressing and a sprig of parsley to finish it.

"How's The Dick?" she asks as she approaches our open concept kitchen. "He's been gone forever."

I grab two forks out of the drawer and hand her one. "It's only been a few days."

She spears a piece of sweet potato. "Do you miss him?"

I take a bite of the food from my bowl as I move back toward the living room. Usually, we'd sit at the dining room table and eat, but I'm hoping the noise from the television will distract Sinclair enough that we won't talk about Dominick.

"He'll be back tomorrow," I say before I take a pepper into my mouth. I chew slowly.

We eat in silence while someone on the cooking competition we're watching spills salad on the floor. They curse, but all we hear is one long-draw-out beep.

We laugh in unison.

"You're in love with him."

My head snaps in my roommate's direction. "Sinclair."

"How could you not fall in love with him?" She smiles. "He's gorgeous, and he treats you right."

"It's more than that," I confess. "He has a good heart."

"That makes him even more perfect for you."

I think he's perfect for me too, but there's a lot he doesn't know about me. There's a lot I don't know about him either. Learning what he's done for Brooks is proof of that.

"What if it doesn't work out?" I ask softly. "What if something happens and he doesn't want me anymore?"

Her hand moves to cup my knee through the sweatpants I'm wearing. "You can't think about that, Arietta. Focus on the here and now. You have fun together. Enjoy that, and whatever else happens is meant to be."

Nodding, I pick at the food in my bowl with my fork.

"I'm not an expert in love." She chuckles. "I do know that he looks at you the same way my brother looks at Maren. I never thought Keats could love a woman, and then he met her, and boom, he was a goner."

"You think Dominick loves me too?"

"I think he's falling hard and fast." Her eyes close before they pop back open. "Enjoy every second of it because one day you may be telling your grandkids about the time you fell in love with their granddad."

That's so far in the future I can't wrap my mind around it. I can't think about anything but the moment I see Dominick again.

***

"Tell Dominick that I had a great time last night."

I wish I were having a nightmare, but I'm not.

I'm at my desk. It's just past nine a.m., and I'm on the phone with a woman named Kallista, who apparently spent at least part of the evening with Dominick.

For the first time since I started working at Modica, I can't bring myself to write the message down.

"I wish he hadn't rushed off this morning." She giggles. "Add that onto the message."

I don't make a sound. There's no affirmation from my end that I even heard a word she said.

"Are you there?" she questions in a louder tone. "It's Kallista Montgrew. Should I spell that for you?"

Finding the will inside of me, I jot her name down along with the message about how she wanted more time with him after their night together.

"I'll pass this along to him," I say through clenched teeth.

"Perfect!" she exclaims. "He has my number."

That bites harder than it should.

I want to ask her if he requested it or if she was the one offering it after they fucked.

Tears prick the corners of my eyes.

I'm foolish. I was naïve to think that he'd stop doing what he's been doing for years.

I hang up the call before she does because my stomach is threatening to send my breakfast back up.

I push back from my desk just as Bronwyn rounds the corner.

"Arietta." My name snaps off her lips. "Why do you look like that?"

Since I have no idea what jealousy looks like on me, I take a deep breath. "I don't feel well."

Her hands drop to the front of the navy and white dress she's wearing. "You're not pregnant, too, are you?"

I process that one word at a time as I stare at her beaming face. Tears fall from my eyes, but it's not because I'm happy for her.

I'm upset that I let myself fall for my boss.

I shake my head. "No. I'm not. You are?"

She takes me in her arms for a big hug. "I'm due in seven months. I just found out this morning."

I cling to her, wanting to feel her happiness, but my sorrow is drowning that out.

"I guess I can finally tell you who my boyfriend is." She laughs.

I step back to look at her. Her cheeks are wet with happy tears, so I grab a tissue from the box on my desk and hand it to her. "Tell me who it is."

"Judd's cousin. It's Theon." She shakes her head. "I'm going to be a Corning."

My gaze falls to the diamond on her left hand. "Are you marrying him?"

"He proposed the second we found out we're expecting." She looks down at her flat stomach. "We're telling Judd and Judith tonight. I can't believe Judd and I will be family in a few months."

I suck in a deep breath. "I'm really happy for you."

"I'm happy for me too." Another tear slides down her cheek. "All of my dreams are coming true, Arietta."

I push away my sadness and smile. "You deserve all of this."

"You deserve to be happy too." She cradles my cheeks in her hands. "You're still pale as a ghost. Let's get you something to eat, and we'll talk about Theon's friend, Dawson. He's perfect for you."

I'll listen, but I'm not interested.

There is only one man on this earth who is perfect for me. He's also the only man capable of shattering my heart. He did that last night when he took another woman to bed.

Chapter 49

Dominick

I know something is wrong as soon as I spot the empty chair behind Arietta's desk.

She hasn't answered any of the text messages I've sent her since I arrived at the airport in Miami for my flight to New York.

Before that, I was consumed with business, so I only sent a few emails and text messages since I've been gone. The majority of those were centered on work.

"Mr. Calvetti," Bronwyn calls to me as she appears from the corridor that leads to Judd's office. "Welcome back, sir."

I toss her a curt nod. "Where's Arietta?"

It's nearing three p.m., so unless she's taken a late lunch, she should be behind her desk.

"She was feeling under the weather, so she left." Bronwyn gestures toward Arietta's desk. "She forwarded her desk phone to my phone. I have a few messages for you. I can run and get those now."

I don't give a shit about the messages. I want to know what's wrong with Arietta.

"Under the weather in what sense?" I ask.

That stops Bronwyn mid-step. "It's hard to describe. She was very pale. This may sound odd, but Arietta has this joyfulness about her, and that wasn't there. I told her some good news, and I could tell she was trying to be happy for me, but I don't think her tears were happy tears."

"She was crying?"

"A lot." She sighs. "We had tea in the break room. I even tried to set her up with someone. I thought that might brighten her mood."

"She doesn't need that," I snap back.

Her head pops up. "She hasn't had the best luck with men."

Until now.

I'd crawl across this earth on my bare knees to see her smile. I'd hand my fortune over to her if she agreed to spend the rest of her life with me.

I love her.

If I didn't realize it before this trip, I sure as hell do now.

"When did she go home?" I glance at the pile of messages sitting atop Arietta's desk.

"A couple of hours ago."

I don't stop her when she turns to march back up the corridor toward Judd's office.

Sliding my phone from my pocket, I bring up Arietta's number and press to connect the call. It rings five times before her voicemail picks up.

It's a generic greeting asking the caller to leave a message, but it's the first time I've heard her voice in days. I savor it before I ask her to call me as soon as she can.

I round her desk. Everything is in order.

My gaze centers on the messages.

I read the one on top.

"Fuck," I say under my breath. "Just fuck."

I pull out her chair and drop my ass into it. I reread the message, taking note of the caller's name.

The words written beneath Kallista's name could easily be misinterpreted: *Tell Dominick I had a great time last night. I wish he hadn't rushed off this morning. Please have him call me.*

I drop my gaze, pissed that I didn't get here before Arietta left so I could explain this to her.

My eye catches on the bottom drawer of her desk. It's slightly ajar. I tug it open when I spot a manila envelope inside.

I yank it out and spill the contents all over her desk.

Messages. There are more than a hundred goddamn messages here.

All marked with a woman's name and a note asking me to call back.

Some are more pointed than others, but they're all looking for the same thing. They want more of what we shared.

I curse under my breath, knowing that Arietta has been subjected to this for so fucking long.

I grab the messages, including the one from Kallista. I shove them back into the envelope, drop all of it the wastebasket next to her desk, and I take off toward the elevators.

I need to make this right before I lose the only woman I've ever loved.

Chapter 50

Arietta

I step out of the shower after my hour long walk with Dudley. I needed the fresh air and the time to think.

I was going to confide in Sinclair when I came home from work early, but she's interviewing someone for the next book she's working on. She told me she doesn't expect to be home for at least the next few hours.

After toweling off, I apply scented lotion to my skin.

I need the self-pampering time. It's not only helped me think more clearly, but it's a way for me to care for myself.

I haven't always done that.

Moving to Manhattan was my first step in putting myself first.

I need to do that now too. What I had with Dominick was great while it lasted. It might have been short-lived, but it taught me not to undervalue myself.

I need more from the men I sleep with. Dominick taught me how great sex could be, and I'm not wasting time on anyone who doesn't see my pleasure as important as his own.

Sprinting across the hallway naked, I hurry into my bedroom.

I tug on a pair of black yoga shorts and a matching tank top.

After I run a brush through my hair, I look at myself in my full-length mirror. I'm still wearing my contact lenses, so I'm not blindly staring at my blurred reflection the way I was the morning I took my lingerie selfie.

I laugh to myself when I think about that. I stumbled over my own feet the first time I tried posing for the image. My second attempt was more successful, although I didn't know it until I slid my glasses back on and looked at the photo.

A knock at the apartment door sends me in that direction.

I ordered pizza twenty minutes ago. They have a thirty-minute free pizza promise, so I curse as I pad across the floor in bare feet.

The last two times I ordered it, it was free because the delivery person wasn't familiar with Tribeca. It seems she's found her bearings now.

I swing open the door.

The delivery person is there with a smile on her face, but it's the man standing behind her that I can't take my eyes off of.

Reaching into the inner pocket of his dark gray suit jacket, Dominick slides out his wallet. "I'll take care of this."

The delivery person shoots him a look over her shoulder. "She already paid for it."

He pulls two hundred dollar bills from his wallet and hands them to her in exchange for the pizza. "Here's a tip."

"She already tipped…" Her voice trails as she gets sight of the cash. "Wow. Thank you, sir."

"You're welcome." He smiles at her. "Now, if you'll excuse us, I need to tell this beautiful woman that I'm crazy about her."

***

"The kind of pizza a person loves says a lot about them." Dominick steps into my home even though I haven't invited him in.

I'll play along with this game since I sense that he's using it as a diversion. It won't work, but I'll humor him. "What is your favorite kind of pizza?"

"Hotdog."

I work to hide a smile because I don't want to give him that. I won't give him that after what happened in Miami.

"You like hotdog pizza?"

He nods. "It's an acquired taste. I acquired it when I worked at a pizza place for a day when I was fourteen."

"You only worked there for a day?" I question.

"The owner knew Marti, and when my grandmother found out I went to get a job in a kitchen that wasn't at Calvetti's, I got supreme shit."

I stare at him. Why does this feel so easy, yet so hard?

He drops the pizza box on the dining room table. "I would never cheat on you, Arietta."

I thought he might figure out where my head is based on the message I left at the top of the stack on my desk.

"Kallista is Orson's lawyer," he explains. "He told me if I could work out a deal with her, I could have the contract."

Relief hits me like a tidal wave. I feel my bottom lip tremble.

He stalks toward me, keeping his hands at his sides. "Working out all the details on a deal that large takes time."

I smile. "You didn't do anything while you were gone?"

"I didn't do anything but work." He shakes his head. "And think about you. I can't tell you how hard it's been not being this close to you."

I bite my lip. "You didn't break the contract."

He huffs out a laugh. "I don't need that fucking contract to be faithful to you. I don't want anyone else, Arietta. I don't need anyone else. If you didn't feel the need to have that contract to secure your job, I'd rip it up now to show you that I'm not going anywhere."

I scrub a hand over my forehead, pushing my still wet hair aside. "I misunderstood what she said when she called."

"Because you've been screening my calls for too long." He drops his gaze to the floor. "I'm sorry you've had to do that."

I reach forward for his hand. He gives it to me.

"I don't have a clue about how to be an open book." He locks eyes with me. "If you want to know my secrets, I'll confess them all. Ask me anything."

"What do you think my favorite pizza is?"

His gaze flicks across the top of the pizza box. "What the hell? You ordered from the same place I worked at for a day."

I point at the box. "Open it. My favorite pizza is inside."

He flips open the box before his head falls back in laughter. "I think you and I are the only two people in this city who love hot dogs on their pizza."

Chapter 51

Dominick

I take her into my arms again.

I ate her out after we had pizza, and then I fucked her from behind with her ass in my hands and my cock buried deep inside of her.

She whimpered and cried out when I pumped harder. Her pleas were for more, but her body was craving my touch.

Not just the drives of my dick into her, but my hands on her flesh and my lips on her neck.

I held her like that, close to me, as I emptied my release inside a condom. I wanted to rid myself of it and drive back into her to feel her wet heat wrapped around my cock, but I stopped myself.

I need to ask for that.

I have to reassure her that I'm clean before we discuss birth control. If she's comfortable with that, I want to take her bare.

"Arietta," I whisper her name into her neck. "You're so fucking beautiful."

She lets out a stuttered laugh. "I think I had pizza sauce on my face the entire time we were doing that."

I move so I can look at her. I dip my mouth to the corner of her lips to lick the tiny speck of sauce that settled there.

She uses that to her advantage to kiss me.

It's slow and deep. I feel it in every part of me, but it takes my heart by surprise. I belong with her. Wherever she is, I need to be.

"I was scared," she confesses in a soft voice.

I kiss her forehead to reassure her that I'm here and I'm listening. "Of what, beautiful?"

"That I wasn't enough." She breathes heavily. "I haven't always been enough."

If a man in her past made her feel that way, that's on him. It's a reflection of his insecurities.

"My first boyfriend wanted me to change."

"Change how?" I ask.

I want to look into her eyes for this conversation, but I sense she needs this more. She needs to feel protected by me. She has to feel me wrapped around her, shielding her from her past pain.

"How I look." She exhales. "The way I dress. My hair. The glasses."

"You're perfect the way you are," I tell her honestly. "I think you're the most beautiful woman on this planet."

That draws her away from me far enough that she can look at my face. I'm grateful that she has her contact lenses in, so there's no mistaking the desire in my eyes.

"You do?"

"You're mesmerizing. No one this earth comes close to being as breathtaking as you."

Tears gather in the corners of her eyes. "I believe you."

I kiss her on the mouth. "Good, because it's true."

"Have you always been drop-dead gorgeous?" She gazes at my face. "You're so good-looking that it's kind of distracting."

"Is it distracting now?" I stick out my tongue.

"More so." She wiggles next to me. "I know what that tongue feels like on my body. If this building were burning down right now, I wouldn't notice."

I inch down her body, trailing kisses along her smooth skin.

I stop to take her right nipple in my mouth. I circle it softly with my tongue before I shift my focus to the other.

"Am I going to have another orgasm?" she asks quietly.

I shake my head as I drop my tongue to her stomach. "Two."

"Three?" she asks hopefully. "In a row?"

I stop what I'm doing to press a kiss to the top of her mound. "Are we negotiating, Miss Voss?"

Under heavy lids, she looks at me. "Is it possible to have three in a row?"

I've never focused my attention on a woman long enough to know the answer to that question. "We're about to find out."

I dip my tongue down to draw a lazy path over her cleft. Her legs fall open, revealing her pretty pink pussy.

My breath catches when her hand drops into my hair. "I love when you do this to me."

I love what you do to me.

I hold those words on the tip of my tongue as I pleasure the woman I love, hoping that tonight is the first of a lifetime of moments just like this.

Chapter 52

Arietta

"Get dressed," Dominick whispers in my ear. "Now, Arietta."

I fumble around in the darkness trying to find him. I must have dozed off after he ate me out. He proved that it's possible for me to have three orgasms in a row.

I finally find the light next to my bed. I tap the base to turn it on.

I shake my head when I realize that everything is crystal clear. I'm still wearing my contact lenses. My eyes are going to hate me in the morning.

I look to where Dominick is standing next to my bed. He's wearing his pants and white button-down shirt. The collar is unbuttoned, and the sleeves rolled up.

His hair is mussed.

"Come back to bed," I purr, rolling over.

His gaze drops to my ass. "You have no fucking idea how tempted I am to do that."

"So do it," I challenge.

"After you come with me." He holds out a hand.

"Where?"

He takes both my hands to pull me up to my feet. He picks up my tank top and yoga shorts from the floor. Silently, he guides me to put them on, tugging the fabric of the shorts up my legs.

"I'm tired." I laugh. "You left me with no energy."

"I'll carry you," he says before he scoops me up like a bride.

Swatting his shoulder, I shake my head. "No. Tell me first where we're going."

He kisses me so tenderly that time stands still for the briefest of seconds. "We're going to the roof."

"Why?"

Moving toward my bedroom door, he motions to the doorknob. "Open the door for me. "

He dips me in that direction, so I do as asked. Dudley greets us immediately with a few jumps that land against Dominick's legs.

"I took him for a walk," he says casually. "He was whining by the apartment door."

I glance at the floor but only catch a fleeting glance of Dudley's back as he circles Dominick's feet. "I didn't hear him whining."

"You were asleep," he points out. "I found his leash and your keys on the foyer table, so I took him down for a walk and then paid Ricky to give me a key to the door that leads up to the roof."

"Wait," I say. "Back up."

Dominick does exactly what I say. He backs up one step. With a huge smile on his face, he kisses me.

"You paid the doorman to give you a key to the roof?"

He nods. "Five hundred dollars."

My eyes widen. "Five hundred dollars? Why would you do that?"

"You'll see," he says with a wink of his eye. "Dudley will wait here for us."

He turns to the dog and orders him to sit in a soft tone.

Dudley listens for the first time ever. I laugh.

I hang tightly to the man I adore as he takes us out of my apartment and to the elevator that leads to the top floor and the door marked '*ROOF*' that is always locked.

***

238

I'm grateful for the pouring rain because I know that Dominick can't tell that I'm crying.

These are tears of joy.

I hold tightly to him as he spins me around in a puddle. We both have bare feet, but the smooth concrete makes for a perfect dance floor as the moon shines down on us through the rain.

The thunder in the distance is muted by the music streaming from the phone in Dominick's pocket.

I recognize the song immediately.

It's Precious Beats by Asher Foster.

I listened to this song on repeat during the bus ride that brought me to New York City from Buffalo.

Dominick clears his throat. "You're the arrow I follow."

My lips part. This can't be real. He's singing along to the lyrics.

"I'll take my chances on you over and over again."

I mouth the words as he belts them out in a strangled, off-pitch tone.

He swings me around again, making me feel as though I'm light on my feet and in the middle of a movie scene.

"Don't tell me this isn't right!" He screams into the rain. "I know what I feel."

I join him for the next line. "Tomorrow will be ours forever."

He gazes down at me through the pelting rain. "Don't tell me this is your favorite song, Arietta."

I nod, unsure if I can answer that question because he's making one of my dreams come true, and he doesn't know it.

"It's mine too," he says.

I rest my head against his chest as he leads me into the chorus with his arms wrapped around me. His deep voice fills the air as he sings every word of the song with me.

Chapter 53

Dominick

Last night was one for the record books.

I sang my heart out, and then I handed it over to Arietta Voss. It belongs to her whether she wants it or not.

I'm not in control of any of this. I don't want to be. All I want is to feel this way forever.

I take a seat behind my desk and stare at her empty chair.

She's at home.

I left her there an hour ago to go home to change and toss my pants in the trash. They're ruined, but I don't give a fuck. I'd throw all my clothes into the Hudson River for the chance to dance with her again.

A knock on the doorjamb of my office draws my gaze up.

"Judd," I say his name even though I can tell he's itching to talk. "Let me guess what you're here for."

He steps into my office but leaves the door open. I take that to mean we're talking business, not personal.

"Did you catch that storm last night?" He glances at the window to his right. "It kept my boys up."

"It kept me up too."

It's not a lie. I made love to Arietta after we warmed up in her shower. It was tender and slow. She fell asleep in my arms before I drifted off feeling like I'd found the treasure I've been searching a lifetime for.

"You and the woman you don't fuck?"

"Me and Arietta."

240

That snaps his head back toward me. "You're shitting me."

I lean back in my chair. "I danced in the rain with her last night. I spent the night at her apartment. I've been apart from her for an hour, and I miss her."

He shakes his head. "Damn, Dominick."

I can't tell from his expression what he thinks. It doesn't matter because this is it for me. I don't care that she works for me. I don't give a shit that she's twelve years younger than I am.

"I didn't see that coming." He huffs out a laugh. "But it makes perfect sense."

It does to me too, so I don't ask him to clarify the remark.

"Are you in love with her?"

I glance past him to the corridor. I don't want Arietta to hear those words coming from my mouth unless they're directed at her and her alone.

"I need to discuss that with her first."

"So that's a solid yes." He smiles. "I'm loving this. It's about damn time you fell in love."

It's been thirty-four years.

It was well worth the wait.

"When's the wedding?" He glances at his watch. "If it's an outdoor ceremony, I can tell you the days of the year it's least likely to rain, and you'll want to avoid February. It's the windiest month."

I'm not there yet, but I can see it on the horizon.

"Let's slow this down." I push to my feet. "She's young, and I'm in no hurry."

It's a lie, but I'm not going to push Arietta on anything.

"You and Arietta will go the distance," he says matter-of-factly.

That's what I want.

"You didn't tell me what brought you here."

He laughs. "Bronwyn's knocked up. She's going to marry Theon."

I chuckle. "No shit?"

"No shit." He shakes his head. "It looks like I'll need a temp to replace her for a few months. You wouldn't happen to want to share Arietta with me, would you?"

I know we're talking business, but that's not happening.

"You'll find a temp."

"I will," he assures me with a brisk nod. "It's all good, Dom. Things around here are changing, and I couldn't be happier for all of us. Especially you."

I thank him with a smile. "The future is looking good."

"Better than you think." He taps the corner of my desk. "I heard that Vernon Greenwalt is in town. It's time for us to make our move."

Signing a deal with him would be the icing on the cake.

"I'll call him."

"Bronwyn's on it." He laughs. "I told her we'd match what we gave Arietta for landing Clarice, so let's let her take a swing at it."

I have yet to hand Arietta the check for twenty-five thousand dollars for her integral part in getting Clarice on board.

As wary as I am, I agree to his terms. "I'll leave it in Bronwyn's hands."

Until tomorrow, I don't add.

Vernon Greenwalt is too important of a potential client for me not to give this my all.

***

An hour later, Arietta takes a seat at her desk.

She's wearing a yellow and red striped dress. Her hair is braided today to the side. I have no idea if it's supposed to be as messy as it is, but I fucking love it.

She turns in my direction to wiggle her fingers at me.

I smile as I watch her adjust her glasses on her nose.

"I appreciate the call," I tell one of my clients as he drones on about a half a percent interest rate drop that's going to cost him peanuts compared to the fortune he just made cashing in some bonds. "We can go over this at lunch tomorrow if you like."

He agrees to it because he knows I'll reassure him in person while I treat him to a premium steak alongside a glass of expensive red wine.

Once I end the call, I curve a finger luring Arietta in my direction.

She's on her feet in an instant. Without a word from me she closes my office door behind her.

I watch in silence as she rounds my desk to deposit herself in my lap.

I roll back my chair to give her the room she needs.

"I'm sorry I'm late," she says before planting a soft kiss on my jaw.

My cock instantly comes to life beneath her. "You'll make it up to me."

"Will I?" She bats her eyelashes. "How?"

I'd order her onto her knees now, but I have work to do.

"That happens in my bed."

Her eyes skim my face. "Can I ask you something?"

I cup her cheek before I answer. "Anything."

"Did you negotiate a deal with Kallista?" she asks.

"I did."

"Would you say she's a good lawyer?"

That's an unexpected question, but I answer honestly. "No. She didn't hold her ground. I would have given up some of my commission if pressed just to land the deal."

Her eyes hone in on mine. "She didn't read you right."

I agree with a gentle nod of my head. "You're right. She didn't."

"It takes a long time to learn that." Her fingers dance over my shoulder. "I'm learning how to do that."

I study her eyes. "You want to be a lawyer."

She leans closer until her lips skim the curve of my ear. "One day."

She's more remarkable than I even imagined. Her goals are high as they should be. "You'll do it."

Planting a kiss on my neck, she nods. "I know I will."

"I have something for you." I point at the top drawer of my desk. "Reach in there and get it."

Hesitation dictates her movements. She stops before she touches the drawer pull. "Is it something good?"

"Yes," I reassure her with a kiss on her cheek.

She slowly pulls open the drawer to find a white envelope with her first name scribbled hastily across it.

Picking it up, she weighs it in her hands. "Did you amend our contract?"

I want to shred the fucking thing because I don't need a piece of paper to tie me to her. My heart is doing that for me.

"Open it," I direct her.

She does it slowly.

I watch her face intently as she slides out the check I wrote to her just moments before she arrived. Judd co-signed it making it official.

Her eyes scan the check. "What?"

"That's your bonus for bringing Clarice on board," I whisper.

Her gaze jumps to my face. A tear rolls down her cheek. "This is mine? I earned this?"

"Every penny of it."

Her bottom lip trembles under the weight of what she's feeling. "I can't believe this. Thank you, Dominick. You have no idea how much this means to me."

Based on the look in her eyes, I have a pretty solid idea. "You're welcome."

She seals the deal with a soft kiss on my mouth, leaving me wanting more the way she always does.

Chapter 54

Dominick

I wanted Arietta in my bed tonight, but she promised her roommate she'd have dinner with her.

I can't blame Sinclair.

There isn't a soul on this earth that I'd rather spend time with than Arietta.

I glance across the restaurant to see my grandmother talking to an older gentleman. My family has always encouraged her to find a new love, but she's told us repeatedly that my late grandfather took her heart with him when he died.

I couldn't understand what she meant until now.

She tosses me a wave and a smile. I offer the same in return. That sets her in motion in a sprint toward me.

"Why are you happy?" she demands as soon as she's next to the table I sat down at five minutes ago.

"What?" I laugh. "What kind of question is that?"

"The kind that I want an answer to." She pats me on the cheek. "You're smiling a lot."

I can't wipe the fucking smile off my face, so I motion for her to take a seat across from me. "What should I order for dinner?"

"I'll bring you the lamb stew."

That hasn't been on the menu for years. "What's the special occasion, Marti?"

"Your dad requested it." She heaves a sigh. "He came in earlier but had to leave. He's volunteering tonight."

That sounds like my dad.

He's been putting in time helping with little league coaching since I was a kid. It was some of the best days of my life. I took a ball to my ankle during a game late in the season when I was twelve.

It wasn't a career-ending injury. I hobbled around for most of the off-season, but when it came time to sign up again, I declined. I wanted to focus on getting to bed extra early so I could be up at dawn to deliver newspapers before school.

I'll always regret not having that extra time on the ball diamond with my dad.

"You didn't answer my question," she persists. "You seem too happy."

"Is it a crime to be happy?"

"Did you make a lot of money today?"

That's an obvious question since the only reason I've ever smiled for years was because I landed a huge deal.

"I make a lot of money every day," I answer with a straight face.

She studies me. "Are you going to tell me you're in love?"

I'm spreading this news around too much. I need to tell Arietta how I feel before Marti hears it. Otherwise, half of Manhattan will know about it by midnight.

"I like someone," I say quietly. "A lot."

She leans back in the chair and crosses her arms over her chest. "It's Arietta."

I perk both brows. "What?"

"Don't try and lie to me," she warns. "You don't think I have eyes? I saw how you looked at her when you two were here together."

Was it that fucking obvious back then?

"When will the wedding be?" She looks toward the kitchen. "I'll get champagne for us to toast. Call Arietta. Tell her to come."

I stop her with a hand on her wrist before she can get out of her chair. "I think I should tell her how I feel first."

That earns me a light swat across my hand. "You haven't told her yet?"

"I'm working on it."

She moves her hand to cup mine. "Tell her, Dominick. Do it now."

"Right now?" I joke.

Her face goes stoic. "No one can guarantee you another minute. Why waste even one when you can be with the woman you love?"

She's damn right.

"At least give me a bowl of lamb stew and a glass of wine before you boot me out." I tap on the back pocket of my jeans. "I brought my wallet. I can pay for it."

That sends her up to her feet. "My grandchildren don't pay for food here."

Shaking her head and mumbling to herself, she takes off in the direction of the kitchen.

I'll enjoy my meal and another hour with her before I stop by Arietta's place to tell her how I feel.

***

I step out onto the sidewalk outside of Calvetti's into the warmth of the evening.

The daytime temperatures are creeping up. I don't know by how much. Judd is the one who has a pulse on that. He may claim he never wanted to be a meteorologist, but I've always wondered if that was his true calling.

"Mr. Calvetti?"

I turn at the sound of a deep voice.

I shake my head because I swear to fuck I'm seeing things.

"Vernon Greenwalt?" As much as I want his name to come out in a calm statement, it sounds more like a confused question.

He extends a hand to me. "One in the same."

I shake his hand, noting the expensive watch on his wrist. It's a custom piece crafted by hand. He made mention of it in an article a couple of years ago.

While I try and find the words to ask him what the hell he's doing outside my grandmother's restaurant, he points at the windows that look into Calvetti's. "I stopped by your office. The doorman in the lobby suggested that I might find you here."

It's pure luck that he did. I glance down at the phone in my hand.

"I didn't call," he explains. "I wanted to talk face-to-face."

I wish to fuck I wouldn't have stopped by my apartment after work. I ditched a three thousand dollar suit for a pair of faded jeans and a sweater with a small hole near the bottom hem.

He doesn't seem to notice.

I won't offer him an invite to talk to me inside of Calvetti's. My grandmother tries to make everyone feel at home to the point that business gets buried under the stories she tells.

I learned that the hard way when I brought Mr. Morano here for dinner one night.

"Let's grab a drink," he suggests. "I'm looking for a smooth glass of bourbon."

I know there's a bar around the corner that will have something to quench his thirst. This wasn't how I envisioned my first meeting with my long-time idol, but life is full of surprises, and this is one I'm more than willing to roll with.

I've rehearsed my pitch to him thousands of times. I know word-for-word what I want to say to him.

"There's a bar not far from here." I gesture in the direction we're about to head. "I'm eager to discuss what I have to offer."

He stops mid-step and looks me straight in the eye. "I'm eager to discuss something too."

Something?

He jabs a finger into my shoulder just hard enough to keep my attention focused on him. "Don't mistake this for a business meeting, Mr. Calvetti. I'm here to talk about one thing and one thing only."

What the fuck is going on?

Just as I'm about to ask that, he answers my unspoken question for me. "Let's talk about my granddaughter."

That's so unexpected that I take a step back. I've never paid attention to his personal life because he never mentions it in interviews. I had no idea he had a child or children. I sure as fuck didn't know he has a granddaughter.

"Your granddaughter?" I perk a brow, hoping I didn't fuck and flee and leave her hanging.

If that bites me in the ass, so be it.

I'm not that man anymore.

He steps closer to me, keeping his icy blue eyes locked on my face. "That's what I said. We need to talk about what it's going to take to get you out of her life."

Chapter 55

Arietta

I glance in the direction of Dominick's darkened office again.

It's just past eleven, which means he's technically over two hours late. He isn't scheduled to sign anyone to a new contract today, so I don't think he's with his dad enjoying a celebratory breakfast.

The two calls I've made to him since last night have gone unanswered. So have the three emails and two text messages I sent.

I hear footsteps behind me, but I don't need to turn around to know who is on the approach.

Mr. Corning has been to see me three times already today.

The first time he brought me a chocolate chip muffin because he said Bronwyn turned it down because of her morning sickness.

His second visit was all about Dominick. He wanted to know where he was. He had a goofy grin on his face while we talked. I'm not sure if Dominick has told his business partner about our relationship or not, but I won't say anything.

"Arietta," Judd calls from behind me. "Any word yet."

"None." I steal a glance at him over my shoulder.

The smile that was pasted on his mouth earlier is gone. It's been replaced with concern. I see it in the way he keeps volleying his gaze between me and the empty chair behind Dominick's desk.

"Did he say anything to you about his meetings today?"

Pointing at the screen of my laptop, I shake my head. "I have his schedule here. You can check for yourself."

He moves to stand behind me. "He has a two p.m. with Mr. Morano. Do they typically meet here?"

I hear the hope in his voice.

"Yes. Almost always."

I glance over my shoulder to find him checking his watch. "He'll show up for that."

He says it to reassure himself, but I need more.

"Do you think something might have happened to him?"

He drops a hand to my shoulder to give it a reassuring squeeze. "He's good. For all we know, he's out chasing Vern Greenwalt around town."

I stare at him, unsure if I heard him correctly. "What?"

He moves to stand next to me. "A friend of a friend works as a doorman at the Bishop Hotel in Tribeca. He knows we've been after Vern Greenwalt for years. He spotted him at the hotel yesterday and gave me a heads-up. Dom's eager to get a meeting with Vern, but I told him we're going to let Bronwyn take her shot."

That can't be true.

We had an agreement. I didn't tell him I was in Manhattan.

I push back from my desk. "I need to go, sir. Can I take my lunch early today?"

His gaze flicks over my face. "What's wrong, Arietta?"

"I need to go see someone." I run a shaky hand over my forehead. "Please, sir. I'll be back."

"Take your time," he says softly. "Take all the time you need."

This won't take long.

My granddad broke another promise to me. I only have one thing I need to say to him. I hope that I can do that before Dominick discovers the secret I've been keeping.

***

I stand outside the hotel suite where my granddad is staying.

The woman working the reception desk at the lobby called him as soon as I requested his room number. He told her to send me right up.

I hate that he has a heads-up. It gives him a chance to weave another lie to feed me.

Before I have a chance to knock, he swings open the door.

"Arietta." He stretches his arms out to me. "There she is."

"Here I am," I whisper as he takes me in for an embrace.

I used to find comfort in his touch. When I was a young girl, I'd sit on his knee while he read stories to me.

It didn't matter if it was in his mansion in Buffalo or the beachfront house in Nantucket, he was always wearing a three-piece suit and a tie, just as he is now.

"Come in," he says as we break the embrace. "Let me look at you."

I brace myself for the inevitable comment about my appearance. It started when I was a teenager. I chose vintage clothes over the designer brands he bought me. I always told him I didn't want to wear the things he picked for me, but he kept picking them.

Just as he thought he could choose my life partner.

Baron Guidry is the grandson of my grandfather's best friend.

He was my first everything – kiss, lover, heartbreak.

Baron wanted me to change too. His idea of perfection is the two of us married running the businesses our grandfathers built from the ground up.

"You look lovely today."

I glance down at the red and striped sheath dress I'm wearing. I covered up on my way over with a white cardigan. My hair is pinned into a bun that has slid half-way down the back of my head.

"What?"

He steps back. "I said you're beautiful."

A lump forms in the back of my throat. I've never heard him say that to me. "Thank you, granddad."

"I've missed you," he confesses. "Very much."

I glance around the immaculate suite. Something doesn't feel right. This man has my grandfather's face, and he's wearing the same cologne that he's always worn, but he's different. He's kind, and there's softness in his eyes that I haven't seen in a very long time.

"You said you wouldn't try and find me." I sigh. "You agreed that you'd give me time to decide what's right for me."

He gestures toward a seating area. I settle into a big brown leather armchair. He sits in a matching one across from me.

"When you left Buffalo, I was angry," he admits.

The last conversation we ever had was proof of that. He told me that unless I returned to Buffalo soon, I'd lose my trust fund and any chance I had to take control of his business when he retires.

I told him to keep both.

Being the only grandchild of Vernon Greenwalt was too much pressure for me. I needed an out.

I'd gone to college to get the business degree he wanted me to have, but when I told him that law school was my dream, he listed the reasons why it was a waste of my time.

We reached an agreement that I would leave Buffalo to find my feet before I made a final decision about my future.

The day I arrived in Manhattan, my mind was made up.

I belong here in this city. I want to follow in my mom's footsteps to become a lawyer. I want to build a practice here helping people who don't know where to turn when they have a legal issue.

"I know," I say softly. "I'm sorry, granddad, but I needed time."

"No." He shakes his head. "You needed a chance. You needed a chance to find out what makes you happy; who makes you happy."

"Baron doesn't," I confess.

He leans back in the chair. "I see that now."

I study his face. "Did mom tell you where I was?"

He nods. "She came to see me yesterday. She told me you were working in Manhattan. She told me about him."

Him.

Dominick.

I had called my mom to tell her that I danced in the rain with a man I was falling in love with. She knew how much that meant to me. On my sixteenth birthday, she was with me when I'd written my life to-do list and tucked it into the poetry book she bought me was when I was ten-years-old at a vintage store near her office.

I was allowed to choose one thing from all the treasures in the store.

I had chosen that book because the title of the first poem in the Table of Contents spoke to me in all my awkwardness.

Her Beauty Within.

I read that poem until I memorized every word, and then I lived it, owning who I am - never apologizing for it. Instead, celebrating it.

"He's a good man, Arietta."

That lures my gaze to my grandfather's face. I nod. "He is."

"We met."

Panic sends me to my feet. "What? When?"

My granddad pushes until he's standing. His movements aren't as graceful as they once were. Leveling his stance with his hand resting on the arm of the chair, he takes a deep breath. "I met Dominick Calvetti last night. We talked."

I hadn't told him about my granddad. I didn't want that to influence my position at Modica or my relationship with him.

I knew it was a conversation I needed to have with him soon, but I thought it could wait. I fooled myself into thinking it could wait, but now it's too late.

"He knows," I whisper.

"He didn't until I told him who I was," he admits.

I step closer to my granddad, looking for the comfort he used to offer when I'd fall and skin my knee, or a nervous stomachache would land me in bed.

He holds out a hand, and I take it.

"What did he say?" I ask, even though I don't know that I'm ready to hear the answer.

"I think you need to talk to him, Arietta." He squeezes my hand. "I don't know if you took that job to spite me or to learn from him so you can handle your trust fund on your own. I do know that he loves you. He loves you with a might I've only seen once in my life. It's the same love that I felt for your grandmother until the day she died."

"He loves me?" Tear flood my eyes.

"Deeply." He takes my hand and holds it to the center of his chest. "Dominick wants a future with you. He's determined to help you achieve everything you're meant to accomplish, and all that man wants in return is your love."

Chapter 56

Dominick

I toss the baseball back to my dad. He catches it in his worn glove without a problem.

He pitches it back to me, aiming it directly at my glove.

When we first started this routine, I was five-years-old and completely uncoordinated. I'd fumble the ball every time he threw it in my direction, but we practiced, again and again until I could catch it with my dad six inches in front of me.

That changed to a foot apart and then two feet.

He's at least ten feet in front of me now, standing on the baseline on one of the little league fields at the ball club he volunteers at.

Once he catches my last pitch, he drops the glove and the ball on the ground.

His hands jump into the air, so I watch them intently as he signs to me. *Are you ready to tell me what's going on with you?*

I tuck my glove under my arm. *What makes you think something is going on with me?*

He steps around the ball and glove. *It's the middle of the day. You're not at the office.*

I needed time to sort through what I want to say to Arietta. Her life in no way mirrors mine. She had it rough growing up, trying to conform to the daydreams her grandfather had for her.

Her mom and aunt both passed on the opportunity to take the helm of their father's business, so all of that was put on Arietta.

She was Vernon Greenwalt's only hope for keeping the business in the family.

That's a type of pressure I've never felt.

I thought Greenwalt was living the dream. It turns out he was creating a nightmare for the woman I love.

I told him as much last night as we sipped bourbon in a crowded bar.

He offered me the chance to handle his entire portfolio if I fired Arietta and walked out of her life. I laughed that off and told him to look at his granddaughter for the brilliant, accomplished woman she is. She's more than capable of making her own choices.

Once my dad is within a foot of me, I raise my hands. *I'm in love.*

The look on his face is camera worthy. I stare at it, hoping I'll never forget it.

I watch his hands when asks the question I knew was coming. *You're serious?*

"Dead serious," I say under my breath as I sign it to him.

He rushes at me, and even though he's at least six inches shorter than me and lighter by fifty pounds, he scoops me up and tries to twirl me around.

I laugh.

The joy on his face is his laughter.

That turns to tears.

I feel that too, so I sob.

Is it Arietta? He signs when we scramble apart just before we fall to the grass.

I nod.

I love her. His hands keep moving. *Like a daughter. Like she's mine.*

"I love her too," I sign as I shout the words for all of Manhattan to hear.

258

You make her happy forever. He signs before he pats my cheek.

That's my plan, and it starts today.

***

The questions that were thrown at me when I pushed my two p.m. meeting with Mr. Morano on Judd were priceless. He wanted to know where the fuck I was and whether I was doing anything that would hurt Arietta.

I assured him that I'd cut off my left hand before I hurt her.

He laughed before filling me on the fact that Arietta shot out of the office like a rocket before lunch and after he mentioned Greenwalt's name to her.

I suspect she went to pay her dear old granddad a visit.

Vernon told me all about their agreement after I turned down his offer to push Arietta out of my life.

He was supposed to keep his distance until she decided on her future.

She was willing to walk away from a trust valued at close to forty million dollars to chase her dreams.

I admire her and cherish her, and I'm going to make that clear to her today.

A knock at my apartment door sends me in that direction.

I swing the door open to find a young woman with light brown hair and a smile on her face.

"Mr. Calvetti?" She glances at the flowers in her hands. "I'm Athena Millett from Wild Lilac. We brought the flowers you ordered, sir."

"It's Dominick." I take the vase from her hands. "You brought them all?"

"As many as I could find." She glances over her shoulder. "My fiancé, Liam, is helping me out today. I told him it was all hands on deck. I've never had this large of an order before."

I have no fucking idea how she pulled this together in the limited time I gave her.

"I think I purchased every pink and red rose in the five boroughs, New Jersey, and a few other places along the Eastern seaboard."

I laugh. "The place is yours to work your magic."

Her gaze settles on the room behind me. "I'll make it beautiful for her."

That's all I can ask for. "I'll be in my den if you need anything."

She nods. "Tonight must be a very special occasion."

"It is," I answer.

It's the night I tell Arietta that I love her and my future belongs to her. I'll sign whatever the fuck she wants me to sign. I'll do cartwheels down Fifth Avenue in a dinosaur costume if she adds that to her to-do list. I'll do what it takes to prove to her that I'm in this forever. I hope to hell she is too.

Chapter 57

Arietta

I glance down at my phone's screen as I walk into Past Over.

I just got off work, and I still haven't heard from Dominick. I did hear from Sinclair an hour ago. I gave her a brief explanation of what's going on.

When I first told her about my grandfather months ago, she didn't say very much. I know that she didn't want to influence my decision about my future either way, so today when I explained that I patched things up with my granddad, she let out a sigh of relief.

She only wants what is best for me.

She thinks that's a distraction from Dominick, so we're meeting here to find a couple of new outfits for me to wear to work.

I have every intention of keeping my job at Modica until my contract expires.

By then, I will have saved up enough to help get me through law school. My granddad called me earlier to tell me that he'll release my trust fund to me regardless of whether I choose to take over his business.

I want to do this on my own though.

If I invest that money wisely, I can work as a lawyer pro-bono for people who can't afford legal advice.

"Arietta!" Lynn calls from where she's standing behind the check-out counter. "Aren't you a vision?"

I'm still wearing the same striped dress I was when I saw my granddad. I gave up on my hair mid-afternoon, so I tugged it out of the bun it was half-pinned in.

"How are you?" I ask as I approach her.

"Swamped." She laughs.

Since I'm the only person in the store, I can't tell if she's joking or not.

I err on the side of caution. "Can I help you?"

"You can," she affirms with a nod of her head. "There's a book on that table over there I need brought up here. Can you grab it?"

Since we're standing less than twenty feet away from the table she's pointing at, I take a breath. "You want me to get a book for you?"

"Please." She cups her hands together in front of her. "I'd be forever grateful."

Shrugging, I set off toward the table, wondering why the hell she needs help with that. "Which book is it?"

"You'll know it when you see it," she calls after me.

I take one last look at the screen of my phone before I drop it in the tote slung over my shoulder.

I approach the table. My gaze hones in on a poetry book that looks exactly like the one I have at home.

It even has the same torn edge in the left hand corner.

I pick it up and notice immediately a piece of paper sticking out of it.

Curiosity drives me to open the book. I thumb through the pages stopping when I see one has been taped back into place.

This can't be right.

I keep turning pages until I spot an all too familiar paper folded into quarters.

I glance back to find Lynn gone. "Lynn?"

My call to her goes unanswered, so I drop my gaze back to the book.

I tug out the paper and carefully unfold it.

It's my life to-do list. I read it before I tuck it back into place.

With my heart pounding in my chest, I keep thumbing through the pages until I reach the spot where a piece of paper has been shoved between the last two pages.

I yank it out.

I unfold it slowly.

I can't fight back more tears as I read what's written in masculine handwriting. It's the same handwriting I've become familiar with since I see it all the time.

Dominick wrote this.

My To-Do List

> *1. Live in NYC! My home. The place I belong with my love.*
>
> *2. Live in an apartment that's filled with fresh red and pink roses!*
>
> *3. Dance in the rain again and again. Splash my feet. Sing along to the music!*
>
> *4. Adopt a dog named DICK!*
>
> *5. Be kissed by Arietta every fucking day of my life.*
>
> *6. Fall in love! Deeply. Passionately. Forever. WITH ARIETTA!*
>
> *7. Propose to Arietta on the roof in the rain.*
>
> *8. Get married to Arietta in the fall with the leaves turning colors.*
>
> *9. Have a baby…or two. Maybe 3… or 4?*
>
> *10. Never stop smiling because I'm the luckiest man in the world.*

With trembling hands, and a face full of fallen tears, I sob aloud.

"Arietta?"

I spin around when I hear his voice behind me. "Dominick."

He's wearing the suit and tie that I love. I tripped over my feet the first time that I saw him in it.

"Come with me." He holds out his hand. "Come home with me."

Nodding, I take a step toward him, worried that my legs won't support me because they're shaking so hard. "Hold my hand."

"That would be my honor," he says as he reaches for me. "I like this place."

I look up and into his face. "Me too."

"I guess you know that I saw your to-do list." He chuckles. "My sole goal in life is to make all of that a reality."

"Everything on your list too?"

Scooping an arm around my waist, he leads me to the door. "Yes. That starts with the surprise I have waiting for you at our apartment."

I stop. "Our apartment?"

His response is a soft kiss on my mouth before he ushers me out the door and into the back seat of a waiting car.

Chapter 58

Dominick

They say a picture is worth a thousand words, but the look on Arietta's face is priceless.

I brought her into the apartment with the promise that I'd let her open her eyes as soon as we crossed the threshold.

I wanted to carry her over it like a bride, but that will come.

When the time is right, I'll drop to a knee on the roof and ask her to marry me.

Today, I want something just as monumental from her. I want her to move in with me.

She stares at me before her gaze wanders the perimeter of the living room. Her hand jumps to her mouth.

"Dominick," she says my name breathlessly.

I'm tempted to whip out my phone to capture this moment in time in photographic form, but I won't.

I know I'll never forget her expression as she takes in the thousands of red and pink roses gathered together in bouquets in vintage vases set around this room.

I supplied most of the vases. I found the majority at Past Over earlier when I stopped there after I played catch with my dad.

Lynn had boxes and boxes of vases packed in her storeroom.

Sinclair offered to come to help me pick some out when I called her to tell her my plan. She brought a few vases, and the others were treasures Athena had at her floral shop.

I needed to give Athena the extra time to set up the flowers, so I took the poetry book Sinclair brought me to Past Over right before Arietta was supposed to arrive. I set it on that table, and then I watched the love of my life read my life to-do list.

It's heavily focused on her, but *fuck*, that's what I want.

She's all I want.

I step into Arietta's sightline. "Live here with me."

Her gaze trails over my face, landing on my lips. "What?"

I lean closer. "I want you to move in with me. I want to wake up every day next to you and fall asleep wrapped around you. I want to adopt a dog named Dick. We'll take him for walks after I cook dinner for you. He can watch us dance in the rain on the roof."

She studies me as she takes in each word. Her voice comes out in a trembling whisper. "When, Dominick?"

"Now."

"I'm…it's… so much has…" she stumbles her way through that.

"If you need me to sign something that promises my heart to you forever, I can have a pen in my hand in the next five seconds." I cup my hands over her cheeks. "I want to protect you and love you. I want to watch you become the woman you want to be."

"I want to be with you," she whispers.

"Sinclair can have your stuff packed up in an hour." I chuckle. "She's not eager to see you go, but she told me she wants you to be happy."

Nodding her head, she leans in to kiss the corner of my mouth. "I am happy."

Wariness is wrapped around those words, so I rest my lips against her forehead. "Tell me to slow it the fuck down if you need to."

That lures a laugh from her. "I should have told you about my granddad."

If guilt is causing her hesitation, that stops now.

"You would have," I assure her because I know it's the truth. "You made a decision to wait to tell me, and I respect that. I respect the hell out of that, Arietta."

"You do?"

"If I'm totally honest, I don't know what I would have done if you would have told me you were Vernon Greenwalt's granddaughter when we hired you on."

"You would have used that information to get me to arrange a meeting between you two."

It's not an accusation. It's an observation, a correct one.

"I wanted to come to New York City and make it on my own. I wanted to learn how to handle wealth," she explains. "In Buffalo, I was always that Greenwalt kid. My friends knew my granddad was rich, even though we didn't live that way. He didn't help my mom when she told him she wanted to go to law school. He cut off my Aunt Cressida when she went away to college and never came back."

To think I looked up to him for most of my life. Vernon Greenwalt was the person I most wanted to be like.

He tried to trample the dreams of the people who loved him because the almighty dollar was the most important thing to him.

"He's changed," she says softly. "I don't know what happened, but he's different."

I can't take credit for that, but I know what I said to him last night resonated deeply. I helped him see that his granddaughter is unique and there isn't a price tag on her happiness.

No one on this earth can plan Arietta's future for her. I sure as hell want to marry her and be the father of her children, but whether or not that happens depends on her.

"Things are better between you two?"

She nods. "We'll talk again soon. We'll sort all the details out."

I stare at her as she takes another glance at all the flowers. "If I move in, I want to pay rent."

I won't argue with her even though there's no mortgage on this place. "You can pay me what you pay for the apartment you're living in now."

I'll tuck that money away for college for the children we'll have.

She nods. "That's fair."

"I'll do the cooking."

She smiles. "I'll cook too."

"We'll make love every day," I counter.

"And every night," she adds. "Starting…"

"Now." I scoop her up into my arms. "Our bed awaits."

"Our bed," she whispers into my ear. "Our home. Our life."

"Our forever, Arietta. This is just the beginning." I press a kiss to her mouth. "I love you."

"I love you too," she whispers those words to me for the very first time.

Epilogue

Three Months Later

Arietta

"Sex without a condom is next level."

Dominick cracks open one of his eyelids to look at me. "You're telling me. Nothing feels as good as being bare inside of you."

It's a decision we made together a little over a month ago.

I've been on birth control for a few years, and after we were both tested to make sure we were clean, we decided that it was time to make love without a condom.

We've been taking full advantage of that ever since, including just now.

"Tell me about your lunch with Vern today."

I rest my head on my pillow. "We may have come to a compromise."

He turns to me, covering his semi-erect cock with the sheet. "What compromise?"

After my granddad and I discussed my future, we came to the mutual agreement that his right hand man would carry on with the business.

I'll go to law school, and if my granddad ever needs my services, I'll do the work for free. It's the least I can do since he's releasing my trust fund in its entirety to me on my twenty-third birthday.

"One that lets me achieve my dreams without having to worry about money."

Dominick smiles. Even though he's offered numerous times to give me the money for school, I've turned him down. I also passed when he asked if I wanted to work out a loan arrangement.

Money is part of our relationship, but it's only a fraction of it. On the day I officially moved in, we tore up the contract we signed before making love for the first time. Dominick insisted on signing a document that will protect my trust fund. I didn't want that, but he assured me he did. He told me it's important that I know that my money has no bearing on what he feels for me, just as his money doesn't matter to me.

Our love binds us together.

"You'll go to law school?" He questions as he rubs the scruff on his jaw.

I nod my head. "Don't do that when we're talking."

"Do what?" He shoves a hand through his mussed-up hair.

"That."

He shrugs. "How can I stop if I have no idea what I'm doing?"

I crawl on top of him.

That lures a moan from deep within him. "I can go again, beautiful."

I know that. This man can fuck me senseless, and within twenty minutes, we're making love in the most tender and gentle way.

"You're what women call devastatingly handsome," I say before I kiss him.

"I'm what they call desperately in love," he counters.

"With me," I whisper.

"Forever," he adds.

We sit in silence staring at each other until Dick, our Yorkshire Terrier, breaks that with a loud bark.

"A storm must be coming," Dominick glides his hands on my thighs. "That gives me just enough time for a triple treat."

I laugh at the name he bestowed on his pussy eating abilities.

I reach down to cup my hand over his cock. "It's my turn."

His tongue darts over his bottom lip. "I'm here for that."

I slide down his body to take him in my mouth. The groan that escapes him flows through me as a clap of thunder fills the air.

***

I wake in the darkness with the sound of rain hitting the windows.

It hasn't rained in weeks.

I've missed the sound and the smell of a summer storm, so I slip on my glasses and walk across the hardwood floor to crack open the window.

I look back to the bed to find it empty.

I'm not surprised. Judd and Judith's daughter, Kinsley, was born just a few weeks ago. Since then, Judd's been touching base with Dominick each night to talk about what's going on at the office. I use that time to check in on Sinclair and Maren. Sinclair is interviewing potential roommates. Maren is anxiously awaiting the arrival of her son, Weber.

Moving closer to the bedroom door, I listen for Dominick's voice, but I'm met with silence. I peek around the corner to see darkness in his den.

Just as I'm about to make my way down the hallway, the sound of fingernails on a chalkboard stops me in place.

I laugh aloud and rush to where my phone is sitting on the nightstand. I smile at the subject line.

Subject: Singing in the Rain

Dear Arietta,

Join me on the roof?

I can offer you a dance and a song for the price of a kiss.

I love you.

Signed,
Your Dominick

XOXO

I reply immediately with a light touch of my fingers over the screen of my phone.

Subject Re: Singing in the Rain

I'm on my way!

I love you too.

Arietta xoxo

I tug on a pair of lace panties before I slide one of Dominick's T-shirts over my head. I race out of the penthouse to the door at the end of the corridor that leads to the roof.

Taking the steps quickly, I burst onto the roof to find him standing in a suit.

He hasn't worn a suit for our dancing since the first night we did it at my apartment.

I stare at him and the strings of small white lights decorating the perimeter of the roof. Red and pink roses are everywhere. The petals of all the flowers are glistening from the rain shower.

"Dominick?"

He drops to one knee in what feels like slow motion.

My hands leap to cover my mouth.

"Beautiful, come here," he beckons me closer with a curl of his index finger.

I do as asked and pad on my bare feet through a puddle. I reach for his hand. He takes it, holding it gently next to his cheek before he kisses my palm.

"You are what happens when good flourishes within a person." His bottom lip trembles. "You've taught me so much about myself and others. I am honored to know you and humbled to be loved by you."

I try desperately to hold my composure.

"I love you more than I can express, Arietta." He bows his head. "Every day I wake up and question why I'm this lucky. What did I do to deserve this much happiness with the most remarkable women on earth?"

I want to tell him it's because he's just as remarkable. He's good, and kind, and loving. He may be driven, but he's done so much good with his wealth. He's helped his family, and friends, and our community.

"Marry me, Arietta." His free hand dives into the pocket of his suit jacket. He tugs out a small box. "Marry me when the day is right for you. I don't care if it's this fall or a year from now or a year after that. I need to be your husband. I want to grow old with you. Loving you forever will make my life complete, and I promise you that I will always cherish you for the woman you are."

I stare at the box when he opens it.

I lose it because it's the ring. It's the ring that I've dreamed of wearing since I was a little girl.

The diamond is tiny, the white gold surrounding it worn in places, but it means everything to me.

"Your grandfather gave me his blessing and this ring today." He glances down at it. "It was on your grandmother's finger for most of her life. I want more than anything to place it on yours for the rest of my life."

"My life," I repeat as I sob.

"No," he whispers as he slides it onto my finger. "I can't live without you. I want you to be my wife until I leave this earth."

"I want that too," I say as thunder smacks in the distance.

Dick barks from where he's been sitting in the corner, shielded from the rain by an awning.

Dominick glides to his feet. "Is that a yes?"

"Yes!" I scream. "Yes a million times."

He sweeps me into his arms and twirls me around again and again.

"Let's dance to that." He laughs as he sets me down on my shaky feet.

He drags his phone out of his pocket and starts Precious Beats, our favorite song.

Under the rain and close to the stars, we dance and sing, knowing that our love story with all of its twists and turns is just beginning.

Preview of Plucked

PLUCKED, a sexy standalone from New York Times Bestseller, Deborah Bladon.

Roman Hawthorne is tall, devastatingly handsome, and has a jawline that is so sharp that it cut could glass. He's my dream guy on paper but let's just say Roman is arrogant with a capital A.

When I meet him in a bar on a random Tuesday, I think I'll never see him again.

But I do.

Every time I show up at that bar, Roman is there with his perfectly styled hair, dark brown eyes, and megawatt smile.

Soon our innocent flirtation turns into more.

He brings me daisies, encourages me to chase all of my dreams, and we do things that make even me blush.

When he looks at me, I swear he can see into my soul.

Roman is everything I've ever wanted in a man. In fact, I soon realize that with him, I get a whole lot more than I bargained for.

The problem is that I'm not sure I'm ready for any of it.

Chapter 1

Bianca

"The world could do with fewer men." I shove my hand into a plastic bowl filled with peanuts only for it to topple over. "Screw you."

"Screw me?" A man's voice growls next to me.

It growls. The type of deep and raw sound that enters your ear, but then it crawls down your body lighting up every nerve ending.

I turn because who wouldn't want to see what this guy looks like?

The face outdoes the voice tenfold.

He has dark brown hair that's too long on top to be corporate but stylish enough on the sides to be contemporary.

I look into brown eyes that are a shade lighter than a great espresso.

His nose looks like it was gifted to him courtesy of a Greek God, and his jawline is so sharp that other men must question their masculinity when they're in his presence.

I may be exaggerating, but I've known a guy or two who would hide in a hole after seeing the man sitting on the barstool next to me.

The gray suit he's wearing is next level, as is the silk tie that has thin lines of lilac thread crisscrossing through it.

"I wasn't talking to you," I toss back because I'm not single.

What a waste this encounter is going to be.

"I thought I heard an invitation." He pops a dark brow. He evens that out with a smirk.

Full pink lips and a tongue that I get a hint of when he licks his lower lip only add to his *whatever-the-hell-it-is*. It trumps charisma by miles, and attractive isn't even in the ballpark.

This man could charge money for women to sit and stare at him.

I raise a finger when the bartender approaches because, truth be told, this is not my first time in this questionable establishment.

I have to pick and choose where I show my face in this town.

Manhattan is vast, but my stepfather's reach surpasses that.

I glance at the hands of the man sitting next to me. I tell myself it's because I want to see what he's holding. (A glass half-filled with top-shelf bourbon, from the looks of it.) But, size does matter when it comes to doughnuts and dicks.

If you're going to indulge, satisfaction should be guaranteed.

The suit sitting next to me has large hands.

They are strikingly larger than my current boyfriend's. Kieran's hands are average. They do the job, or they used to.

Some say you can't judge the size of a cock by the owner's hands. I say you can. My research has proven it.

A glass with a little too much vodka and not enough cranberry juice is set just to the left of me. "Thanks, Rolly."

Rolly knows what I like down to the two lime wedges he's propped on the glass's rim.

"I'll add it to your tab, Miss Marks."

Apparently, Rolly has never seen an episode of Dateline. Identifying information in a bar is a no-no. With a discreet shake of my head, I roll my eyes even though I doubt that Rolly will see it.

I'd estimate that the prescription for his eyeglasses dates back to the nineties. He tosses a kiss in my general direction thrown from his palm because Rolly is a kind soul. He makes a mean drink too and strong. It's very strong.

"Go ahead and put it on my tab." The man next to me leans closer, and I get my first scent of him. I can't tell if it's cologne or just his skin, but it makes me think of his lips in places other than the rim of his glass.

There's no harm in letting him buy me a drink, so I smile. Pushing my long brown hair over my shoulder, I look at him. "Thank you."

He stares into my blue eyes as if I'm going to share my deepest secret with him. "You're welcome, Miss Marks."

Thanks a hell of a lot, Rolly.

"I'm Roman Hawthorne." He extends a hand, and I get a glimpse of an obscenely expensive gold watch peeking out from beneath the arm of his suit jacket.

My stepdad would be jealous, which makes me think this man might be even richer than the Marks brood is.

I take his hand for a brief shake. "Miss Marks."

He lets out a chuckle that vibrates through him. "Tit-for-tat, Miss Marks."

My gaze drops to the front of the royal blue blouse I'm wearing. I'm all buttoned up. I'd make a comment about my breasts, but there is no need. Mr. Hawthorne is getting his fill of what they look like, although he can't see the pretty lace bra they're bundled up in.

"A first name," he says as though it's a question.

I sip on the drink even though I want to down it in one large gulp. I haven't forgotten why I'm here, although the five o-clock shadow on this guy makes me almost forget I have a boyfriend.

The last time Kieran went down on me, he had a beard.

That was weeks ago.

Lately, it's been one minute of foreplay in the form of a swipe of his finger over my clit, three minutes of thrusting before Kieran comes, and ten minutes with my vibrator after I get back to my place.

"I have one," I bounce back.

He laughs, and time in all its infinite wisdom stops. Even Rolly looks in our direction to see where the glorious sound is coming from.

I take another drink.

"Let's start again," he says through a lingering chuckle. "You said something about the world needing fewer men. What was that about?"

"That was about one John Smith."

That is my boss's name, but Roman can't track me down based on that. That's assuming that he'd want to track me down. For all I know, he's in here drowning his sorrows because his girlfriend left him.

I laugh out loud at that.

What woman in her right mind would leave him?

Roman's brows pinch together. "Was that a joke?"

"No," I sigh. "My boss passed me over for a promotion today."

"Bastard," Roman snaps the word off his tongue.

I'd call John worse, and I have, but I did that on the trek here in the sweltering New York City heat.

I'm all cursed out, for now.

"He gave the job to one of his cronies." I edge my manicured, pink-tipped nail around the rim of my glass. "If that's what you call an old friend who has much less experience than me."

"I call it favoritism." Roman finishes his drink. "John Smith made a mistake."

For someone who has no idea what I do for a living, I admire his commitment to taking my side.

"I think it's time to look for a new job," I say half-heartedly.

I've been working at Packton Properties for three years. The senior project manager's job should have been mine. Once John's BFF was put on staff, my chance for any advancement went up in smoke. You'd think that eighty-year-old men would be ready to hang up their hats and hit the retirement path, but not John and Jim.

"If you have a background in law, I'd consider offering you a position with my firm."

That has to be the smoothest humble brag I've ever heard. I don't take the bait because my only experience with the law was a warning for crossing against a light when I was seventeen. I've stayed on the straight and narrow for the last ten years.

I take another sip of my drink, waiting for Roman, the gorgeous, but not modest attorney, to ask for my number. My ego hopes he will, even though I can't share it because of Kieran.

I am many things, but I'm not a cheater.

He takes a look at his enviable watch. "It's been an experience, Miss Marks. I hope the employment situation sorts itself out."

"I'll sort it out." I catch his eye one last time. "Thank you again for the drink, Mr. Hawthorne."

"Roman." He taps his fingers on the top of the bar. "It's Roman to you."

He stands. All six-feet-two-inches of him are breathtaking.

I'll never see him again after today, so I take one last, very long look at him.

"Until we meet again," he says, buttoning his suit jacket. "Good day, Miss Marks."

Taking a deep breath, I turn back to my drink and whisper, "You made it a very good day, Mr. Hawthorne."

Coming soon!

THANK YOU

Thank you for purchasing and downloading my book. I can't even begin to put to words what it means to me. If you enjoyed it, please remember to write a review for it. Let me know your thoughts! I want to keep my readers happy.

For more information on new series and standalones, please visit my website, **https://deborahbladon.com**. There are book trailers and other goodies to check out.

If you want to chat with me personally, please LIKE my page on Facebook. I love connecting with all of my readers because without you, none of this would be possible. **www.facebook.com/authordeborahbladon**

Thank you, for everything.

ABOUT THE AUTHOR

Deborah Bladon has never read a romance hero she didn't like. Her love for romance novels began when she was old enough to board the bus, library card in hand to check out the newest Harlequin paperbacks. She's a Canadian by heart, and by passport, but you can often spot her in New York City sipping a latte and looking for inspiration for her next story. Manhattan is definitely her second home.

She cherishes her family and believes that each day is a gift for writing, for reading, and for loving.

Made in United States
North Haven, CT
26 October 2021

10603267R00157